Praise for
the Resurrectionist

"The best novel I've read in years, and absolutely the best first novel I've ever read. . . . Surprising, compelling, moving, shocking, and satisfying."   —Chris Offutt, author of *Kentucky Straight*

"I just finished Matthew Guinn's fine new novel *The Resurrectionist* with a rare sense of excitement. It's relentlessly compelling, thoughtful, intelligent, and just plain wise. It's a shame Robert Penn Warren is no longer with us, because this is a book he would love."   —Steve Yarbrough, author of *Safe from the Neighbors*

"*The Resurrectionist* is a spectacular novel that seamlessly connects fact and fiction, past and present. Matthew Guinn is a novelist who possesses that rarest and most underrated of literary gifts—how to tell a story in such a way that the reader surrenders completely to its power."   —Ron Rash, author of *Serena*

"Guinn's fascinating, occasionally macabre, and engrossing novel offers a story of redemption and renewal while revealing the uncomfortable details about the historical practice of procuring human cadavers for doctors in training."
—Historical Novel Society

"The enigmatic body thief Nemo elevates the pulse rate on this haunted history lesson."   —Tray Butler, *Atlanta Journal-Constitution*

"An engrossing tale . . . weaves crime, social commentary and revenge into a moral parable of the South."   —Susan O'Bryan,
Clarion-Ledger

"Creepy and macabre (in the best possible way). . . . [A] curious yet highly satisfying brew."   —Alabama Booksmith blog

"Matthew Guinn makes books like they used to. . . . [B]y remaining mindful that literature is both entertaining and academic, he's created something fresh."   —Sam Suttle, Portico magazine

"A noteworthy debut of an author from whom we will hopefully read more, and soon." —Joe Hartlaub, BookReporter.com

"Guinn provides a lot of twists and an effectively ominous mood, thanks partly to some not-for-the-squeamish medical scenes."   —Kirkus Reviews

"Strong pacing, interesting lead characters, well-framed moral questions, and clever resolutions to both prongs of the story are the hallmarks of this winning debut that shows that in matters of race and American history, navigating to 'truth' and 'right' is almost always a complex journey." —Neil Hollands, Library Journal

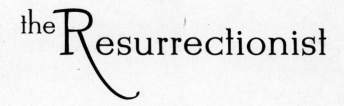

W. W. NORTON & COMPANY   NEW YORK   LONDON

the Resurrectionist

A Novel

MATTHEW GUINN

For information about permission to reproduce selections from this book,
write to Permissions, W. W. Norton & Company, Inc.,
500 Fifth Avenue, New York, NY 10110

For information about special discounts for bulk purchases, please contact
W. W. Norton Special Sales at specialsales@wwnorton.com or 800-233-4830

Manufacturing by RR Donnelley, Harrisonburg
Book design by Ellen Cipriano
Production manager: Devon Zahn

Library of Congress Cataloging-in-Publication Data

Guinn, Matthew.
The resurrectionist : a novel / Matthew Guinn. — First Edition.
pages cm
ISBN 978-0-393-23931-7 (hardcover)
1. Medical Students—Fiction. 2. Secrets—Fiction.
3. Corpse removals—Fiction. 4. African Americans—Fiction.
I. Title.
PS3607.U4856R47 2013
813'.6—dc23

2013003760

ISBN 978-0-393-34881-1 pbk.

W. W. Norton & Company, Inc.
500 Fifth Avenue, New York, N.Y. 10110
www.wwnorton.com

W. W. Norton & Company Ltd.
Castle House, 75/76 Wells Street, London W1T 3QT

1 2 3 4 5 6 7 8 9 0

For two who kept this one alive:

JOE HICKMAN

and

BRAIDEN GUINN

resurrectionist n. (**a**) *Hist*. A body-snatcher; a resurrection man; (**b**) *gen*. a person who resurrects something (lit. & fig.); (**c**) a believer in resurrection

fernyear n. & *adv*. (**a**) *Obsc*. A past year, olden times

In whatsoever houses I enter, I will enter to help the sick, and I will abstain from all intentional wrongdoing and harm, especially from abusing the bodies of man or woman, bond or free. And whatsoever I shall see or hear in the course of my profession in my intercourse with men, if it be what should not be published abroad, I will never divulge, holding such things to be holy secrets. Now if I carry out this oath, and break it not, may I gain forever reputation among all men for my life and for my art; but if I transgress it and forswear myself, may the opposite befall me.

—HIPPOCRATES

Educational institutions . . . are peculiarly sensitive to outside criticism, and particularly to any statement of the circumstances of their own conduct or equipment which seems to them unfavorable. . . . As a rule, the only knowledge which the public has concerning an institution of learning is derived from the statements given out by the institution itself.

—ABRAHAM FLEXNER (1910)

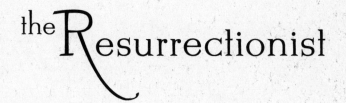

Monday

DOG DAYS AND THE FRESH BODIES are arriving once again. Always, Jacob feels the old stir of anticipation when the baked stillness of August is broken by their return to campus, these young people crackling with energy in the last sullen days of summer. The first-year students are always the first to arrive, fresh-faced and with eyes narrowed toward the bright future, intent on the four years ahead of them in laboratory, classroom, and clinic; painfully earnest, the noble words of Hippocrates echoing in their minds. They come from every corner of the state and the nation and from eighteen foreign countries, even Kazakhstan this year. He'd had to pull down the globe to find that one, working late in this drafty office last winter, poring over the registrar's report. Each of them from the top tier of their college classes, a crowd of overachievers prepped, tested, vetted, screened, admitted, and financed. And each of them consumed with a single, burning goal: to leave this South Carolina campus a doctor.

The view from the top floor of the old administration building offers a vision straight from a recruiting brochure: serene live oaks dropping shade over the rich green of the Bermuda grass, the campus walks bricked in stately order. Every inch of the old campus meticulously maintained, a fit and proper welcome to the incoming class, this one hundred and fortieth group of doctors to be graduated by the South Carolina Medical College. All that history, he thinks, renewing itself annually. A long tide of beneficent humanity ushered forth to heal the rest. And generation after generation of venerated MDs defeated, ultimately, by the immutable fact that human life is still a terminal sentence.

But today is no time for morbid thoughts; there is too much to be done. At the base of the building, just within Jacob's line of sight, Dean Jim McMichaels stands before a group of reporters and photographers doing what he does best: pressing the flesh of anyone within his reach. Or, as the dean puts it behind closed doors, shooting the shit. He excels at it. In the year that Jacob has served as the school's public relations director, McMichaels has made his job almost too easy; the dean himself is the real PR man.

The dean is dressed for the role, in a white hard hat and Wellington boots no less, the boot leather caked with red clay from the exposed walls of the building's foundation, threatening to soil the cuffs of his Brooks Brothers pants. He gestures and points as though he were the foreman of the crew, and Jacob can easily imagine the spiel he is laying out for the press. No doubt a good deal of play on the metaphor of foundations, from the antebellum brick of this old building under renovation to the role of the Medical College in the state's past and future. "Foundations for the Future" is the catchphrase the dean happily announced for this year's campaign, and Jim McMichaels having said it, it was so. The newspapermen are probably jotting it down in their notebooks now.

McMichaels takes hold of a gold shovel and gazes at it significantly. Jacob knows the shovel. He bought it and the metallic spray paint that now coats it yesterday, at Five Points Hardware. There are traces of gold back at his condominium, on the concrete patio where the paint drifted past the newspapers he'd set out before spraying it.

There is the sound of applause as the dean takes aim at the ground with his golden spade. He settles the shovel on the school's hallowed ground and gives it a hearty kick with a Wellington heel, grinning to beat the band while the cameras flash.

Grinning himself, Jacob settles at his desk and begins to leaf through the morning's paperwork, a small stack of press releases to be cleared for the university's website. Most of them are pro forma, this year's versions of news of the Class of 1999 rewritten from last year's texts. An agenda for the white-coat ceremony to be held in the Chapel Clinic that afternoon, another for the opening-of-year gala at the Dean's Mansion Friday night. No edits except for the first of the external releases, announcing

Dr. Austin Malloy's promotion within Admissions. Jacob strikes the phrase "will assume the position of associate dean" from the text, though he knows the school's alumni will have Malloy grabbing his ankles soon enough.

The last release gives him pause. From it, a black-and-white photo of a stunning young woman stares back at him. Her features are regal—aquiline nose and luminous eyes, black hair cascading around a face so perfectly featured that it might have been carved from stone. He reads her name and sees that this is the Presidential Scholar from the University of Virginia he has been hearing so much about.

Jacob had picked the young man from Kazakhstan as his diversity star for the class profile this year, but now he has a bona fide poster girl. Daughter of an Egyptian diplomat, childhood in Cairo followed up by high school outside D.C. before her years at U. Va. and Oxford. A rare case: the academic record is as beautiful as her portrait. *Yara Nasir, I will have to be careful not to overexpose you*, he thinks as he places the release in his out-box, marked *high priority*.

His desk phone rings and he grabs it, is greeted by the voice of Elizabeth, the dean's secretary and the de facto receptionist for Administration; every call goes through the dean's office first.

"Kaye Siegel for you, line one," she says in her Charleston accent, the low-country cadences still pronounced after twenty years in Columbia. "*International call*," she adds. He can picture her raising an eyebrow as she says it.

"Thanks, Elizabeth," he says, and presses the blinking red light on his phone. He speaks over the faint buzz of long-distance static. "*Guten Tag*, love."

Kaye laughs. "Closer to *Guten Abend* here, Jacob."

"How's Munich?"

"A German conference room bears a striking resemblance to a Columbia conference room, especially after the third straight day. At least the coffee's decent."

Jacob smiles into the phone. Kaye is, as his late father would have described her, a woman in a man's world. Bavarian Motor Works began courting her before she even graduated from international law at Carolina, and she has been with the company since, with the plant in Spartanburg running full steam now and talk of expansion all but constant. A woman in a man's world perhaps, but Jacob knows his father would have walked out of West Columbia Textiles midshift for the kind of job the German automaker has brought to South Carolina.

"And how are you?" she asks.

"Good. A little first-week mania, but it's seasonal."

"Pressure is pressure, Jacob. Are you handling it?"

He looks at the stack of press releases on his desk and cannot see how his day's work could be much less significant.

"Handling it fine. Even keel. Really."

There is a pause on the line. He knows that she is, by training, thinking of pursuing an alternative line of questioning. Instead she sighs.

"Even keel, huh?"

"Yep. Even. Keel."

"Keep it that way, all right? Look, they're starting the next meeting without me."

"How do you say 'wait' in German? Can you tell them to hold up a minute?"

Again she laughs. "You don't say 'wait' over here. Corporate policy. It's a four-letter word. Take care of yourself, Jacob. I'll see you Wednesday, okay?"

"Can't wait."

He would say more, but Kaye has already rung off. He places the receiver back in its cradle and thinks that he is grateful for her checking on him. But even more grateful, perhaps, that she did not say why. At least by name.

He steps to the window to monitor the dean's progress. No one is left on the lawn. Remarkable efficiency. Had Jacob joined the photo op, he would still be down there, buttonholed by some bored metro writer telling one bad joke after another to forestall going back to the newsroom. But McMichaels has dispersed them like a class at the end of a lecture. Even the shovel is gone.

Jacob checks his watch, looks over at the bookcase that lines one wall of his office. He scans the photographs propped on the shelves. Most are shots of himself with Kaye, interspersed with a couple of awkwardly posed Polaroids of his late parents. But it is another photograph there that catches his eye, and he pulls it down. Old sepia daguerreotype, faded, a portrait of the school's graduating class of 1860. Men from the foundations, as

McMichaels would say. Taken on the front steps of this building all those years ago. Two rows of stern-looking faces, all male, all white, staring the camera down in the moribund manner of the nineteenth century, this gathering of plantation gentlemen setting out to do what they could in the bleak era before penicillin, asepsis, or the X-ray. Their bearded faces seem to scowl at him. One dark smudge of an African face peers over a shoulder in the second row, probably caught there while running an errand into the building, trying to get out of the photographer's way.

Standing by the bookcase, he can just make out the graceful lines of the face of Yara Nasir, class of '99, on his desk. Things are different now from what they used to be, thank God. More room at the inn.

AT EIGHT-THIRTY ON this August morning the Chapel Clinic glows like an emerald, its bright glass façade giving back the morning sunshine to the city around it, casting the greenish light refracted from its mirrored windows on the palmettos and the concrete, bathing everything in underwater hues. But Jacob hardly notices; he is going to be late for his monthly meeting with Kirstin Reithoffer, his sponsor from the Physicians' Task Force, and Reithoffer is a doctor for whom all trains run on time.

He double-times it past the great fountain toward the building's front entrance. In lean-budget years the fountain is shut off to save on electricity and maintenance, but lately, with the economy booming, it sprays forth its two-story-high jets of water almost exuberantly, just as the famous architect envisioned it: a perfect counterpoint to the clinic's glass walls. Patients passing the last minutes before their appointments sit on the concrete walls that frame the fountain's pool, some of them staring vacantly at the traffic, most of them smoking. A black man in the school's physical plant uniform walks the edges of the pool with a net, skimming out the cigarette butts tossed in the water.

At the entrance Jacob takes his place in line as the doors are opened for the busy day. It is a bad spot to be in a hurry. Nearly all the patients filing into the building are disabled in one way or another, a crowd of the sick and lame moving into the clinic through clouds of smoke from their discarded cigarettes. Jacob steps aside to let a woman with a walker go in front of him in a slow, shuffling gait. The woman is easily fifty pounds overweight, and is escorted by her husband, a thin man with skin weathered like old leather, wearing a feed cap with the logo of a local co-op embroidered on its front. Country osmosis, he has always called it: this strange process by which the women of the rural South seem to take on the weight lost by their men in hard labor. When the walker creaks past the granite walls of the foyer and into the open atrium, Jacob is free, and slips past the patients creeping toward the elevators. He moves to the escalators instead, where he takes the moving steps two at a time.

He spies an old face from his intern days coming toward him on the down escalator. Parker Hauser, a real hotshot back then and a rich kid, probably heading down from the parking deck to the dermatology clinic on the first floor, where he now runs one of the most coveted practices in the clinic. Jacob remembers him as the first person he'd known to own a cellular phone. Jacob had kicked it once, accidentally, where it sat on the floor of the interns' lounge, and Parker had exploded. "Do you know how much a bag phone costs, dickhead?" he'd shouted, and one of the nurses had burst into laughter. Jacob smiles and says hello to him as they pass on the moving stairs, but Hauser, caught up in intense conversation with one of his residents, seems not to have noticed him.

At the vascular surgery clinic on the third floor Jacob is ushered back to Reithoffer's office by the administrative assistant, who shuts the door behind him. She is the new one; Reithoffer replaced the entire staff within six months of coming south to Columbia, claiming they were too inefficient for a first-rate clinic. None of the new people are local.

Reithoffer is on the phone, but she nods at Jacob and motions for him to take a seat. While the surgeon talks, Jacob looks around the office, taking in the framed diplomas and citations. Though her residency brought her stateside, Reithoffer's other accolades are international: certificates from surgical associations in Germany and the Netherlands, a commendation from the University of Edinburgh for lifetime achievement. How she finds time for her committee service to the school has always mystified him.

"So, how are the cravings, Jacob?"

Jacob looks down from the walls and into Reithoffer's pale blue eyes. He has not heard the doctor finish her phone call; he has been reading a framed proclamation from the American Academy of Surgeons, trying to make out all the fine type. He clears his throat.

"Fine, thanks. Except that there isn't much doctoring in Administration. I'm ready to get back into practice."

"Of course you are. But the cravings?"

"Nearly gone."

"Nearly?"

"There are times . . ." Jacob says, his voice trailing off. "There are times when I think about it. That freedom from anxiety."

Reithoffer nods. "Understandable. But you fully realize that this freedom is illusory?"

"Yes."

"That is the key to avoiding relapse, you know. And the craving is the key danger of Xanax, why every course of medication should be carefully monitored." Reithoffer waves one hand in the air, the gesture casually European. "Only in America would we imagine life without the bother of anxiety. And that is why these tranquilizers are so completely overprescribed here."

There is an awkward silence; they both know that Jacob never got his tranquilizers from a prescription. As if to break the tension, Reithoffer begins flipping pages in the chart spread out on her desk. "How about alcohol?" she asks.

"Same as before. Just the social drink."

"Fine. But remember that it's all of a piece with addiction. Alcohol is the prime avenue of relapse for those in tranquilizer recovery. It's cheap. Easy to come by. Similar effects on the nervous system. Be careful."

"Right. I've got you."

Reithoffer rises and takes a blood-pressure cuff and stethoscope off the coat tree behind the office door. She sits on the edge of her desk and motions for Jacob to raise his arm.

"And the Klonopin? How long have we been off that?"

"Three months now. I started tapering it in March."

"Which you will remember I advised against."

Jacob nods. "I remember. But I'm not a junkie, Kirstin."

Reithoffer shoves the cuff up over Jacob's bicep and cinches the strap tight against his arm. "No. Not a junkie." She breathes through her nose as she arranges the strap to her satisfaction. "No junkie could have finished a residency here at Carolina. If one ever does, the school will have my resignation promptly." She smiles. "What you are—were—was a resident under great strain, working long hours. A resident who made a mistake. I am under strict confidentiality regulations from the Physicians' Task Force, but I can tell you that you are not the only one to make such a mistake."

"That's good to know."

Reithoffer slips the stethoscope under the cuff. It is steely cold against Jacob's skin. "Let's review it once more, the error. Tell me again why you broke your oath."

Jacob shifts in the chair, but Reithoffer grips his arm more tightly and begins pumping the bulb of the blood-pressure cuff. Her fingers are long, delicately tapered, but strong.

"Again? What's the point?"

"To know your weakness. To face down the wolf so he doesn't come again."

Jacob takes a deep breath. He knows that Reithoffer will take at least three readings of his blood pressure as he talks. There will be time.

"The last year was the hardest," Jacob begins. "I had a lot of debt, just piling up, and the moonlighting was the only way out of it. I was getting stretched too thin. I was getting tired."

Reithoffer studies the gauge of the cuff. Jacob can hear the starch in her white coat crackle when she moves. She nods for Jacob to continue.

Jacob takes a deep breath, closes his eyes, and remembers.

That third year of his residency, something had slipped, some cog in the turning wheels of his ambition had sprung loose. He'd been working like a dog at the little county hospital out in Newberry in between shifts at Memorial, trying to stay ahead of his rent and the enormous student loans. Some weeks that meant two to three days with no sleep, the seven-to-seven shift in Newberry sandwiched between his schedule at the university and his ancient Honda overheating on I-26 as he floored the pedal to make it from one ER to another. It had started out as hard as he could imagine. Then it had gotten harder.

It was especially bad in Newberry that fall. He lost three patients in November—two of them goners that he could have let go easily enough, but the third a woman of thirty-two whose breast cancer had metastasized at a rate beyond any even the oncologist could comprehend. Jacob had diagnosed the tumor and consulted with the oncologist throughout her treatment. Everyone knew it wasn't his fault and couldn't have been. But still there were her eyes, sinking into her skull in the last two weeks she was alive, which would never accuse him. And that, somehow, was the worst of it, the last indictment of his incompetence as her physician.

Her chemotherapy had been aggressive and it had taken its course on her body. A week before Thanksgiving he had stuck his head in a door on rounds and apologized to the woman in the bed.

"Wrong room," he said. "Sorry."

"No, right room, Doctor Thacker," she said as he looked down to recheck the name on his chart. "Wrong life, I guess."

Jacob froze. He felt that he could never again look up from the clipboard, so great was his shame, his disgust with himself.

"It's all right," she said softly from the bed. "It's okay."

When he looked up, she was smiling. Her weary face wore an open expression, already past this latest indignity. Not as though she were anticipating some long-shot good news from this visit, but simply that she was glad to see him. Her expression was simply, impossibly human.

He understood then that she knew this Friday afternoon to be her last, and tomorrow's Saturday afternoon to be her last.

He sat down on her bed and they did not talk about the cancer or her regimen but simply talked. Yet her approaching death was in every unspoken word, fusing the conversation and charging it with meaning, with a new significance of the mundane. Later it would strike him that it was something like grace in the room, but then he could see it only as death, a thing she had somehow transcended while it crippled her healer.

After that it was as though his horizon had shifted, then dimmed. The bright goal was still there but now with less luster. The woman died on Thanksgiving Day. Jacob was at the hospital, midway through his twelve-hour shift, when he heard. He had eaten a Thanksgiving meal of cold turkey and store-bought dressing without tasting any of it.

Later that evening, a farmer had come in with his hand mangled to hamburger from attempting a thresher repair after too much holiday cheer. The man's wife was hysterical to the point of shock, so once Jacob got the farmer stabilized he went to the supply closet to get her a Xanax. And there in the supply room, his hand paused with the bottle of sedatives in it, as if by its own will. He knew the dose was .5 milligrams. He had shaken out two pills and swallowed one of them dry.

Reithoffer shifts on the desk and turns the valve of the blood-pressure cuff. The bulb hisses as the air drains from the cuff, and Jacob feels the pressure loosen against his arm.

"So where was the error, Jacob?"

He attempts a joke. "Not sending a nurse to the supply room."

But Reithoffer does not smile, only fixes her flinty eyes on Jacob as she pulls the stethoscope from her ears.

"The error was a confusion of compassion," Jacob says, sighing. They have been over this same ground for months.

"Exactly. Patients die, Jacob. They die when they should not, when we are unprepared and when their medical records indicate any other feasible outcome. College athletes in the prime of health suffer massive infarctions. Twenty-year-old mothers die of postpartum stroke after routine deliveries. And young women get cancer."

"Her name was Varina Payton."

"Let it go, Jacob. Our concern is with the survivors. The living."

Jacob thinks to tell her again about the woman's eyes, the depths of suffering and endurance in them, but knows it is no use. He suspects Reithoffer has witnessed too much of it to really see it anymore.

"You cannot be a doctor without achieving the proper distance from your patients. Every physician must face the terminal cases and move on. Some are beyond our reach. Move on."

Jacob nods. Reithoffer pulls the cuff off his arm and hangs it on the wall. When she turns back to him, the flinty eyes seem to have softened a degree.

"Jacob," she says, "how did you lose your mother?"

He looks up more quickly than he had intended. "Not breast cancer. Emphysema. Dad too, three years earlier. They both worked in the mills all their life."

Reithoffer nods, bends over her desk to make a notation in Jacob's chart.

"Last week I had to reply to a memo on conserving printer paper, Kirstin. *Office supplies.* I should be handling charts, seeing patients. Some days I look up from that computer, that desk, and I don't even know who I am anymore."

"Blood pressure is one-thirty over ninety-two. Not too good. You need to be getting more exercise."

"I haven't gotten down to the gym much lately."

"Make it a priority. We are all busy." Reithoffer closes the chart and puts it into a filing cabinet behind her desk.

"How is everything otherwise? We're at the midpoint now, right? Will I get a good report?"

Reithoffer locks the filing cabinet and drops the key in her pocket, checking her watch as she does it. She steps around the desk to where Jacob sits and rests a hand on his shoulder; Jacob can just make out the neatly manicured fingernails in his peripheral vision.

"These things take time, and the task force feels it can never be too careful. Get some exercise. Get some rest. You look tired." The hand grips his shoulder. "Recovery is one day at a time. And today I have a long line of patients to see."

Then the hand is gone and Jacob can hear the office door opening. Before it shuts, Reithoffer speaks again.

"You left a urine specimen with the technician?"

Jacob drops his head. "Not yet, ma'am," he says.

Two hours later he is back in the office, finishing a set of interview questions for Miss Nasir's profile in the next issue of the alumni magazine. Interviewing the new med students is usually awkward for him, but he feels a bit of genuine anticipation this time. He prints the document and sits back while the printer whirs.

Something is happening downstairs. The old building's central stairwells and open banisters cannot hide much from one story to the next. The racket of the construction has been building steadily for nearly a week, but now its timbre has changed; there is still noise, but not machinery, no hammering or sawing. Only voices charged with a current of intensity beyond the daily banter.

Below him, three black men emerge onto the front lawn clad in the khaki uniforms of the physical plant, their legs slathered with clay. One of them slings his hard hat back toward the building and stomps off toward the crosswalk at Gervais Street, and the others look after him for a moment before lighting cigarettes. They gesture expansively as they talk and drag deeply on their smokes. He recognizes one—Lorenzo Shanks—as a familiar face from the gym on Beltline Avenue, Jacob's occasional spotter on the bench press. He has never seen Lorenzo's face so intense, almost frightened.

A few minutes later, Jacob is down on the main floor, brushing aside the plastic sheet that has guarded the presidential offices from the dust of the foundation work in the cellar.

His loafers sound emptily on the wooden stairs as he descends to the droplights that gleam against the red walls hewn from the dirt of the cellar. The foreman, Bowman, stands near one corner of the basement, shaking his head over the raw clay and smoking a cigarette of his own—an express violation of code inside a state building.

"You should know there's no smoking in here," Jacob says as he approaches, but the man seems not to hear as he kicks at the dirt and a small collection of ivory fragments upon it. Bones.

"What I've got to work with," he says. "Jesus Christ. If you-all had let me bring in my men, we'd be half done by now." Smoke billows from his nostrils as he grunts. "White crew wouldn't have spooked at no pile of cat bones."

Jacob squats at his feet. He prods at the bones until he arranges them into the metacarpus and phalanges of a small hand, human. He cradles the bones in his palm and rises with them in his hand like porcelain, until he is toe-to-toe with Bowman.

"Turns out your crew is smarter than you thought," Jacob says, breathing evenly. "This is a second-shaft metacarpus and a first-row phalange. Which to you means the pointer finger of a small child, maybe five years old."

Bowman backs up a step. "Shit," he says.

"No shit. How many have you found?"

"They're all over the place. One of the boys looked in that vat yonder and just about ran out of here screaming. Rest followed him."

Jacob looks where Bowman has nodded and sees an ancient cask of wooden slats bound in iron bands at the edge of the electric light. It is half buried in the dry earth of the cellar, like something that has washed up on a beach, then been partly reclaimed by tides. He's heard stories of old times, of the school contained in this single antebellum building, anatomy lab and all. He thinks he knows what might be in the cask. The old familiar smell in here underneath all the other odors, beneath the scents of raw earth and dry rot, is formaldehyde.

"We need to seal this area off. You and your men can take the day until I notify you."

"Losing a day's going to cost us, you know. It'll fuck everything up."

"I'm aware of that. Leave it to me."

"I stand to lose a lot here, getting set back."

"I said I'm aware of that. I'll speak to the dean personally."

Bowman drops his cigarette and snuffs it with a boot heel. Almost as an afterthought, he spits on the ground before turning toward the stairway.

And then Bowman too is gone and Jacob is left with the clay and the musty darkness and the scattered bones. Like shards of ivory littering the earthen floor, so many of them.

THE FIRST CHANCE Jacob gets to meet with the dean is no chance at all—McMichaels has breezed into the auditorium of the Chapel Clinic at three minutes to one o'clock, when the white-coat ceremony is set to begin. He presses Jacob's hand as he passes the dais of faculty and administrators and steps to the podium. He does not need to call for order; after the immediate burst of applause that greeted him, the assembly has quieted to a funereal hush. After flashing them all a big-toothed smile, his face assumes a somber expression, and he begins.

"Ladies and gentlemen, we have convened today for a sacred rite: the ceremony that symbolizes your first step on the journey that will culminate—for many of you, but not all—in the realization of a dream dear not only to your hearts but to our faculty's as well, and beyond that, to the hearts of our state and our nation. Those of you who prevail in the next four years will emerge as physicians, as healers. It is a great responsibility—indeed, a universal one. For there is no man so lofty that he does not welcome the presence of the physician in his hour of need.

"To those of you who seek fortune, I counsel another path, because ours is a sacred profession, ladies and gentlemen, and I do not use the word lightly. History has enshrined physicians in the roster of humanity's greatest achievements: Hippocrates, Galen, Lister, Pasteur, and Salk. The very names echo with the gravity of their contributions to the human family. It is our responsibility, however meager our means may seem compared to these men, to uphold that tradition and carry it forward."

McMichaels pauses for a moment, letting his words sink in to the bright minds seated in front of him.

"We may note with some pride that our own institution has

played a role in that great tradition. The state-of-the-art clinic in which we have gathered is named for but one of many illustrious forebears at the Medical College of South Carolina—George Chapel, who performed the first open-heart surgery in the South, a bold operation carried out with characteristic precision in spite of rudimentary equipment and daunting odds. Seated behind me—and still very much among the living," he adds with a smile—"is Kirstin Reithoffer, author of the internal medicine textbook you will soon be using as the manual for your first year—a text used in every medical school in the nation as a benchmark of medical scholarship. More distant to us through the mists of time, but no less important, is the figure of Frederick Johnston, the founder of our institution. Our present administration building, once the school's sole facility, bears his name in tribute. For it was Doctor Johnston, casting the long shadow of his influence, who assembled in this city a faculty of intrepid physicians committed to advancing the medical arts. We can thank those pioneering men for our presence here today."

McMichaels pauses again, taking a moment to look at each expectant face before closing. "It is time now for you to step forward and join our tradition."

Awed to silence, the first-years begin to file down the aisles as the new associate dean of admissions, Malloy, assuming his position, steps forward to hand McMichaels the first of two hundred lab coats he will dispense this afternoon. The speech, even by McMichaels's standards, has been a good one. And it is made more so for Jacob by his seeing that there is nothing on the podium before the dean but a creased and grease-stained takeout menu from Pete's Barbeque. The students begin passing in line, the dean draping a starched coat on each set of shoulders, one by one. Jacob smiles, then his face sobers—not only out of a sense of decorum, but because he is thinking again of the basement. Telling McMichaels about it, he knows, is going to ruin the dean's banner day.

Fernyear: 1857

FREDERICK AUGUSTUS JOHNSTON STRODE down the aisle, savoring the sound of each creaking board beneath his feet. With his mustache waxed, the gold chain of his pocket watch gleaming, and his hands hooked into his vest pockets, he looked the very embodiment of the best the Carolina College of Medicine and Physic could produce. Behind him, the faculty entered the room in double file, all six of them, and took their places against the walls of the room, flanking the incoming class seated in the center.

The new class was raw material, to be certain. Country boys, most of them, arrayed on the rude benches in various attitudes of untidy poise. Johnston was pleased, however, to note that most of them straightened as he made his slow progress toward the front of the room, their crimson necks flushing a shade deeper to be in the presence of the noted Doctor

Johnston, who had studied under the great Benjamin Rush at Pittsburgh—now one of South Carolina's leading medical men, lately arrived in the capital to found the new school. They had come here expecting him to shape and mold them after his model. And that he would do, God willing. Provided they could endure ten months of rigorous study and training, they too could attain the heights of medical science.

As Johnston neared the first row, one of the boys leaned over and expelled a long stream of tobacco juice onto the new plank floor, not even bothering to aim for the spittoon placed at the end of each row expressly for that purpose. Johnston flinched. *Raw material,* he reminded himself, *and each of them important to our mission.* Indeed, a good deal was riding on this class. The new building, impressive as it was, was threatening to sink the young college in a sea of red ink. The faculty needed every tuition dollar these boys could bring them.

Johnston took his place in front of the slate chalkboard, leaning back a little on his heels. "Gentlemen," he began, "you are the third class of the Carolina College of Medicine and Physic. It is my privilege and honor to welcome you here today. You come seeking an honorable trade, and we are prepared to supply you with one. Our mission is to provide this great and sovereign state with as many doctors as we can produce, within reason, and to make open the road for poor boys to learn a lucrative profession. To that end, we can offer you the finest facilities in Columbia for medical instruction. Allow me to elaborate.

"Our Negro hospital is the first of its kind in the South and the envy of the region. Through it we have access to a range of patients offering you a wealth of clinical experience, ranging from gunshot wounds to childbirths. Administered by Doctor Evans"—Johnston nodded toward his bearded colleague—"the hospital will advance your education most expeditiously."

Johnston stepped to the corner of the room, where a microscope and a half-dozen slides rested on a small table set in front of a skeleton suspended from the ceiling. "Our chemical equipment is of the latest manufacture from London," he said, resting a hand on the fragile-looking piece. "I trust several of you have had the chemistry course in high school?"

One of the boys nodded.

"Very well, then. Doctor Winston will guide you through the mysteries of chemistry." Winston's spectacles winked in the light as he nodded to the young men.

"Last and perhaps greatest, taught by the entire faculty collectively, is the ancient art of human anatomy." Johnston placed a hand on the skeleton's shoulder. "This fellow, along with our female manikin for obstetrical instruction, will soon become a close associate of yours as we guide you through the intricacies of skeletal and muscular structure." He noticed that a few of the students were looking out the windows, their interest flagging. He turned the skeleton around so the bullet hole in the back of its skull came into view. "A veteran of the Mexican War, gentlemen," he said, "and unfortunately for him, a Mexican."

As the laughter subsided, Johnston strode across the room to a closed door adjacent to the slate board. "First things first, however. Today you embark on the road of dissection—this morning, this very hour. Your course of study begins in the room beyond, our dissection room, where you will first taste the exquisite elixir, the sublime experience, of gross anatomy." As he expected, the students were on the edge of the benches now. With a sweep of his arm, Johnston threw open the door.

If the third class of the Carolina College had been bracing for their first sight of a human cadaver, they were soon either sorely disappointed or vastly relieved. What greeted them in the next room was the sight of a half-dozen slate tables on which had been arranged the bodies of as many dead goats. Some lay on their sides, staring out toward the lecture hall with glassy eyes, but most, already stiffened from the embalming process, lay on their backs, short horns against the slate, little hooves pointing to the ceiling.

Johnston could almost feel the silence behind him. "We begin with small mammals," he said under his breath, then, turning to face the students, he cried, "Gentlemen, to the goats!"

TWO HOURS LATER the faculty was again convened. Despite Johnston's efforts, two of the incoming class had stomped out of the dissecting room within minutes of making the first cut on their animals, muttering about dental school. Four others had followed, leaving him half his original enrollment. Worse still, the last defectors had thought to ask for a refund of their tuition, which Johnston reluctantly granted. Now he was embroiled in the first heated faculty meeting of the year—on the first day of the semester.

"Gentlemen," Evans was saying, "this day's debacle has convinced me that small mammals simply will not do for a proper anatomy course."

Ballard, the new man from Boston, sniffed. "I must say, I had no idea conditions were so primitive in the South."

"We are not alone in using animals for the anatomy course," Winston said. "Mississippi has used pigs for years."

"Cats in Chattanooga, I have heard."

"Chattanooga is a third-rate diploma mill, Stanton."

"Which places us in the second tier, I suppose?"

Ballard's voice rose above the others in his clipped Yankee accent. "At some point these boys will be turned loose on bipedal mammals. We must have cadavers. Human cadavers."

"And how will you get them?" Stanton said between puffs on his meerschaum. "Mister Ballard, you may be too recently arrived to be aware of the fact, but the South Carolina legislature made human dissection illegal years ago."

"It is true, Ballard," Evans said. "A lamentable fact, but we are limited by law to executed convicts and deceased slaves. I provide what I can from the colored hospital, but that procurement is difficult work. There is the matter of discretion, and this is not a large town."

The room fell silent for a moment. Then Johnston spoke for the first time.

"Today's misfortunes lie entirely at my feet, gentlemen. We have had a run of bad luck with the unseasonably cool July and August. In a normal year we could expect two or three fresh cadavers from malaria or sunstroke, but Doctor Evans's charges have been few, and as of late, fatalities nil. We've fared no better with dead hands from the plantations out of town. I hazarded on the goats, and lost. Although I maintain that a lower mammal is perfectly sufficient for limited instruction, our students quite clearly think otherwise."

Ballard drummed his fingers on the table. "What about the Scottish way?"

Evans snorted. "These boys? They come here to put an end to physical labor, digging included."

But Ballard would not be dissuaded. "Edinburgh as recently as the twenties required each student to procure his own cadaver—it was viewed as a sort of rite of passage. Each man brought his own *Gray's* and his own body to the course."

"And you, in Boston? Did you?"

"I would have, had it been required."

"Our boys would revolt at the idea."

"What about a Negro?" Winston said in his quiet voice. "I mention it because we seem to be at an impasse on the issue of the labor of the thing. I too doubt the boys would find the task agreeable, nor can I imagine any of ourselves doing the work. But a boy procured for the purpose —"

Evans laughed. "Bully for you, Winston! A nigger body snatcher! An African sack-'em-up man!"

"I want no part of my own remuneration sacrificed to buy a slave," Ballard said. "Entirely too much expense."

"Expensive, no doubt," Winston said, "but also a permanent solution. Our present trouble would be resolved in perpetuity."

"A boy fit to do the work of cadaver procurement could cost a thousand dollars."

"True," Johnston said, and the others turned to look at him. "Goats are cheaper. But we also lost half of our student body this morning. Their tuition money followed them. I think Winston's proposal is valid. These are desperate times, and may require desperate measures."

"So we will recruit again," Stanton said, shaking his head. "No one has been across the river in a year or more, nor to the coast. Simply recruit as we have done, I say, and the cost-to-profit ratio will remain in our favor."

"You know well that Chapman's running a school in Charleston that offers the degree in six months," Evans said. "We cannot compete with him. And Georgia . . ." He trailed off, as though Georgia were beyond explanation. "Perhaps this cuffy could also serve as a kind of manservant, or as janitor for the school. Would that not improve your ratio?"

"It might. A butler for functions would enhance our profile in the community."

"I saw a notice yesterday of an estate auction near Camden," Winston said. "Rock Meade Plantation, a total loss after the fire. There will be upwards of two hundred slaves on the block."

Johnston cleared his throat. "Colleagues, if we move to proceed on this proposal, no vulgar display at auction will be necessary. I had a wire not an hour ago from All Saints Parish, Windsor Plantation. An old friend of mine with whom some of you have acquaintance, Robert Drake, has lately had a rough encounter with a fox trap and requests my attentions immediately. He owns four or five hundred hands and may be able to spare a boy for a reasonable amount."

Stanton laughed and twisted his fingers into his beard. "Ah, Johnston," he said, "you are always a step or two ahead of the game. What dealings do you have in mind at Windsor?"

"Drake's telegraph mentioned gangrene. He may find himself increasingly amenable to a fair transaction."

"At Camden they will be selling some by the pound," Winston said worriedly. "The notice said as much."

"If the faculty will vote their trust in me, I will bring back someone ideal for the job, whether priced by the pound or in a round figure. We yet have some credit remaining with the Columbia Bank."

Stanton relit his pipe, smoke clouding his face. "All right, then, damn it. I had my heart set on a new barouche for the springtime, but I suppose it can wait another year. I stand with Johnston and move to vote. Any further discussion, gentlemen?"

A second motion was made for a vote, and Johnston emerged victorious. He would leave for Windsor in the morning in the school's two-horse phaeton, to see what could be done about bringing back in it a school slave.

THE SANDY ROAD wound through the outskirts of All Saints Parish under cypress and live oak that hung low enough to form a cavern of branches over the white lane. The sun, so fierce elsewhere, was here subdued, filtered through the millions of dense small leaves so that the road at midmorning seemed steeped in twilight. Crickets chirred in the shadows, a soft counterpoint to the hissing of the wagon wheels in the sand and the muted plod of the horses' hooves out front of the phaeton.

On the bench, Johnston slept. In one hand he held a volume of Cicero, a finger marking the place where he had acceded to sleep. He held the reins loosely in the other. His head nodded in time with the bobbing of the horses' manes. Like any good country doctor, he could ride for an hour or two at a stretch like this, letting the pair of animals yoked in front carry him to whatever house call awaited at whatever distant hamlet and back again. And like most of those country doctors, he had known the bemused dislocation of waking before a strange tavern or commissary, the sonorous motion of wheels replaced by the sound of his mares lapping at the trough out front, only to find that he had a mile—or two or three—to retrace back to some crossroads where his equine pilots had taken the wrong fork in the road. But for now he slept in the soft doze of the low-country afternoon.

The phaeton rounded a bend and the road split before it, a hand-painted sign adorned with the legend WINDSOR pointing to the left. The horses tugged right.

Presently the branches overhead began to thin and the soft undulating sound of flowing water ahead hastened the animals' steps. The wagon dipped into a small hollow and rose on the other side to a low bluff a hundred yards from the Waccamaw River. The horses stopped and snorted, nostrils flaring as a breeze off the river brought to them the coppery scent of blood.

Johnston opened his eyes slowly, expecting to see before him the inspiring grace of Windsor's twelve-columned façade. What he saw instead was an imposing structure of a different sort: a hard-weathered lodge propped ten feet above the marsh ground on stilts of cypress trunks, a set of bowed plank steps leading up to a high porch that bristled with the antlers of perhaps three dozen whitetail bucks. They were nailed to the wall beneath the gabled roof as densely as the clapboard wall could accommodate them, from twelve-pointers down to spikes, so that the front of the old building looked to his sleep-clouded eyes like either a wall of outsized thorns or the many-tined skeleton of a prehistoric beast.

"Hallo there, master!" a voice called. "Good day, sir!"

The greeting was robust, but when Johnston's eyes separated the man who issued it from the shadowy space beneath the lodge, the greeter seemed markedly less than glad for the company. A slave nearly six feet tall stepped from the shadows, wiping a blood-smeared knife on his trouser leg. Behind him hung the carcass of a fat doe hamstrung on two hooks fixed to the lodge floor above. He slipped the knife into his pocket and shrugged his shoulders. Johnston smiled.

"Ah, me. I am not so lost as I feared I might be. If I know my man, you are Drake's Cudjo, head huntsman of Windsor and guide extraordinaire. Am I mistaken?"

"No, sir."

"And that fine specimen of venison behind you would be one of your master's prime herd, taken—let me think—a good two weeks before Windsor's season begins. Again, am I mistaken?"

"Again, sir, you ain't."

Johnston slipped down from the phaeton seat like a man ten years younger. "Cudjo, you are still a boy with appetites beyond the limits of his master's beneficence. But I must say I am pleased to see you nonetheless." He stepped to the carcass and felt of it, glanced into the tub set below to catch the entrails. "Still warm, Cudjo."

"Yes, sir. She was a pretty thing."

"I'd guess her weight at a hundred and twenty."

"No more than hundred, hundred and ten, master, this back say. I can't lie, Doctor Johnston. She was a pitiful sight, caught up in the worm fence a half mile down the river. When I saw her neck was nearly broke, there weren't much else to do."

Johnston held up a hand. "You may as well save that for Mister Drake. Carry on," he said, and sat down on a section of log. He had always held Cudjo's skill at dressing deer in the highest esteem and had watched him each year cleaning the gentlemen's kills with a regard bordering on envy. Put him in another country, perhaps in another era, Johnston would tell his friends over their evening whiskeys, and Cudjo could have stood with the most senior of Johns Hopkins surgeons in an operating theater. Not in this country, they would say, laughing, and sure as hell not in my era.

After a moment of Cudjo's shuffling, the knife reappeared and continued slicing against the hide, shearing it from the crimson muscle as precisely and smoothly as though it were working through butter rather than tissue. As he had always done—and as none of the other skinners bothered to attempt—Cudjo cut the fat from the muscle as he went, long ribbons of the pearl-like material falling to the tub in gossamer sheets. Johnston realized that the slave had been talking for several moments as he worked, his voice as raspy as the blade on the hide, hints of Senegal in the cadences and lilt of his words.

"Shame, shame about him. Say it ain't getting but worse. Say he ain't left the house in a week."

"Drake? Drake will be better on the morrow, I assure you. There will be adjustments, to be sure. Perhaps no hunting for him this season."

"Say they had to open the windows on his study, even with the mosquitoes so bad, on account of the smell."

"That is the nature of gangrene."

"He going to lose the foot?"

"Impossible to say without a proper diagnosis, of course. It's likely. Say, may I take a look at your knife there?"

Cudjo halted his methodical work and wiped the blade on his trousers before handing it over heel-first.

"Extraordinary," Johnston said, balancing the blade across his fingers. "What manner of knife is this? The heft is nearly perfect." He scraped the blade against his forearm and sheared more hair than he had intended.

Cudjo chuckled, the sound like wind in corn husks. "Ain't nothing but an old butter knife, sir. Took the emery wheel to it. See, your old hunting knife got too much shaft to it, don't bend. Butter knife'll ground down thin, so she'll bend. Little flex in the blade makes the cutting easier."

Like a scalpel, Johnston thought. But with an extra three inches of cutting edge and a tang strong enough for it to double as a tendon blade. He handed it back to Cudjo and nodded toward the deer. "You're nearly finished here, are you not?"

"Yes, sir. She just ready for the smokehouse now."

"Well, put her in, then. I will wait for you in the phaeton."

Cudjo stared at the doctor blankly. "You aim to turn me in?"

Johnston turned on his heel. "I've never answered questions put to me by a slave, Cudjo, and don't intend to begin now." He stopped a few steps short of the carriage. "You can handle a two-in-hand, can't you?"

The slave had the doe over his shoulder, but he turned to face Johnston before he spoke. "I can, sir, and a four-in-hand just as well."

"Very well. Put the venison in the smokehouse and then you shall drive me to Windsor, where no person shall be turned in for alleged deeds I did not witness." Johnston climbed into the phaeton's passenger seat and shut the little door. "And Cudjo, make sure to bring that knife of yours."

"Yes, sir!" the slave said, moving more briskly now.

"We shall retrieve the venison on our way out of the parish this evening," Johnston said, though he knew that Cudjo, enveloped in the smoldering smokehouse now, was beyond the range of his voice.

DRAKE'S LIBRARY AT Windsor was paneled in English walnut, wood imported on the same ship that had brought the pewter chandelier hanging above the shelves of leather-bound classics that reached to the twelve-foot ceilings. Johnston noted that the books were ordered in the meticulous manner of an owner who never bothered to read them. Drake, he knew, was not a man for poetry or essays—not a man for books of any kind, in fact, that were not ledgers or accounts; he had probably never delved further into his library than to glance at the engraved frontispiece of Scott's *Ivanhoe*. These books, like the library itself, were but part of the grand image of the planter-scholar so beloved in the low country—a creature as rare in Johnston's experience as the fabled albino alligator of the Waccamaw Swamp.

Whatever kind of man Drake was or purported to be, he

was at present a man in considerable discomfort. His face was drawn, his eyes hollowed, his neckerchief soaked with the acrid sweat of sickness. He sat in a leather armchair by the fireplace, a half-empty decanter of bourbon beside him and a glass in his hand. Propped on an ottoman in front of him was the gangrenous left foot. A blind man could have located it by the olfactory sense alone, Johnston thought. It was well that Drake had not waited another day to send for him. The big toe had already swollen and blackened around the raw cut. It turned a bruised green at its root, then shaded into yellow at the sole, with crimson runners of infection stretching across the arch of the foot. Drake's houseman, Caesar, stood behind the chair, slowly fanning the air with a palmetto branch. He looked rather green himself.

"Don't get up, Robert," Johnston said with a faint smile as he set his bag on the floor.

"Goddamn it, you know I couldn't if I wanted to. I can't bear to put any weight on it. Every time Caesar gets close to it, I flinch. I can feel the air on it, Johnston, like a pressure."

Johnston traced the tip of his finger down the arch of the foot. Drake groaned and sipped from his glass.

"We will attend to it this morning. Caesar, all the windows shut directly, if you please. It will not do to operate with the swamp miasma permeating the room."

At the mention of operation, Drake motioned for more whiskey. Caesar filled his glass and began lowering the windows in their casements.

"You mentioned a fox trap in your telegraph," Johnston said. "I'm grateful it did not catch you at the ankle."

"That goddamned Cudjo has set them out all over the place. It would have caught me, by God, but I was just dismounting when it sprang. He sets them with a hair trigger."

"A most enterprising boy, he is. I met him on the road."

Drake grunted. "That figures. His task this morning was to go down by the shore to see to the crab traps. Never where he should be. Look for him south, he's north. Look east, and he's west."

"He is what the hands call a stray nigger, sir," Caesar said.

"Be that as it may, he is in the yard now. I suppose I rounded him up for you. Caesar, help me move your master to his desk, will you? We will arrange him facedown."

Caesar stepped forward and hooked his hands under Drake's shoulders. Johnston took the legs as gingerly as he could.

"Bring that whiskey with me," Drake said.

Before they could lay Drake out to Johnston's satisfaction, the lord of the manor had downed another glass of bourbon. He lay breathing heavily as Johnston took his materials out of the leather bag, careful to array the scalpels, saw, and glass cups on the desk out of Drake's vision. Frowning, Johnston chipped at a smear of dried blood on a scalpel blade with his thumbnail.

"Should we bother with unbuttoning your shirt, Robert? Or would you prefer that I cut it?"

"Cut it down the back, damn it. I'm not moving another inch." He held out the empty glass. "Caesar, again."

"And Caesar, a tallow, after you've replenished Mister Drake."

Johnston sliced at the broadside cotton while Caesar poured. When Caesar came around the desk with a candle, Johnston handed him a bell-shaped glass cup slightly larger than a shot glass.

"A delicate thing, isn't it? And in and of itself hardly an impressive apparatus. But one of the cornerstones of modern medicine, nonetheless. I will place them on Mister Drake's back, two at a time. You will hold them in place while I administer heat with the candle." Caesar looked at him with horror. But Johnston, disciple of Benjamin Rush, would go to his grave convinced of the salubrious effect of blistering and bloodletting. It was inconceivable to essay surgery without this preparatory treatment to draw out the infection. "You are capable of that small task, are you not?"

"I will endeavor my best, sir," Caesar said.

"Excellent." Johnston set two cups on Drake's white back below each shoulder blade. "Hold them by the rim, fast to the skin. Do not lift them until I say so. Take another drink, Robert."

While Drake gulped the whiskey, Johnston bent the candle to the peak of the first glass cup, one hand spread out beneath it to catch dripping wax. After thirty seconds, Drake began to groan as the flesh beneath the glass reddened. When the skin began to rise Johnston moved the candle to the other cup. Wax dripped on his palm and he blew at it. When the skin once more rose into a welt, he set the tallow aside and pulled his watch from its vest pocket. The second hand completed three quarters of its circuit and he nodded to Caesar, who removed the cups and set them on the desk blotter abruptly, one of them nearly rolling off to the floor. On Drake's back now were two perfect circles, each the size of a silver dollar. The red flesh seemed to glow angrily above his twitching muscles.

"Excellent," Johnston said with satisfaction. "Two more and we are done."

Caesar cleared his throat. "I don't believe I'll be able to assist you again, sir."

"That's my good man, Caesar," Drake said. His speech was beginning to slur. He waved the glass over his shoulder and murmured, "Pour."

Johnston looked at Caesar coldly. A glance revealed the butler had lost what little stomach he may have had before. The close air of the room seemed to be affecting him.

"I cannot perform the surgery without aid. Caesar, since you are unable to provide assistance beyond libation, step outside and send in that Cudjo. The fresh air may renew your vigor."

"Cudjo!" Drake spat. "Do you mean to kill me, man?"

"You know my opinion of his abilities, Robert. He is quite adept."

"At skinning a fucking deer! I'll not have him in here at my back with a knife, by God."

"He will only assist, Robert, nothing more." Johnston nodded at Caesar, indicating the foyer. "Would you like some laudanum?"

Despite his pain, Drake nearly turned over on the desk. "You've had laudanum all this time? Blistering my back with nothing but whiskey, and you've had laudanum?"

"I can only give you ten grains. I intended to conserve it until the moment of greatest need."

"I am in great need, I assure you."

Johnston took a pewter tin and a pack of papers out of his bag. He shook the tin over one of the papers, much as he would salt a delicacy, and handed the paper to Drake. "Under the nose, Robert. Sniff it vigorously."

Drake needed little encouragement. He snorted the powder, sniffled twice, and sipped from his glass. "All you doctors, God. I never send for you if I can help it, because things always get worse after you arrive."

"Surgery without pain is a chimera, Robert," Johnston said as he set two more cups on Drake's lower back.

"Surgery is just shit, I say."

"You'll be at greater ease presently," Johnston said as Caesar and Cudjo entered, the former ushering his taller and darker companion into the room with a sardonic flourish.

"Hold these cups where they are, Cudjo, firmly. I will attempt to move at greater haste." Cudjo took his place as Drake muttered. Johnston set to work with the candle again, Cudjo watching intently as the skin puckered and reddened. As he touched the flame to the last cup, Johnston looked at Cudjo appraisingly. "Doing all right?"

"Capital, sir," he said, his lips thinning into a smile.

"Robert, feeling pain?"

Drake said only, "Oh, mammy."

"Fine, then. We will remove the foot with dispatch, at the ankle. Cudjo, take firm hold of the heel and toes. Hold them fast."

"Mammy, mammy," Drake said, the words rising to a falsetto singsong as the slave grasped his foot.

Johnston picked a scalpel from the small array on the desk. At the first incision, low on the Achilles tendon, blood spurted onto his shirtfront, crimson on the starched white. He worked the blade around and under, to the front of the foot, then rose again to complete the circle. Arterial blood shot into his eye and he paused to wipe his face with a handkerchief. At the corner of his vision he saw Caesar stumbling out of the room.

"Your knife, Cudjo."

"Sir?"

"Your blade, quickly." He snapped his fingers.

Cudjo loosened his hold on the rapidly blanching foot and produced the knife. Johnston set to with it on the remaining ligaments, cutting each with a precise nick of the blade, realizing that this humble tool would speed his already efficient amputation regimen—a point of considerable pride—by as much as ten seconds.

"Bone saw," he said.

He was pleased to feel the slave set the saw into his outstretched palm without further prompting. He made six vigorous passes, the saw blade first grinding, then singing as it picked up speed, and the foot came off in Cudjo's hands. Johnston retrieved his needle and sutures himself, selecting a number-four catgut. Three minutes later the arteries were closed and the stump swaddled in the remains of Drake's shirt. Johnston and Cudjo carried the semiconscious Drake back to the armchair. Johnston propped the foot up with two volumes of Ralph Waldo Emerson, watching the spread of the bloodstain on the bandage. After a moment he added Emerson's *English Traits* to the stack, then, convinced the elevation was suitable to stanch the blood flow, sat down himself.

"Cudjo, be a good man and bring me a glass of whiskey. Ask in the kitchen for rags to clean up this room." He sighed as Cudjo handed him an amber glass. He hoped the day's roughest work was now behind him.

AN HOUR LATER, the room cleared of the operating debris, which Cudjo had carried out in a single bloody bundle, Drake showed signs of reviving. His mood was uplifted considerably after a second dose of laudanum, which caused him to giggle intermittently as Johnston collected his equipment.

"How much of that dope do you carry with you on a call, Johnston? I would like to procure a bit more of it. You can roll the cost into your fee."

Johnston smiled. "I've left four more powders here on your desk, Robert. One dose every six hours for the next day, then back to the whiskey as you need it."

"All right, then," Drake said, and giggled. "Oh, mammy."

"As to the fee, there is none. How could I bill the man who has been my host for so many memorable hunting seasons?" Johnston snapped his bag shut. "I would, however, like to engage you in a business transaction."

The host stopped giggling. "What business?"

"Cudjo. I would like to purchase him for the medical school."

"What in hell for?"

Johnston looked out the window. "As a valet. A butler and custodian. The faculty needs a man. I'm prepared to offer you a promissory note, drawn on the Bank of Columbia, for eight hundred dollars."

Drake bellowed with laughter. "A business transaction, indeed! You're no businessman, Johnston. That nigger's run off six times in four years. Eight hundred dollars! I'll be glad just to get shut of him." He wiped his eyes. "Cudjo's half wild. Those Senegalese never tame. I'd have let him go at six hundred."

"Six hundred, then. As men of honor."

Drake's eyebrows narrowed. "Seven hundred. Seven hundred and you leave me a bit more of that dope. My foot is killing me."

CUDJO RECEIVED HIS initial anatomy lesson under moonlight, in the open air of the phaeton as he guided it to Columbia, urging the horses over roads winding farther north than he had ever ventured. The carcass of the doe lay splayed

44

between him and Johnston in the rear seat, skinned naked in the starry night air. They had retrieved it at the doctor's urging from the hunting lodge smokehouse that afternoon, while the news of Cudjo's sale still hung over the slave like a fog of ambivalence; he was delivered from Drake and the malarial heat of Windsor, but to what new fate? As Johnston strolled along the bank of the Waccamaw, seeming delighted that his transaction had proceeded so smoothly, Cudjo had gathered up his scant belongings from beneath the lodge. It was short work. He had loaded the doe into the phaeton and trundled it to the river while the doctor still mused, looking down into the tea-colored waters, the slave having said his last goodbye to Windsor and All Saints Parish.

But now, near midnight, they were approaching the outskirts of Columbia, well into the foreign elevations of the South Carolina Midlands. As they crossed the wooden bridge over the Congaree River, Cudjo looked over his shoulder, trying to follow the tics of Johnston's riding crop as it pointed out the musculature of the doe's carcass. Johnston had said that one mammal could substitute as well as another for an extempore general lecture and was now making good on the claim. While the wheels lumbered over the last bridge planks, the tip of the crop stopped once more, hovering over the base of the doe's spine.

"Recapitulation now, Cudjo. This is?"

"That's the loin."

"No. *Gluteus maximus.*" The crop rose as though to indicate the heavens above. "Sound it out."

Cudjo repeated the Latin slowly. The crop rose and fell with each syllable, then dropped back to the doe.

"Much better. And this?"

"Flexor."

"Very good. *Flexor longus digitorum*. And here?"

"Semitendinosus."

"Excellent." Johnston smiled, his teeth gleaming in the moonlight like the bone nubbins of the doe's severed limbs. "You are a most extraordinary Negro. I cannot help but feel I've made a bargain today. Seven hundred dollars for a man of your capabilities and a month's worth of venison thrown into the bargain—whether Drake knew of the deer or not," he added, as though troubled by his conscience on the matter of the doe. He fell silent for a while.

Cudjo had lapsed into a doze when the crop prodded him gently on the shoulder.

"Say, Cudjo. I've been thinking that Cudjo is no name for an adjunct to the faculty of the Carolina School of Medicine and Physic. We need something with a bit more élan."

The slave seemed to pause thoughtfully before he spoke. "Cudjo always been all right with me."

"Fine, but Cudjo is a name fit for an animal, not for a person of some stature."

"Cudjo is African," he said quietly.

Johnston seemed not to have heard. "How about something biblical? We need something with a few syllables to it. Solomon? Nebuchadnezzar. No, too grandiose. Simeon is plain, but it would do. Saul. Theophilus. Both are good, though I am inclined toward Theophilus."

The slave's shoulders seemed to have drooped as Johnston ran through his catalogue. So low that his voice could barely be heard, he said a single word: "Nemo."

"Nemo? You know Latin, then? Nemo means 'no man.' Can you read Latin?"

"Slave can't read."

"I asked if *you* can read."

"I reads a little, when I can."

"Excellent. That will be one less thing to teach you. Nemo, then? Why not? Fair enough. You should have some say in the matter. Nemo it is, and will be from the moment I introduce you to your new masters in Columbia."

Why not, indeed, the slave thought as the phaeton rumbled toward its destination and his new home. After it all, after his faint memories of Africa and the black pirate ships, one transfer of ownership to another, from Senegal to South Carolina—why not "No Man"? In his homeland, the matter of a name could incite a fight to the death. But he was not there now, and had not been for decades. If not only his body and soul but his very name was at the behest of other men, why not become No Man?

After this long day, begun on the soft banks of the Waccamaw and set to end in a strange place, he saw no point in resisting it. Today he had in fact felt the tug of becoming no man at all. Yet he had countered it, and thus had another reason to be drawn to a new name. There at the lodge, with the doctor down by the river, he had made a gesture of protest. He figured his ties to Windsor were cut permanently now, unless Drake came looking for him—after the hunting season had begun, after the guests began to arrive at the lodge for the annual pursuit of big game. It was a ritual farewell in the African style, a last missive. With a rock and a tenpenny nail, Cudjo had pounded Robert Drake's severed left foot into the front wall of the lodge. There, among the antlers, it would drip off its flesh and bleach white in the autumn sun like the other bones—one more trophy, one more memento of conquest.

Nemo: it was a name that could serve its owner well. No man could be a good man to be indeed.

Tuesday

THE DISSECTING LAB IS IN THE Chapel Clinic, but as if in a nod to the bygone days when human dissection was frowned upon by church and state alike, even this postmodern building of oblique angles and mirrored glass has placed it in the basement. Even in the twilight years of the twentieth century, it wouldn't do to have sidewalk-level windows looking in on a room where such work is done.

Jacob takes the steps down two at a time, trading the morning sunlight outside for the sterile gloom of fluorescent light on tile. He is still smarting from the Internal Review Board meeting that just adjourned and is anxious to see the friendly face of Adam Claybaugh. Despite the grim nature of his vocation—and his rank as an endowed professor—Adam has always been among the most accessible of the faculty, a living rebuke to the stereotypical notion of the anatomy professor as a vaguely cadaverous old soul. Adam is a triathlete, robust and brimming with energy, as likely as not to appear for a lecture in running shorts, fresh from another of his quick eight-mile runs. Jacob remembers him from his own tenure in the anatomy lab as an apt mentor, a sharp contrast to his subjects—both the cadavers themselves and the pasty-faced first-years charged with taking them apart.

He finds him now seated behind the large desk at one end of the dissecting room, eating a salad. Before him lie the two dozen cadavers that will greet the first-years tomorrow, each covered with a white sheet but still exuding its strange bouquet of preservation and rot. At their feet Adam has set out the dissecting kits in their familiar brown plastic boxes, perched atop the copies of *Grant's Dissector*. Tomorrow morning the sheets will be pulled back and the students will set to work on the back muscles, allowing them in the time-honored ritual to make their first cuts before turning the cadavers over to reveal the dead faces. For today, however, the dead bide the time patiently, like a silent cast awaiting the first act. Their dreadful muteness Jacob learned to abide, but the smell still galls him, invading the nostrils and creeping down into the lungs, like an affront to the living.

Adam's voice booms down the long room. "Young apprentice!" he shouts as Jacob walks past the rows of bodies. "Is it homecoming week already?" He rises and stretches out a hand. "Jake, it's been too long."

Jacob can feel his bones grinding under the handshake. "Go

ahead and finish your lunch, Adam. How you can eat down here is beyond me."

Adam shrugs. "Used to it. But I'm about to make forty-odd vegetarians out of the incoming class. Until the new year, anyway."

Jacob pulls up a chair and looks out over the still forms. "When I finished gross I swore I'd never darken your door again."

"You ought to come back now and then," Adam says through a mouthful of bean sprouts. "Get your bearings reoriented."

"It's not the kind of place you return to for sentimental reasons. Every doctor's idea of the worst patient is a Goner. The patients down here are Confirmed Goners."

"Way Goners. I know all the jokes. But damn, Jacob, the dead are the key to the living. I'm always having to preach that, over and over." Adam's voice, as always, alternates between enthusiasm and reverence, the only tones in which he speaks of the dead. "You get into practice for a few years and tend to forget it. Or, say, get swallowed up in the administration."

"Oh, boy, don't start. I'll be back in practice in a year, I hope."

Adam looks at him thoughtfully. "You got a raw deal, Jake. I'm sorry about it."

"What the hell. Probation's two years, then I'm clear."

"I'll be glad to see you out of Johnston Hall. You're probably the only one left over there with a soul."

Jacob can't argue this, and for a full minute there is only the sound of Adam chewing lettuce. He pokes a fork at his salad. "I saw Lorenzo down at the Iron Horse last night. Hear you've got some bones in the basement."

Jacob sighs. "I hope Lorenzo doesn't talk himself out of a job. But yeah, a bunch of them. I'm hoping you can come take a look. The crew that found them wants us to call the coroner."

Adam smiles. "McTeague? He's a moron."

"A moron who likes his picture in the papers."

"And you don't want the papers in on this."

"Hell, no."

"Why not?" Adam leans back in his chair. "It's the school's dirty little secret. We ought to come clean."

"Are you crazy? We're in the middle of a capital campaign, Adam. It'll send our donors flying."

Adam waves a hand toward the bodies arrayed down the long room. "These are the only donors that count."

"I'm not going to argue abstractions with you, Adam. These guys are crucial, yes, but they don't pay our salaries." In spite of himself, Jacob has allowed his voice to rise. "It's not pure, I know it, but it's necessary. PR is the dirty work that keeps the machine running."

Adam sets his fork down and takes a paper bag out of a desk drawer. He pulls a plum from it and offers it to Jacob. Jacob shakes his head. Adam takes a bite from the plum and looks at Jake for a long moment as he chews slowly. "All right, Jake. I'll help you with your dirty work. I've already got an idea of what's down there, though. You know the full history of our august institution?"

Again Jacob shakes his head. "Some of it. I heard about it all through school. Everybody did. I figured it was just rumors, like a ghost story." There had always been folklore concerning medical students and cadavers and always would be; the morbid symbiosis was as old as the profession itself, a way to maintain the precarious balance between the ghoulishness of anatomy and the higher purpose it served. Five or six years ago, a pair of anatomy students had dressed their cadaver in a suit and sunglasses and left him propped up, sitting, in the waiting area of the emergency room. Tad Bowling and his partner, Jacob remembers. They'd been expelled that very day. But they had all laughed, the students. There was a weird callousness about it, the way you had to set the boundaries between yourself and your cadaver—as though it weren't human anymore. How else could you pop the pelvis like a wishbone, split the nose, saw the jaw off a fellow human being? He remembers, though, that until this week the basement door of Johnston Hall has always been padlocked.

"No rumors, no ghost story. The dissecting room was in the current registrar's office until the turn of the century. I figure when they finished with the bodies for the course, they just took them downstairs and buried them. Quietly. Public perception, you know."

Jacob ignores the jab. "Not too bad, so far."

"No. If that was all, you could call the coroner yourself. But from what I've heard, they were all black. The cadavers. Deceased slaves before the war and freedmen during Reconstruction. Not good enough to be seen as patients but fine for anatomy subjects."

Jacob thinks of the old photograph in his office. The dark face in the back flashes in his mind, featureless.

"You're sitting on a powder keg over there. Have been for more than a century." Adam stands up and stretches, his massive biceps bunching under the sleeves of his T-shirt. "Yeah, I'll help you with your dirty work, Doctor Thacker. But first I want you to help me with a little of mine."

THE HOLDING TANK is a giant cylinder of polished stainless steel, and Jacob and Adam have to climb a set of perforated metal stairs on its circumference to reach the top. This room is off-limits to the medical students, and for good reason: as shocking as the sight of dozens of dead bodies in the dissecting lab might be for the new student, seeing them afloat in a thousand gallons of formaldehyde would be worse.

A week before, this tank was full of the naked bodies, floating vertically in the preservative and crowded close on one another. Now that Adam has set most of them out for the incoming class, their ranks are thinned. A few leftovers are all that remain, their scalps just showing above the surface. Their hair is cropped close to the skull when they are processed, so the tank reveals a half-dozen crew-cut scalps poking from the viscous liquid, most of them gray-stubbled, bobbing in the formaldehyde like a new genus of bad apples. "Players," they had called them back in school, Jacob remembers.

"I'm looking for the thin female," Adam says. "Should be the best demonstrator I've had in years. Beautiful musculature." He takes a last bite from the plum as he manipulates the grapple over the tank like the grab-a-toy game at a fairground. Jacob winces as its tines close around a head. A body comes up out of the liquid, its face set in a grimace and streaming formaldehyde, and Adam lowers it back gently. "Wrong one."

Jacob looks toward the ceiling. "Meant to tell you I met with your former colleague this morning."

"Washburn?"

"The one. He's a son of a bitch. Black-market organ sales? I could hardly believe it."

"He was a bad hire. Never had a proper respect."

"He'd have taken the school down with him if he could."

Adam settles the grapple over a head and lowers it onto the dome of the skull. "Yep. That's why I turned him in."

Jacob is stunned by this admission—the whistleblower rules allow for complete anonymity—but is glad that Adam feels he can confide in him.

"There she is." The cadaver is younger than Jacob expected; small wonder that Adam has given her his top spot for the fall semester. Beyond her prunish hands and the sullen droop of her breasts, she appears to have been a woman in vigorous middle age.

"I think I'll call her Beatrice. Does she look like a Beatrice to you? It seems fitting."

"It is. We named our man Henry. Not very imaginative, I know. I used to have dreams of old naked Henry climbing off the table and chasing me with a scalpel."

"Yep, the revenge nightmare. There's the old guilt. Grab a pair of gloves and help me get her on the gurney, will you?"

Jacob steps down the stairs, pulls two latex gloves from a box on the wall, and tugs them on as he waits by the gurney. Adam lowers Beatrice to him, the body revolving slowly with the grapple, still dripping formaldehyde, in a slow-motion pirouette.

"Put her facedown, Jake."

Jacob takes hold of the ankles and tugs on the legs until the toes are aligned near the foot of the gurney. Adam lowers the head and Beatrice's body meets the metal slab an inch at a time, knees to chest.

"Grab the head, please, so I don't drop her on the face." He does as he is told, careful to keep his shirtsleeves clear of the grapple's tines. He can feel Beatrice's short hair bristling under the latex. As the grapple rises again he turns the head to lay the face on its side. Beatrice's watery brown eyes are open, looking through him.

Adam springs down the steps and pushes the gurney out into the lab. Jacob almost has to trot to keep up. "Want to try your hand again?" Adam says over his shoulder. "See if you've still got it?"

Jacob is beginning to remember that a little of Adam's eccentricity goes a long way. He is ready to get out of this basement. Whether Adam cares to acknowledge it or not, the world moves at a different pace aboveground. "I've got a crisis brewing, Adam. Don't have the time."

"Ah, time. I'm disappointed, young apprentice. You've forgotten the great philosophical lesson of the anatomy lab. Time is *all* you have. Take a look around. If this isn't a sight to keep time in the proper context, I don't know what is. These people are out of time. You have plenty." He brandishes a scalpel at Jacob. "First step is the incision," he says, handing it over. "Proceed."

With a sigh, Jacob takes the scalpel and leans close to the back. But not too close; he remembers well the hazard of cadaver juice spurting into a mouth or an eye. He makes three long incisions through the skin, as if to carve the partial outline of a box on Beatrice's back. The cuts are bloodless. This is the first time in years he has even thought to make a cut without a hemostat and gauze at hand. But God, the feel of the scalpel in his hand.

"Step two: reflect the skin from the posterior musculature."

"Is a buttonhole okay?"

"Absolutely."

He carves a quarter-sized hole in the skin below the neck and pushes it through. With a finger through the flesh, he joins forefinger and thumb and pulls the skin away as though drawing down a very reluctant window shade. The tissue parts with a wet sucking sound. Beatrice's musculature is indeed remarkable. The latissimus dorsi are well formed and even, looking under this exposure like a pair of wings spanning the shoulder blades. He pulls until the flesh is stripped away down to the end of the incisions and lays it over the buttocks, the flap of skin draped over Beatrice's posterior like a miniskirt.

"Well done," Adam says. "Your half of our barter is completed. Glad to see you've still got a light touch." He picks up a ketchup bottle from his desk and sprinkles phenoxyethanol on the corpse before covering her with a sheet. He tucks the corners in under the shoulders almost tenderly.

"Great. When can you come?"

"No time like the present."

Jacob knows he should acknowledge the lesson from his old teacher. "Thank you for making the time."

"Not a problem. What have I got to lose by changing my day? Flexibility's the key to life, Jacob. It's why I'm such a happy fucking camper."

NOONTIME RUSH IS in full swing at the Hub. Waitresses jostle their way through throngs of doctors and lawyers and politicians who have crowded into the narrow alley-shaped café during the hour-long break from clinic, court, and legislature. With the combination of its prime downtown location and its venerable meat-and-three menu, the Hub has been a Columbia institution since the fifties. And it looks it: the paneled walls are covered with the autographed photos of governors and football coaches, its acoustic tile ceiling sooted dark brown from the exhaust of forty years of deep-fried lunches. Jacob has arrived in time to secure a coveted booth underneath the scowling face of Joe Morrison, who had written in black marker on his photo, "Best meatloaf in Dixie." Above Coach Morrison, the ceiling fan spins lazily enough for Jacob to study the quarter inch of dust accumulated on each of its blades.

The cowbell over the front door clangs again and Jacob looks up to see McMichaels making his way in, pausing at every table to exchange a handshake and a few words, stopping longest at those tables where legislators sit huddled and cabalistic. When he finally slides into the booth across from Jacob, he is still nodding and smiling at diners across the room. A waitress appears at the table instantly, although Jacob has been there for nearly ten minutes without so much as a nod from the waitstaff.

"Afternoon, dean," she says as she spreads paper napkins and beat-up silver on the Formica tabletop. "Tuesday special is country-fried steak."

"With gravy?"

"If you want it."

"I do, June," he says, and takes a long look at her. "When are you going to run away with me, June-bug?"

June only rolls her eyes. Jacob gives her his order, including fried okra at the dean's insistence. Once she is gone, he leans closer to the dean, though the din in the Hub probably makes it unnecessary.

"We've got a situation," he says.

"No, we don't," the dean says, spreading a napkin in his lap. "I sent Jake Thacker in to handle it, and I know it got handled right. I'd bet good money that Internal Review Board meeting went off without a hitch. Washburn signed those resignation papers, I know, Jake, because I sent the right man to do the job."

"He signed the papers."

Now McMichaels leans over the table, grinning. "I hope you roasted him a little."

Jacob would like to tell him so, but it had been Washburn, imperious as ever, who had very nearly done the roasting. Even with the entire Internal Review Board ringed around him at the closed meeting—and Kirstin Reithoffer chairing the proceedings in her stern Austrian manner—Washburn had refused to buckle until the very end. From the outset he had challenged Jacob's presence, snorting when Jacob said he was there in an advisory role.

"I don't see how you have any advice worth contributing," Washburn said. "The rest of us here, you will note, are *scientists*."

"Doctor Washburn, you are a scientist who has been found selling cadaver organs to research interests for personal profit. Whatever title you claim, the man in the street—the taxpayer— would call that graft and corruption. Even those of us who fall short of scientific status can see the serious breach of medical ethics you've committed. The dean sent me here to see that you don't wind up in legal custody and disgrace the school any further."

"Disgrace," Washburn spat. "You speak of disgrace, with your record."

Jacob had been rising before he realized it, but felt the cool hand of Kirstin Reithoffer on his chest. Reithoffer had taken over then, and within a half hour Washburn had signed the confidentiality papers that severed all his ties to the Medical College of South Carolina, banished to a future in chiropractic science for all Jacob cared.

The dean is still looking at Jacob expectantly. "He got a little of what he's due," Jacob says. "We took his lab keys and sent him packing."

June is back now with sweet tea and their lunch, everything balanced precariously on her suntanned arms. The dean thanks her and digs in.

"You did the right thing, Jake. Remember, I'm a holistic man. Got to maintain the health of the entire organism. If a part is bringing down the whole, away it goes." He holds a speared piece of fried okra aloft on his fork, regarding it as though it were a rare diamond. "Trans fats. They'll kill you quick, but damn, it's worth the trip, isn't it?"

"Right. But Washburn's not the situation I mean. Bowman's crew found bones in the cellar yesterday."

"Medical waste, sure. It's an old building."

"More than waste. Bones. They're human. Adam Claybaugh and I took a quick look this morning. Most of them show signs of dissection. We found a skull with a trepanation in it."

"How many of them?"

"Can't say yet. Some are still partly buried, but Adam thinks maybe remains of forty or more. We found an infant still mostly intact. Pickled in an old whiskey barrel."

McMichaels seems to have lost his appetite. "Why didn't you tell me this yesterday?"

"Couldn't get past your entourage."

"You tried the house?"

"Twice. Two messages."

"Ah. The help." McMichaels waves a hand in the air as though swatting at something. "God, God," he says. "We'll have to keep a very tight lid on this."

Jacob forks a piece of baked catfish into his mouth. Baked, the menu claims, but it is swimming in butter. "We will. There were three on the crew. I know one of them. I'll talk to him. Bowman's too dumb to think much about it so long as he's billing us by the hour."

"Good. Put them all to work on something else—painting, whatever. Keep Bowman happy and don't miss a payday."

"Jim, did you know about the basement?"

McMichaels mops at the splatter of gravy on his plate with a roll. "Back in the day, we used to sneak down there at night in the fall. Halloween. A little hazing ritual, back before the school was coed. Harmless kid stuff, letting off steam. But I saw some of it, yes, and I should have had it taken care of before we called in the physical plant." The dean's eyes have gone distant. "For fuck's sake, Jacob, why were they *digging* down there?"

McMichaels takes another bite of steak and pushes his plate

away. "It would be a shame if this came out. We've done so much good work, so much. People wouldn't understand. Those were good men, Jacob, no matter how that basement may have looked to you today."

"It didn't look too much different from Washburn to me."

"You're wrong about that. Standards were different then."

Jacob shrugs. He knows that the public would not see the distinction. Anyway, the dean is rising to leave.

"What about the bones?"

McMichaels rests a big hand on Jacob's shoulder. "I need you to take care of it for me. We need for it to go away."

Slowly, Jacob nods. The hand pats his shoulder. "I'm behind you a hundred percent."

Then he is gone, making his way toward the door, stopping again at tables occupied now by recently arrived customers. Before McMichaels has made it out the door, Jacob realizes he has left him with the check. When June shows up again, he slides his corporate AmEx card across the table.

June shakes her head. "Don't take credit cards, honey."

OUTSIDE THE HUB, Jacob pauses on the sidewalk, the tinny sound of the restaurant's cowbell echoing in his ears. The day is humid but otherwise clear, and the scorching concrete of the sidewalk throws back the sunlight as brightly as bleached bone. He checks his watch and decides to squeeze in an hour at the school's archives.

He can feel the sweat threatening to soak through the armpits of his coat by the time he rounds the corner onto Pendleton Street and his destination comes into view. Beaupre Hall, despite its august name, is an ugly bunkerlike building that looks squat even at its height of four stories, a nightmare of poured concrete built in 1966—a low point from Columbia's architectural dark ages. So long as its air conditioning is blowing full-steam, though, he will register no complaint.

He takes the elevator to the top floor, fanning himself with his portfolio as the elevator climbs. The doors open to the mortuary hush of the archives, and he steps out onto the deep carpet directly in front of the curator, Janice Tanaka, whose desk faces the elevator doors as though in preparation for an attack from those quarters. She looks over the top of her glasses and her eyes seem to narrow when she recognizes Jacob.

It has been nearly a year since Jacob was last on this floor. Just before McMichaels kicked off the capital campaign, he charged Jacob with putting together a photographic retrospective of the school's physical plant through the ages. Because McMichaels would not be satisfied with photocopied images from the school history book, Jacob had had to spend a long weekend here arranging photographic duplications of the original materials. He'd realized early in the weekend that Janice Tanaka was like a terrier over forms and paperwork; he'd left the building late Sunday night reeling from her intensive supervision—as if not only the school's documentary past but its very history were solely her domain.

After a second's hesitation, Janice's face relaxes from its wary expression and she rises to greet him, a full foot shorter than Jacob, which always inclines him to stoop when they shake hands. He remembers the story that Janice's father enlisted in the U.S. Army just prior to World War II (good timing, he has always thought) and ended up stationed at Fort Jackson, fifteen miles east of the university, where Janice was born. Janice is as American as he is, but he can never help feeling that there is some reserve of samurai in her, some native allegiance passed down in the genes, that views him as the foreigner every time they meet. And now that he has once again broached her kingdom, he supposes it is so in some way.

"Hello, Janice." He speaks too loudly; his voice booms out in the quiet room like a football booster's at a tailgate party.

"Doctor Thacker," she says quietly, precisely. "How may I help you?"

Jacob's voice is lower when he speaks again. "I need some information on the administration building's history."

Janice looks almost chastened. "Were the photographs not satisfactory?"

"Oh yes, fantastic. What I'm looking for now is a little less public-oriented," he says, thinking, *Interior stuff. Subterranean, even.* "This is sensitive, Janice. I'll have to ask for your discretion on this. I'm trying to find out some background on anatomy instruction in the building. Dissection. How it was done back in the day."

Jacob thinks he can almost see her eyes, behind the glasses, beginning to tick off files.

"You'll need primarily nineteenth-century materials," she says.

"I hope that's all."

"Yes," she says, nodding, and moves off to a wall of file drawers and begins pulling one out. It requires a bit of a heave from her; the drawer finally trundles out a yard or more, revealing a neat row of folders that he is certain are arranged with meticulous precision. He takes a seat at one of the oak tables set perpendicular to the filing cabinets, opens his port-folio, and flips until he reaches a blank sheet.

Janice returns with a handful of manila folders and sets them on the table. He glances at the label on the first of them—*1850s: Curricula*—and opens it. It contains mostly administrative minu-tiae, course syllabi and enrollment records, grade reports and a small sheaf of recorded minutes from faculty meetings, set down in a flowing hand in ink that seems well along in the process of fading from the paper.

He sets it aside and looks up to see Janice standing at his shoulder, frowning down at the folders and his hands on them. From her own hand dangles a pair of white cotton gloves. She holds them out to him.

"Please put them on," she says. "To preserve the documents."

Jacob pulls the white cotton, thin but pristinely clean, over his hands as Janice makes her way back into the stacks of cabi-nets. The second file, labeled *Misc.*, seems more promising. He finds in it first a newspaper clipping advertising the school in the September 18, 1858, edition of the *South Carolinian*. It touts Dr.

Frederick Augustus Johnston's name boldly at the top and in heavy typeface promises "Income Potential and Expeditious Advancement." Not the kind of recruitment currently in favor.

As he sets it aside he finds himself staring into the face of a black man sitting for a posed portrait, a daguerreotype. The man is sitting formally erect and dignified in spite of his rather dandified getup of a paisley cravat and matching pocket square carefully arranged in the pocket of his black coat. He holds a bowler hat on his lap, and one hand is draped over the gold handle of a walking stick. His beard is neatly clipped and flecked with gray; the portrait reminds Jacob of images he has seen of Frederick Douglass, although this man is less hirsute, his eyes more distant.

He turns the daguerreotype over. The photograph beneath it is a group portrait taken on the front steps of Johnston Hall, the same picture he has framed in his office, of the class of 1860. In the back he notes the lone black face, caught on celluloid hurrying past the group, as though trying to dodge the camera's lens.

He is looking back and forth between the daguerreotype and the class photo when Janice returns with a stack of slim ledgers, years printed on their spines in faded gilt. He sets a white fingertip on the black face.

"Janice, who is this man?"

She seems to stiffen slightly. "He was with the school for a number of years—1857 to 1866, I believe."

"In what capacity?"

"His duties were rather vaguely defined," she answers

slowly. "It appears he was brought on as a general custodian. Over time he became an integral member of the staff, it seems. You'll find his record here," she says, and rests her small hand on the ledgers.

"Did he have a name?"

"Nemo Johnston."

"His name was *Johnston*?"

"He took the name of his owner, as was the custom."

Jacob looks at her for a long moment before he speaks again.

"Eighteen fifty-seven, you say."

"Before the war."

Jacob shakes his head slowly as he looks back at the daguerre-otype, the group portrait. *Context*, he thinks. *Context is everything*. His skills as a diagnostician have grown rusty.

"But why stay on? I mean after the war?"

For answer Janice leans over and begins flipping through the other photographs in the folder, several of them showing Nemo Johnston in the anatomy lab and the other downstairs rooms of the old building. No cellar shots. There is one photograph in which he appears with his namesake in the lecture hall, Professor Johnston holding forth with a pointer in front of a skeleton, the slave and a young nurse looking on almost rev-erentially as Doctor Johnston addresses his students. Jacob pauses for a moment over the face of the nurse. It is turned in profile, but even so he sees that she was beautiful, with pro-nounced cheekbones and eyes pale and luminescent in the morning light of the lecture room. Even in black-and-white, he can see that her hair was as fair as his own.

There is only one more photograph in the folder, and it arrests Jacob's attention immediately. Another one taken inside Johnston Hall, he quickly determines. At the borders of the frame he can make out stark white light shining down through the tall windows of the current bursar's office. But the men in the center of the photo seem swathed in shadow, the object on the table before the four students little more than a mass of darkness save for the bright gleaming bones the dissectors have laid bare of the ebony skin. Yet clearly no snapshot. This portrait was posed, the men dressed in dark frocks, each of them wearing a sort of Shriner's cap on which is embossed a skull over two crossed bones. The students are grinning like hunters posed over a trophy, shoulder-to-shoulder behind the dissecting table. One of them has spread an anatomy book—probably *Gray's*—across the cadaver's pelvis and is gesturing to another who holds a scalpel. The young man at the other end of the table is smirking, his hand over the cadaver's mouth.

The image, despite its medical accoutrements, reminds him of photos he has seen of lynchings. Except that in front of the table, smiling like a minstrel, his dark face split by teeth bared white, kneels Nemo Johnston. The slave holds up the cadaver's right hand—most of its fingers stripped of the flesh down to the bony knuckles—in a playful wave for the camera.

The poor, dumb bastard. Jacob feels a stirring of disgust in his stomach. He wonders what Adam would think of this, how he would interpret this photograph as any part of coming clean about the bones in the basement.

"The Skull and Crossbones Club," Janice says. "That photograph is probably from the 1860s. Nemo Johnston was a sort of unofficial mascot for the club in its early years."

"I always thought Skull and Crossbones was just a legend. People talk about it, but nobody ever claims to be a member."

"Isn't that the nature of secret societies?"

"You think it's real?"

Janice shrugs. "There is scattered evidence in the record of Skull and Crossbones surfacing in some years. It's probably no more than an old boys' club now, but the *South Carolinian* mentioned members trying to suppress Abraham Flexner's report on the school at the beginning of the century."

"From what I know about Flexner, I can't say I blame them."

"Really? His report to the Carnegie Foundation was epochal. He transformed medical education in this country." Her eyes seem to light up talking about the man. "Abraham Flexner had a historian's soul."

Jacob stares down at the grisly photograph. "God knows what he would have made of this."

Janice almost smiles. "I am an archivist, Doctor Thacker, which means I am a completist. What good is the historical record if it is not complete?"

"I don't see any good coming out of any of this, Janice. In fact, an *incomplete* record sounds pretty good right now." Jacob sighs. "But I should have a file on it. Can I get copies of the photographs?"

"You have to sign them out."

"But I'm not taking them anywhere."

Janice merely closes her eyes and shakes her head. With her eyes still closed, she reaches out to a wooden box on the table, pulls a form from it, and pushes it across the polished surface to Jacob.

"I don't remember this from last time."

"The policy has changed."

Jacob looks at the form. It is nearly a page long, a triplicate carbon with copies beneath the original in canary and pink. "The whole thing?"

"The whole thing."

"This could take a minute," he says, and pulls his Waterman pen from his jacket pocket.

"Some things do," she says.

She waits patiently until the form is completed, then takes it and the file folders from him, back toward her desk, moving soundlessly over the carpet.

When he picks up the first of the ledgers he can see the need for the cotton gloves. It is bound in calfskin but fragile-looking, its pages yellowed and brittle with age. He tries to hold it carefully—not an easy task for a doctor, used to handling books like the *Physician's Desk Reference* and the *Guide to Internal Medicine* as mechanics do Chilton manuals.

He turns the pages slowly, following the faded ink from

month to month. The script is delicate and precise, perhaps the hand of F. A. Johnston himself. Some of the expenditures are truly strange. A column labeled *Poultry* for most years, a $300 debit in 1857 for a gelding. Another column for *Anat. specimens*, the amounts paid out varying enough to make Jacob think the school sometimes found itself bargain cadavers one way or another. But most of it is pedestrian stuff, what he would find in this year's report: maintenance costs, materia medica and laboratory supplies, columns of tuition dollars brought in and salaries paid out. On the page for August he finds the purchase of Nemo Johnston, slave: the notation of an $800 loan from the Bank of Columbia, $700 of it marked down to a Robert Drake, the remaining $100 listed under *Sundries*. In the next year's ledger, Nemo merited a column of his own, with his own expenses. Eighty-five dollars for a house in Rosedale, $20 per quarter for "necessities." Telling indeed: beginning with 1858, there is no expense column for cadavers.

Jacob rubs his eyes as he scans through the stacked, open ledgers. It seems to him that the school's finances fluctuated wildly in the old days, a year or two of bounty followed by quarters that showed the school nearly going under. He sees that the school began to pay Nemo Johnston a small salary in 1861, well before emancipation, and that the salary rose every year. He can imagine why. Slave or not, they needed to keep him happy. And quiet.

He flips the pages back and forth, scanning each column

again. He pauses over a page in the 1864 ledger, an itemized list of the curriculum—courses taught and stipends paid to the faculty for each of them. F. A. Johnston listed as preceptor for most, a few other names for chemistry, biology, surgery. Jacob rubs his eyes, then squints at the page. *Anatomy, winter quarter, 1865: N. Johnston, preceptor.* Jacob smiles. Doctor Johnston may have spent too much time in the operating room that day, inhaled a little bit of ether. But as Jacob looks forward to the spring and fall quarters of the year he sees N. Johnston listed again for each of the courses: no separate stipend paid, but the ex-slave's name put down as the instructor of record nonetheless.

The columns and numbers are beginning to blur when Janice returns with a manila envelope holding his photocopies. He checks his watch and sees that he will be late for his two-thirty meeting with the Alumni Committee if he doesn't leave soon. Still, he closes the last ledger, 1866, reluctantly. He hopes that in this last year's record might be found notation of some stipend, some small retirement settlement that could be painted in the school's favor if Nemo Johnston's name becomes public knowledge. If it comes to that.

Jacob taps one white finger on its leather cover. "Janice," he says, "I'm going to need a copy of this ledger."

Janice picks up the book and holds it against her chest. He thinks her eyes have widened behind her glasses. "The whole thing?" she asks.

Jacob only smiles at her as he closes his portfolio. But the smile fades as he sees his own surname on the lined pages of the ledger he just uncovered. "September 3rd, 1867," the faded indigo reads, "S. Thacker. Dismissed. Immoral conduct."

PERHAPS BECAUSE THE name in the ledger will not leave his mind, perhaps because he has not crossed its threshold since Easter, or perhaps only because it is on the route back to the office, Jacob pauses at the wrought-iron gate of the Episcopal Cathedral on Gervais. He checks his watch quickly and decides he can show up for the Alumni Committee meeting a minute or two late. God knows the committee won't be deciding anything fast.

Once through the church's heavy wooden doors he is immersed in the gloomy shadows of the nave. Above him Gothic arches soar to a height of three stories; his steps on the marble floor ring up toward them and echo back before they die somewhere in the side aisles. He opens one of the latched pew doors and sits, his hand lingering on the polished wood for a moment before he reaches for the kneeler and settles himself on it.

This attitude of prayer, ingrained in childhood, has become awkward these last few years. He waits for a prayer to form itself in his mind. Instead he finds himself staring at his hands. He remembers how sometimes his father's hand would settle on his clasped fingers during the prayers, like a secret between them, hidden from the closed eyes of the priest and their fellow parishioners. The gnarled knuckles, the thin gold wedding band, the calluses of his father's palm nearly as rough as sandpaper on his child's hands.

Never in this grand place, though, not that he can recall. His family, like the other lintheads, dispensed instead to a clapboard chapel down the great hill and across the Congaree, its whitewashed modesty a relic of the real old-time mill-town days, its architecture as utilitarian as a commissary. A bit of beneficence from the mill owners—the real Episcopalians—but his father had said the Irish Catholic workers took to it easily enough.

Immoral conduct, he thinks, wondering by what standard such was measured in those bygone days. Like Washburn? Would Jacob's own case have merited the charge?

Rising, he crosses himself reflexively, hoping that that gesture might count for something at least.

As he makes his way back down the aisle he notices the votive candles flickering on the back wall of the nave. He fumbles a few bills out of his pocket as offering and lights one candle each for mother, for father.

HE IS HOME from work by five-thirty, in time to catch the local news and make certain that Washburn's departure has gone unnoticed. In spite of himself, he would almost like to see Washburn on the broadcast, the cameras rolling as he is escorted off-campus and put into a conspicuously unmarked car, campus security loading him into the back seat as the cops do with the more mundane perpetrators. But he knows better; he has long since warmed to McMichaels's binary view of things, in which every event can be placed in one of two categories, like columns on a balance sheet: Good for the School and Not Good for the School.

As he shuts the door behind him he can hear Mary, his housekeeper, shuffling around in the laundry room. Mary has had a summer cold for two weeks now and is moving more slowly than usual, dragging her sandals across the tile. *Oprah* blares from the little television over the refrigerator as he comes into the kitchen, placing his briefcase on a barstool and skirting the ironing board she has set up in the middle of the floor. He takes a cold beer out of the refrigerator and reaches for the TV remote.

He punches buttons on the remote until it calls up the glowing face of Sabrina O'Cannon on Channel 13. Though every renewal of her contract brings with it another morphing of her face closer to Barbie dimensions, she is still the best-looking anchor in town. He presses the mute button and keeps an eye on the screen for a graphic of the school's seal or a live-action shot of the campus. If neither pops up before the weatherman comes on, he knows they are in the clear.

Something is burning. Quickly he steps to the ironing board and lifts the iron laid across the back of one of his Robert Talbot shirts. He winces at the perfect brown outline it has left behind on the yellow broadcloth. At the rate she has been ruining his clothes, Mary may not be a bargain for much longer. When the façade of the Chapel Clinic appears on the screen, he sets the iron on the counter and reaches for the volume control.

"But for allergy sufferers, fall can be nearly as torturous as the spring season," Sabrina is saying. The screen shifts to a clinic shot inside the building, then a close-up of Ben Wheeler talking from behind his desk. Ben looks a little embarrassed as he discusses how "hay fever" is actually a misnomer and goes into a discourse on the multiple sources of allergens, which the reporter has mercifully cut short with some deft editing. It is a thirty-second piece that ends with a suggestion that allergy patients pay a visit to the specialists at Chapel: Good for the School. Jacob has forgotten that he set this interview up last week. Before he knows it, it will be early flu season and he'll have to give Cassandra Stodghill, the ENT chair, a call.

"Why you change my show?"

Mary stands beside him with another of his shirts in her hands, her eyes baggy with cold. Her suffering with common ailments, especially at work, is always conspicuous. When she is sick, she strains toward epic suffering.

"Is that your next victim?" he asks, nodding at the crumpled oxford. He holds the singed Talbot aloft for her to see. She shrugs.

"I'd raise hell if this happened at the cleaners, Mary."

Mary makes a sound of agreement. "Cleaners charge a dollar-fifty each. I charge seven dollars an hour," she says as she smoothes the new shirt out on the board.

Jacob considers the options of taking her up on this line of reasoning, but decides it is hopeless. Mary is prone to finger wagging and neck rolling, so he is wary of being too critical.

Her back is to him anyway as she sprinkles water on the shirt and begins to press it.

He takes a seat behind the breakfast counter and gazes at the television. After a few minutes the local stories are finished and the news crew takes a stab at international affairs with some footage of the Middle East. A swarthy man runs past the camera carrying a child with a head contusion and Jacob trims the volume down a little further, on a level with the squeaking of the ironing board. He takes another sip of his beer.

"Want me to take you home?"

Mary looks at him indignantly. "Can't walk with this cold."

"Did you take the vitamins I gave you?"

"I took some echinacea and ginseng."

"Take the vitamins, Mary. Everything else just makes expensive urine." He picks up his keys from the counter and fingers them, idly pressing the blue-and-white roundel on the car key. In the garage he can hear the convertible's alarm system chirping, activating and deactivating. "Your brother still living with you, Mary?"

"Don't look like he ever going to leave."

"Frank's okay with that?" Jacob has seen Mary's husband only once. He works the third shift at the chicken plant across the river and sleeps during the day.

"They don't hardly cross paths. But one day he going to come home and find Big Junior on his couch watching the TV and kick him on out. I've been telling Big Junior it's time to come up with some rent money."

"He still looking for work?"

"Big Junior mostly just drinks gin. But he say he's looking."
She shakes out the shirt and fits it over a hanger. "What you got
for him?"

"Nothing special. But if he's interested, I can pay fifteen an
hour."

"He'll be interested."

"Good. Tell him I'll pick him up at four. Tomorrow
morning."

"Four a.m.?" Mary shakes her head. "All right. I reckon he'll
still be up then." She inspects the shirt and seems to find it
acceptable. In truth it is perfect, better than the cleaners, no
matter the charge. She takes the ironing board down with a
screech and carries it to the laundry room, moving a little faster
now. She likes riding in Jacob's car with the top down, always
urging him to take the long route to her house in Rosedale. She
steps back into the kitchen with her purse and an empty hanger.

"Mind if I take that yellow shirt home? Yellow look good on
Frank. Only ruined on the back. Suit coat'll cover it fine."

Jacob cannot resist needling her a little. "I was thinking I'd
give it to charity. But I suppose I could take it out of your pay."

Mary stares at him as though he were a simpleton, then
smiles faintly as he throws up his hands.

"Sure. With my compliments."

Mary fits the Talbot over the hanger and leaves him alone in
the kitchen. A moment later he hears the garage door trundling
upward and a car door shutting, but still he lingers, waiting

until the weatherman strides in front of the computerized map of South Carolina and jabbers away, indicating points of interest on a map that seems mostly static. A storm front pushing up from the coast, he says, but otherwise quiet, just the stifling heat of late summer in the Midlands. Some precipitation likely later in the week, but just the heat for now, holding steady.

Jacob switches the television off as the camera cuts back to Sabrina O'Cannon and stares for a moment at the dark screen, her face lingering in his mind. Then sets his beer down, pulls the archives file from his briefcase, and flips through the copies until he finds the shot of the nurse in the lecture hall. He leans close, studying the woman's features, feeling a stir in his memory, then moves to the bedroom, hurrying now.

He pulls a shoebox down from the closet shelf and dumps its contents on the bed, then rifles through the old pictures until he finds his father's service portrait from Korea. By the time he has carried it back to the kitchen, he can hear his pulse beating in his ears.

Side by side, the resemblance is unmistakable. He hadn't seen it before because it was impossible. But the high cheekbones, the sandy hair, the gray eyes, are the same. Except for the distance in time, the woman in the photograph could have been his father's twin.

Fernyear: 1861

T HE WOODEN SPADE SLID INTO THE earth soundlessly, worming into the newly turned soil like a hungry thing. Then rose, its blade full, and swung a swift half circle to the tarpaulin laid across the foot of the grave, where it shook its burden gently onto the canvas. Thus began the second coming of Quash Jones.

Nemo had been at this strange work of body snatching for nearly four years now—four winters since Doctor Johnston first brought him here to Cedar Vale under moonlight—and he had long since caught its rhythms and cadence. In minutes he had cleared the outline of the three-foot square he would dig deeper until he struck the head of Quash's coffin. The exchange of soil from the grave to the canvas tarpaulin, though rapid, was nearly soundless; Nemo was fast, but he handled cemetery dirt as carefully as he did fireplace ash. The twin pillars of nocturnal procurement, Johnston had told him that first night, were swiftness and silence. He had learned the lesson well.

It would be nice to finally see Quash doing some good in the world, he thought as he worked under the faint light of the single open slit in his lantern. Quash was a bad slave and a worse neighbor, a man with a back so ridged and scoured from beatings that the children gaped in horror when he worked shirtless. Whether his perpetual rage was the result of the beatings or the cause of them, no one could agree or dared to ask, but to Nemo it was a pointless debate. Whatever troubles a man had in his work, he should keep them to himself. But Quash had raved about the slave quarters in Rosedale every Sunday like a drunken demon, scattering the gangs of children and shouting filthy words to the women on the porches. The men generally went inside until he moved on—Quash was the biggest Ibo most of them had ever seen—but that changed when the school bought Nemo a house on the corner of Paradise and Harden. He had stayed in his rocking chair when Quash first passed the picket fence out front, but the second time, Quash made the mistake of stopping to exchange words.

"Hey there, conjure-doctor," he brayed, leaning on Nemo's front gate. "You got anything can beat this?" He held his gallon jug aloft, his thumb hooked through its handle, and waved it. He was swaying.

"Got plenty can beat it," Nemo said in an even voice. "What good it doing you?"

"Hanh," Quash said. He took a long pull on the jug and

leaned harder on the gate. The pickets were beginning to weave with him. "If you got something better, why don't you bring it on out?"

The gate broke loose with a crack and fell into the yard, Quash nearly following it. The jug wavered in the air as he caught his balance. When he looked up, Nemo was standing on the brick walkway an arm's reach away, his hand outstretched. In it he held something that arrested Quash's attention immediately: a chicken's foot and crow feathers, bound with wire that had also been run through the palm of a withered child's hand.

Quash seemed to be speechless, and Nemo gave him a long minute to look at the hand of glory before he moved it closer. Quash began to turn, but Nemo snatched the arm that held the jug and lifted it. It was dead weight. He passed the talisman over the mouth of the jug three times, quickly, then looked Quash in the eye.

"Drink it now," Nemo said quietly, "and you'll die tonight."

Quash looked down at the jug as though he held a serpent in his hand. Nemo waited. For a moment it seemed that Quash was sorely tempted to take the risk. But then, like a flame rekindling, his face darkened, his features twisting. He threw the jug to the bricks and walked off while the whiskey soaked into the ground.

Shoulder-deep in Quash's grave, Nemo allowed himself a low chuckle at the recollection. "Quash Jones, you was one dumb son of a bitch," he said.

The shovel resumed its work, the wooden blade making only the slightest of sounds when it struck stones that would have rattled against a metal tool. This was the hardest part of it for Nemo, the stage when he had dug himself down into a vertical coffin of his own. It was now when the claustrophobia came back to him, his legacy from the pirates' barracoon on the Windward Coast, his last home in Africa. Down in the dungeon dug below sea level, he had been terrified at the babble of foreign tongues he now knew were probably Fante, Yoruba, and Ga, but none of them the Wolof of his mother. The strangers' languages echoed and cascaded off the dripping stone walls and quieted only at night, when the shush of waves against the shore hushed the foreigners' snores and murmurs with the taunting sound of freedom outside. He had been buried alive. When they threw open the doors and herded them all down the tunnel toward the waiting ships, he thought it was to be eaten by the whites.

In his hands the shovel vibrated as it hit hard against something solid, and Nemo cursed himself for letting his thoughts wander so. At his feet he could make out the patch of pine board the shovel had struck. He lowered and raised the shovel a half dozen more times until he had cleared the dirt from the head of the coffin, then carefully set the shovel on the ground above, next to the lantern. His crowbar was there, beside the length of rope, and he took it now. Kneeling, he pried at the seams of the coffin lid, putting his shoulders into it so that the boards came apart slowly under the force. The last one he had to bend upward, and the brittle wood broke in his hands, snapping loudly enough to be heard beyond the magnolias and cedars that ringed the cemetery.

He stood up to his full height, his eyes just above the grave's rim, and looked out across the cemetery for five minutes. No movement, no lights approaching. Just the new moon above, full up by now, glowing silver in the sky but no bigger than a rind. A resurrectionist's moon. His hand snaked out to the rope and dragged it down.

Within a minute he had a noose around Quash's neck and was pulling him out of the narrow hole in the coffin with a series of jerking movements. Quash was heavy and he was big; parts of him caught on the splintered ends of the coffin lid and Nemo had to brace his feet against the other side of the hole to heave him free. When he had the body upright and propped against the earth, he began to strip it while Quash leaned against him, head lolling to one side. Nemo squatted to take down his pants and Quash's belly pressed against his face. He put a hand to his cheek, and it came away wet and smelling of rot. In spite of all the spirits he had poured into himself, Quash was going to go fast. Nemo had found that the young ones generally did that, having died early from some long-festering but hidden illness. Quash, dropped dead in the fields yesterday at noon, was no exception. His liver had probably busted at last from all the rotgut whiskey. But Johnston wanted to know for sure; he wanted Quash's liver for a temperance lecture. Nemo stuffed the trousers and shirt into the coffin and climbed out of the hole, the rope in his hand like a leash. He spoke to the body as he pulled it upward.

"Well, Quash, you no-count, you finally moving up in the world. You going to school."

He dragged the earth-laden tarp to the edge of the hole and pushed one end of it over, careful to keep a good grip on an edge of the canvas so he could use it to wrap Quash for the trip back. The dirt slid off the tarpaulin with a hissing sound. In seconds the grave was full again and Nemo was dancing a slow tattoo on the earth, keeping his feet aligned symmetrically as he had seen gravediggers do after the funeral parties had departed. This last step in the process was crucial, as Johnston had told him so many times. "No need to be neat about the job, except at the surface," Johnston would say. "There, Nemo, we must be scrupulous. Not a flower left out of order, not a clod out of place. Should a mourner come to pay his respects tomorrow, he should detect nothing amiss. People have sentiments about these matters, but if they never know the grave is empty, they are just as well off. And the school is a great deal better off."

When he was satisfied that the raw earth matched the image he had burned into his brain before starting to dig, Nemo turned back to Quash. He pulled him behind a wooden headstone and loosened the noose, cutting a length from the rope to bind the body. Roughly he pushed against the legs, stiff with rigor mortis, until he had worked the heels up under the buttocks. He pulled the arms back and tied them to the ankles, pushed Quash's head down against one of his shoulders, and lifted him onto the tarpaulin. He used the remaining rope to truss the bundle tight, until it was the size of an ordinary grain bag that would attract no special attention in the back of the wagon as he trundled through the streets of downtown Columbia.

It was a hard line of work, to be sure, but it was his portion. Take it or leave it, as the white folks liked to say. But he had never heard a slave, who had no choice of leaving anything, use the phrase. So he had taken it. But still, after nearly four years of nighttime visits to this place, he was haunted by ghosts of Senegal, by those wisps of religious instruction he remembered from his mother. Doctor Johnston's maxim—"The metaphysical is entirely secondary to the physical"—had never comforted him much. In Africa he could have expected an instant death for desecrating a grave and disturbing the spirits, and after that death, an eternity of torment from the ancestors and their demons. Here, this work was sanctioned by a group of the most respected white men in town, and there were no demons. Johnston had only laughed when he had expressed his fears of a plateye or angry spirit taking them on that first night in Cedar Vale. And true enough, since then the only glowing eyes he had seen here were those of possums and rats, or the stray raccoon venturing into the city. Night dwellers like himself.

Nemo grunted as he picked up the body. He held it close to his side like an overpacked duffel as he started down the hill toward the mule and wagon waiting to carry his parcel to its postmortem appointment with Doctor Johnston. A slave, he knew, was either a creature of adaptation or just another dead body; Quash could attest to that with mute eloquence. Nemo had adapted.

But one folkway he could not discard. Always he brought along some piece of crockery to leave on the grave, following the ancient ritual of leaving a container nearby to catch the spirit of the departed if it was loosed. This time it was four pieces of cracked ceramic, brown and white, one of them a neck with a thumb hook shaped into it. Though the jagged edges looked raw as broken bone, the kiln-fired smooth surfaces gleamed in the pale moonlight. He left them at the head of the empty grave as Quash's only memorial, tokens from that sunny afternoon two long years ago on his front walk, by the broken gate, in the Carolina springtime.

NEXT DAY QUASH met a hero's welcome in the dissecting room. Nemo had spent the early morning hours embalming him—making the cuts to each side of the groin and the jugular to drain him, then catheterizing the three incisions and pumping in Doctor Johnston's prescribed mixture of turpentine, arsenic, and formalin—and was finishing his sutures when the sun crested the downtown skyline. He could see the first students arriving in the deep shadows of the yard, kicking at the chickens or stopping off at the outhouses in back before coming inside to settle in for the day's work. By seven o'clock there were fourteen men in the high-ceilinged room, crowded around Quash's body like children ringing a schoolyard fight.

"Big bastard, wasn't he?"

"Look at this back."

"How many lashes, do you figure?"

"Never mind that. Go ahead and make the cut. I want to see if the musculature has been damaged as well."

"Hey there, Nemo, hand me a number eight, will you?"

Nemo passed the scalpel to an outstretched hand and stepped over to the body on the adjacent table. "You gentlemens finished with Toby?"

One of the bearded faces peered out of their huddle. "Yes, done. Nothing but hash now," he said.

Nemo gathered up the sheet on which the body lay. As was the custom, the sheet had been twisted to cover the face and genitals, and when it pulled free of Toby's face, he saw that both the eyes had been removed. He was wrapping up the remains when a brown vial landed in the middle of the bundle, clinking against a rib. Its label read F. Brown's Extract of Jamaican Ginger.

"Who threw this bottle?" he asked.

One of the students stiffened and turned a flushed face to him. It was Porter, the one who had lingered longest in the outhouse. "I beg your pardon?" he asked in a clenched voice.

"Mister Porter, this ginger won't do you an ounce of good, if I may say. Have you tried Trommer's malt extract?"

"I have not."

Nemo smiled as he cinched the sheet. "I fetch you some directly. Works twice as well."

The man nodded, and Nemo lifted the remains of Toby from the table. Toby was maybe forty pounds of weight now, reduced by cutting to little more than bone and ligament. He carried him easily in one hand and picked up the full bucket of Quash's blood from the floor with the other. At the cellar door he paused to set the bucket down as he turned the knob. The voices called from the dissecting room almost as soon as he had opened the door.

"Shut that door, damn it."

"My God, what a stench!"

But Nemo paid the voices little heed, for beneath the shouting he heard a light knocking on the front door of the building. He set the bucket on the cellar's top step and tossed the bundled sheet down the stairs, where it landed on the clay with a muffled thump. In seconds he had locked the cellar and was stepping quietly across the foyer to the great doors. He swung the heavy oak open on the morning sunshine and saw a white woman standing on the front steps, a valise beside her.

"Good morning," she said, the sunlight glinting in her gray eyes. Nemo had never seen eyes of so light a shade. A moment later he realized she was holding out her hand to be shaken.

"Good morning, ma'am," he said, taking the hand uneasily and giving it a quick shake. Back at Windsor the penalty for such contact would have been nearly fatal. He wondered where on earth this woman could have come from.

"I'm here about the circular," the woman said. "The advertisement for a nurse?"

Nemo nodded and ushered her into the cool foyer with a slight bow. "Certainly, ma'am," he said, watching the woman as she stood with the valise held in front of her with both hands, her eyes taking in the banister, the sweeping staircase, the tall ceilings. She was hardly bigger than a girl. "May I tell Doctor Johnston who's calling?"

The young woman's eyes had come to rest on a portrait of Benjamin Rush that Doctor Johnston had hung in the front hall. She studied the doctor's features as though she did not think much of what she saw.

"Sara Thacker," she said, looking at him again. Then she sniffed once, her nostrils flaring slightly. "And you may as well tell him that you fellows need a housekeeper as well."

JOHNSTON HELD A CHAIR for the young woman, then took a seat behind his desk uneasily. A nurse, by his definition—or indeed as defined by any of his contemporaries—was by nature matronly and plain. This Sara Thacker, though dressed modestly enough in a simple linen dress, was neither. Her face bore no rouge and her sandy hair was drawn back in the simple ponytail favored by rustic women, but that hair was lustrous and her gray eyes were too bright, he thought, ever to blend into the dull wards of the Negro hospital or settle cheerfully on such menial work as the emptying of bedpans.

Most troubling of all, beneath the linen dress he could detect no corset.

Johnston looked over her letters of reference, nodding from time to time. After a few long moments he peered over the top of the stationery at Sara, his eyes narrowed over his spectacles.

"These are strong recommendations, particularly the reference from Major Anderson. He describes your conduct during the summer's malaria outbreak as 'heroic.' That is high praise indeed from a decorated military man."

The young woman's eyes wandered to the window. "I did what was required," she said softly. "I'm afraid Major Anderson is in for a hard time."

"He certainly is. It is fortunate for you that he deemed it inadvisable to carry women with him to Fort Sumter."

"I would have gone," she said. "There will be a sore need for nurses there."

"Doubtless that is correct." Johnston cleared his throat. "I apologize for the directness of the question, but the hiring procedure at an institution such as ours always requires a degree of indelicacy. You have served in the military's nursing division for over a year. Surely during that time among the men of the service you were presented with opportunities for a less arduous life. Why is it that you have not married?"

The young woman looked at him instantly, light in her eyes. "Would I sound too indelicate, sir, if I told you I found the overtures of eighteen-year-old private soldiers unappealing?"

There was a long moment of quiet before Johnston cleared

his throat again. He smiled faintly. "Frank, perhaps, but not indelicate."

But the young woman seemed not to have heard him. She pulled the circular Johnston had posted from her valise and read from it: " 'All applicants must present letters from at least two persons of trust testifying to morality, integrity, seriousness, and capacity for care of the sick.' " She looked up at Johnston. "I find that order of qualifications interesting."

"Is that so? What in the world is curious about it?"

"I wonder that capacity to care for the sick is not the first consideration."

"I see," Johnston said. He drew a long breath. "But you must understand that the stability of the environment here at the college is fragile and must be maintained. The young men studying here are, physiologically speaking, at their prime. Any feminine distraction would be extremely disruptive. Their vigor, their energies, must be rigorously directed at their studies."

"At caring for the sick."

"Precisely, without distraction."

Miss Thacker tapped the circular against her knee and smiled. "Perhaps, then, they were admitted without adequate testimony to their morality. Or their integrity."

Johnston felt his temper rise. "The circular also states, if I remember correctly, that applicants should be matronly women of mature years." Johnston paused, and his face flushed scarlet. "Begging your pardon, but you seem to possess neither quality."

Her gray eyes never left his face as the long seconds of silence spun out. After a moment, he set the letters on his desktop and spoke again.

"Miss Thacker, I admire your candor. But I cannot help thinking it would be better suited to a more, shall I say, liberal environment. Perhaps you should consider a move northward? My former colleague Joseph Warrington administers an excellent nursing program at the Philadelphia Lying-In Charity. I would gladly write to him on your behalf."

She rose, and as she did caught Doctor Johnston's eye lingering on her waist.

"I can afford a relocation to the north no better than a whalebone corset, sir," she said. "If you decide I'm suitable for the position, please send word to the commissary by Miller's Ferry. I am staying with my people across the river for the time being."

Johnston's mouth was still open on an unspoken word when she shut the door behind her.

FRIDAY NIGHT, APRIL nineteenth, and the booming of Charleston's guns on Fort Sumter seemed still to be echoing across South Carolina a full week later. In honor of the occasion, the faculty had decided to celebrate what they called the Second American Revolution in grand style, with a secession ball. Tonight, nearing eleven, the school glowed with candlelight from every window and its doors had been thrown open to the select society of Columbia, who now thronged the ground-floor rooms in their finery, the sound of their voices jubilant over the whisper of crinoline and starched linen and the tinkling sound of crystal and sterling service put to full use. In one corner of the parlor a hastily assembled group of slaves was flailing away at "Dixie" for the third time, Napoleon Horry scratching his fiddle as though he meant to saw it in half while Ben Smith clawed at a gourd banjo behind him. Ben's son Sam was keeping time for the trio, squatting on the floor and slapping a set of spoons between his knees while pairs of ladies and gentlemen danced, awkwardly attempting to match the song's tempo with a sped-up waltz.

In his dusty suit of tails, Nemo stood behind a bar improvised from a dissecting table and a white tablecloth, nodding and smiling as he refilled glasses. After this long day the line of people in front of the table seemed interminable, but he was happy to celebrate secession with the white folks, since the war would be the end of all of them. He appeared to be the only one here tonight who knew it, though; even Doctor Johnston was a bit tipply, having allowed himself a third glass of punch to toast Abraham Lincoln's imminent defeat. He stood over in the corner talking with Nurse Thacker, who looked uncomfortable in her new dress and touched her neck from time to time as the doctor spoke.

But Nemo had a more pressing concern than the fate of the Union: he was nearly out of whiskey. He had laid in provisions since Wednesday but had grossly underestimated the thirst that secession would elicit in the gentlemen in attendance. And now he saw, midway back in the line, Charles Hampton, coming on inexorably for yet another tumbler of rye. Apparently Mister Hampton intended to drink Columbia dry before departing for Charleston to join the fight; his face burned crimson above the gold lieutenant's stripes of his freshly tailored uniform. Nemo eyed his last bottle of whiskey nervously as he ladled out another glass of punch.

Hampton was tapping his julep cup on the table even before the lady in front of him moved aside. Nemo poured out the last of his whiskey into the cup with a deferential smile. But Hampton did not budge.

"Fill her up, boy," he said, tapping the cup again.

"Can't do it, sir. We fresh out of whiskey."

"Out, you say?"

"Yes, sir. We cleaned out. Ben over there was supposed to bring another barrel this afternoon, but he didn't show up with nothing but his banjo. Can I pour you some apple brandy? How about some gin or rum punch?"

"Rum! Good God, man, we're not sailors. We must have whiskey!"

Nemo held out the empty bottle in response and shrugged apologetically. Hampton's face took on a darker hue of red.

"Don't you brandish that bottle at me, boy. You get those feet hopping and fetch me some more. I don't care a damn if you have to run all the way down Gervais for it."

Nemo looked at his feet and shook his head sadly. "Doctor Johnston told me not to leave my post, sir. He said so specific."

Behind Hampton, the line was growing restless at the delay. Soon Nemo would have a Confederate mutiny of his own to contend with.

Hampton reached out his hand and gathered a fistful of Nemo's shirt in it. He pulled upward until Nemo's eyes met his.

"I'll whip you myself, boy, if you don't fill that tumbler in a minute."

Nemo let his eyes widen as though struck by an inspiration. "Well, now, Mister Hampton," he drawled, "there is one small barrel down the cellar I know of, but the captains tell me it's off-limits." He watched Hampton's face as he spoke. "Tell me it's aged something special. But they told Nemo to leave it alone. Said it was strictly for a momentous occasion."

Hampton's eyes narrowed. "Would you not say this is a momentous evening?"

"Well, sir, I guess it is something special, now, in point of fact."

The hand turned him loose. "Well, get it. I'll watch out for things up here. I can spoon out punch as well as a nigger, I reckon." Someone in the line laughed. Nemo picked up a pewter pitcher and started toward the stairway door while Hampton took up his position behind the bar to a smattering of applause.

Nemo had to excuse himself past a pair of young ladies whispering to one another at the cellar door. As they giggled and moved away, he quickly unlocked the hasp below the glass doorknob. Downstairs, he was glad he had sprinkled an extra layer of quicklime on the floor that morning. The smell was still there, but subtly—little more than a sullen undercurrent to the scent of dry earth, only the hint of decay present beneath the tang of kerosene from the lamp burning on the wall. Tonight the basement looked much like any other, save for the cocky jut of a half-buried rib cage beside one of the brick foundation pillars, dusted with white powder, the last of the cadavers he had cleared for the ball.

He stepped to the corner where the barrel waited, set upright on one end, and pulled off the lid. He dipped the pitcher into the whiskey and let it fill, careful to keep it clear of poor Minnie Jenkins's stillborn baby, who floated upright in the amber liquid. Nemo had not opened the barrel since he had brought the baby down here in August and was pleased to see that the whiskey had worked a marvel of preservation. The little boy looked like an angel, he thought, with his tiny hands balled into fists against his cheeks. His short tufts of curls wafted gently as the pitcher rose from the whiskey, and Nemo placed a hand on them for a moment, saying a silent prayer. Then he put the lid back in place and climbed the stairs.

Hampton was waiting for him in the front room when he hurried in with the pitcher, smiling as he moved through the crowd. Hampton handed a cup of punch to a stout woman in a satin toque and stepped aside for Nemo to fill his cup. Nemo poured with one hand and crushed a sprig of mint into the cup with the other. Hampton took it and tossed it back in a gulp. Nemo cleaned the rim of the pitcher with a napkin very slowly, watching Hampton from the corner of his eye as the white man coughed and wiped his lips. Eyes watering, Hampton stretched out an arm, pointing at Nemo.

"Now that," he said, "is whiskey. Hit me once more."

Again Nemo filled the cup, his smile even broader than before. Hampton turned to the waiting line and raised his glass. "To the Confederacy!" he shouted. The others raised their glasses, cheering, happy to toast everything that was right in the world, the preservation of the old order. Nemo was pleased to see that Lieutenant Hampton drank the deepest.

The FRONT PORCH of Walton's Commissary sagged under the weight of the dozen black men gathered there to while away the hot Saturday afternoon. Summer was coming on strong this year and the cicadas seemed to be singing praises for the heat. Their droning whine all but drowned out the rare comment from the loungers and the murmuring of the milk cows in their stalls behind the store. None of the men complained about the heat. They were glad not to be working in it, with their weekly half day completed at noon, leaving them the welcome expanse of forty hours free of labor until Monday's dawn. Later this afternoon the more industrious slaves, who hired out their Saturday time, would begin to arrive, crowding in the store to spend their new pennies on hard candy and cuts of meat, spreading their aura of prosperity and enterprise. But for now, in the weekend reprieve of hard work, there was only the cicadas' song and the men's lassitude, a quiet time of contentment, of being owned by no man.

Several of them napped in cane-bottomed chairs they had leaned against the front wall of the store. One of these, awakened by a mosquito's bite, opened his eyes and gazed down the road leading to Walton's place. He squinted into the distance, then leaned forward, the chair's legs clapping down on the porch planks. "Here come Nemo Johnston," he said.

The others followed his gaze, knives stopping their carving on sticks of yellow pine, chair legs scraping. In the shimmering heat they saw Nemo coming up the sandy road with his deliberate gait. He wore a black driving coat that set off the white of his boiled shirt, and his head was capped with a Panama hat made of straw dyed black. The heat was so intense in the road that the black shapes of the coat and hat seemed to waver as he came on, his outline shifting in the humid air. But all of the men knew that when he reached the shade of the porch he would have not a drop of sweat on his brow or lip.

"Ain't he dressed fine?" one of the younger men asked.

"Yeah, he dressed fine. He going to dress your ass out someday."

"Won't get me. My brother Abe going to sit up by my grave. We made a deal. Two weeks of nights he'll be there. I do the same for him if he go first."

"Sammy, you a fool. You think Abe going to leave Sally alone nights for two weeks?"

One of the men laughed. "I'll check on her."

Sammy looked uncertain. "Abe promised."

"Sure he did, child. Promise is a good thing. But some promises hard to keep. What if Abe went on first? What would you do if you saw that black bastard coming up on you in the dark graveyard?"

Someone hissed, and the men's conversation stopped abruptly. They looked over at old Renty Tucker where he sat perched on a barrel by the screen door. His wife, Melissa, had died the week just past. Though he sat erect and impassive, a single tear had trailed through the dust on his weathered cheek.

No one heard Nemo's approach until he propped a boot heel on the porch steps. He greeted them, doffing his hat, and began wiping the dust from his foot with a handkerchief. His boots were covered in snakeskin.

One of the men whistled. "Where you get them boots, man?"

"Mister Carlton made them for me. I killed the snake down by the Congaree."

"Mister Carlton?"

"Snake was four foot long. He wouldn't die till the sun went down."

"Mister Carlton a white cobbler."

Nemo nodded. "Still white the last time I saw him."

One of the young men sitting on the porch floor spoke up. "They say a copperhead can put his tail in his mouth and roll after you like a wagon wheel. Run you down." He said it a little too loudly. Some of the old men grunted.

"I'm doing his only rolling now," Nemo said. No one spoke up to contradict him. He climbed the steps and crossed the porch, pausing at the door. He took the Panama hat off his head and turned to old Renty.

"I was sorry to hear about Mrs. Melissa," he said.

Renty Tucker clenched his jaw. It looked as though he were trying to grind his teeth down to nubs.

"Mrs. Melissa was a good woman," Nemo said. "Always kind. She resting peaceful, now, Mister Tucker. I'm sure of it."

Renty Tucker put his face in his hands after the screen door slapped shut. He shivered like a cold wind had just blown over him.

Inside, Nemo set his hat on the counter as he spoke to Walton, who was always glad to see his only customer who had never put anything on credit, always paid in cash. He followed Nemo now as he sauntered down the aisles with his hands clasped behind his back, walking slowly between baskets of dried beans and the tins of crackers and baking powder, sacks of coffee beans and potatoes. Now and then Nemo would pause and nod at a shelf and Walton would sack an item up. His croker sack was getting heavier by the minute.

Nemo stopped in front of the meager toiletries display against the back wall.

"I'll take four of those Ajax collars," he said, and Walton picked up the white crescents gingerly and wrapped them in tissue paper.

Nemo nodded at a pink bottle up on the highest shelf, well out of the reach of children. "How much that toilet water?"

"Dollar-fifty. Lubin's Lavender Water. That's the best perfume I carry."

"Guess it is. Look at the dust on the bottle."

Walton wiped at the bottle with a rag hung from his belt. He grinned slyly.

"You courting somebody, Mister Nemo?"

Nemo almost smiled. "Bag it up," he said, and strode to the front counter. Walton followed him with the croker sack in one hand and the collars and perfume in the other. He reached below the counter and took out a box, began arranging the expensive items in it with another sheet of tissue paper. When he finished he totted up the purchases on the back of a paper sack. His neck flushed when he had the total.

"Ten-fifty, Mister Nemo."

Nemo put a double eagle on the counter. Walton shook his head as he stared at the outstretched wings on the coin.

"Can't change that, Mister Nemo," he said sadly. "Don't have enough in the cashbox."

"Keep it, then. Put the rest down for next week."

Walton's mood lifted. He was bundling up the package when the screen door swung open. Prince Sparkman stood in the doorway, hands propped on his hips. He wore his carpenter's apron, and there was sawdust sprinkled in his black hair. People called him the bishop; he was a freedman who hired himself out as a carpenter during the week and spent every Sunday preaching. He made the rounds of the Midlands churches and came into Columbia every sixth Sunday, regular as clockwork, to feast on the last chicken of some slave family after the services, to consume thigh, breast, and wings while the children watched hungrily.

"Well, well," Prince said loudly. "Seems the devil do walk by daylight."

Nemo ignored him, but Prince walked on into the store. One by one, the men from the porch filed in behind him. Though they made a careful show of examining merchandise, every ear was cocked toward the men at the counter. Nemo saw that Renty Tucker was not among them.

"And here he is spending his ill-gotten money."

"Just came down to do some trading. Didn't come for no sermon."

Prince snorted. "Ain't you the big nigger."

"Only one bigger than you, reverend."

A few of the men snickered.

"Money's the root of all evil, the good book says. I can believe it."

"The book don't say that. Says the love of money is the root of all evil. How long it been since you read it right?"

But Prince would not be put off so easily. "The good book also says the devil can quote scripture like a wise man. What you say to that?"

Nemo shrugged. "Wasn't quoting. Just correcting. And I don't see a wise man here."

Prince stepped up close, as though he meant to strike a blow. When he spoke, his voice had risen to its full oratorical level, playing to the entire store. "I buries good folk every month, every year. Put them into the ground with the word of God. And this hell-spawn brings them back up from their slumbers like so much meat." He looked at Nemo and hissed, "What you doing to your own *people*, man?"

"Yeah, you try that Sunday voice on me, Prince, won't do no good. I know your weekday talk." Nemo raised his voice nearly an octave. "Yassuh, Mistah Smith, I build that corncrib for you right nice, yassuh."

"Don't be misled, brethren. The Lord loves a faithful servant. His reward will be great when the meek shall inherit the earth."

"That the best you can do for your people? I'm a here-and-now man, brother."

Prince shook his head. His face glowed as though he were under an anointing. He reached into his apron pocket and pulled out a small Bible and held it aloft for all to see its sweat-stained leather cover and worn pages. "Bible says the devil can't confront righteousness head-on," he chanted. "And I feel the power of the Spirit in this room, yes, Lord." He held the Bible out to Nemo. "Take it, sinner," he said. "See if it don't burn your hands. You sold your soul to the devil. Tell us you ain't."

"I could tell you that," Nemo acknowledged. "I could tell you I met Old Scratch down at the Camden crossroads in the fall last year. Nine nights—midnights—one after another. And on that ninth night we done the deal. Carry a lucky bone from a black cat with me now and I can put my hexes on anybody I wants to."

One of the men in the aisles dropped a can of sardines.

Nemo took the Bible in one of his long-fingered hands. He lowered his voice and leaned close to the preacher's ear. Prince seemed to shrink back instinctively.

"I could tell you, that, reverend. But I won't. Would be a lie. Only devil I know is white as a sheet, and yes, he walks around in the broad daylight. I works for him and you works for him." He pressed the Bible into the reverend's hand and clasped it. "So maybe you and me are closer than you think."

Prince looked down at the book in his hands as though it were a tool that had malfunctioned. Nemo smiled and took up his package from the counter.

"Walton," he said, "put that credit of mine on the reverend's tab. See if that filthy lucre can't do some of the Lord's work."

He walked out of the commissary in the ensuing silence. Later he learned that the silence had not lasted long, that within days the story of Nemo and the preacher had made the rounds of Rosedale and was acquiring the sheen of a legend. In the weeks that followed, the women began to look at him differently, and the men—they thought often about Nemo's power, whatever its source.

But that afternoon he heard only the slam of the screen door behind him and the drone of the cicadas in the trees. With the afternoon waning, the insects had redoubled their song against the twilight, as if to fight off nightfall by desperately celebrating the brief resurrection from their thirteen-year sleep.

Renty Tucker watched him disappear into the shimmering haze, muttering beneath his breath. "Melissa," he said. "Oh, my Melissa."

Wednesday

IN THE PREDAWN HOURS COLUMBIA IS a somnambulist's dream. It seems that every car in the city but Jacob's is still parked for the night, still sleeping in carport or garage, leaving him to enjoy complete sovereignty over the roads. Most of the traffic lights are blinking yellow, and he wrings the BMW's engine through the intersections, pushing the tachometer up high as he rows through the gears. As he leaves the suburbs he realizes that he has even beaten the paperboys up this morning; today's edition of *The State* has not yet made its rounds. In a half hour or so, the rolled papers will begin slapping down on driveways with news of the city, tidings of the world beyond. But for now there is only the growl of his engine and the silence that trails in its wake.

He punches the engine up to 70 on Devine Street, where the curtains of live oak and crape myrtle give way to the four-lane leading to Five Points. Coasting down the hill to the big intersection, he begins to see signs of life in the college town's main bar district. Here the neon still glows an hour after closing time, and there are indications of recent inhabitance: the glint of empty beer bottles left on the sidewalks, the stray car abandoned in favor of a cab ride home. With the top down and the cool air rushing over his face, he can almost smell the decadent odor of stale beer coming up from the storm gutters. He shakes his head and takes a gulp of his coffee, thinking back to the days when the ER shift would finally end and they would stumble out into the dawning day, sorely missing the carefree undergraduate years when they kept a similar schedule—but drank spirits instead of the tainted coffee of the interns' break room. He takes the right onto Harden and heads up the hill to Rosedale.

Rosedale, it seems, never really sleeps. Though most of the streetlights here have been broken, Jacob can make out dark figures on the corners and on the steps of the old shotgun bungalows even at this hour. In the darkness they look spectral, their movements languid as a dream. But at Mary's house the front porch light is on, the bare bulb shedding forty watts of light on the hulking form of Big Junior in the metal glider chair next to the front door, his outline blurred by the screening Frank has put up between the porch posts. While Jacob idles at the curb, Big Junior rises from the glider, as though by stages, and shuts the screen door behind him softly. When he settles into the passenger seat the car lists toward the curb. Jacob is glad he has opted to put the top down. Big Junior nearly fills the front seat by himself.

"Morning, my man," he says as he pulls the door closed and offers a hand. Jacob takes it and smells the sweetish taint of gin on his breath. It seems to come from his pores as well. "You got you a sweet ride," Big Junior says.

"It's not mine, actually. It's a lease."

"How about that?" he says as Jacob noses the car out into the street. "Mary says you don't commit to *nothing*. Where we heading?"

"The school. We've got what you might call a sensitive assignment."

Big Junior laughs and the car sways. "Man, I like to hear you talk. What you mean by sensitive?"

Jacob looks straight ahead. "We've got to dig up some bones in the basement of Johnston Hall."

"Say *what*?"

"Don't worry. Old bones, from way back. They're buried shallow, just scattered across the floor, maybe a foot down. You won't even have to touch them. You just dig and I'll sift them out of the dirt. I've got a box of plastic bags in the back. I want to bag them up and haul them out later."

With considerable shifting, Big Junior produces a pint bottle from his hip pocket and takes a drink. "Damn," he says. "Mary don't never put me up for any good work." He drinks again. "Wish I had me some Dr Pepper, man."

Jacob almost laughs. "That's it? I was afraid I'd be turning this car around. I thought I'd have to at least talk you into it."

Big Junior shakes his head sadly. "I know about that basement. Half of Rosedale knows. And we know you all know about it. Why you think we don't come up to the hospital unless we're about dying?" He looks out the windshield as if there were nothing beyond it to see. "Used to work with a guy liked to fight. Knives. Every time he was about to scrap, he'd tell everybody around him, 'Don't let 'em take me to Memorial.' Said it like it was a joke, but I knowed he wasn't kidding." Big Junior looks at Jacob intently. "Nobody wants some doctor experimenting on them."

"It's a free hospital, Junior. And nobody does any experimenting on anybody."

"Tell that to them bones. Bet it was a free hospital they walked into."

Because he cannot think of anything to say, Jacob asks for a drink. Big Junior passes him the bottle and he upends it. The liquor is oily and bitter and he sputters as he swallows it.

"Jesus Christ."

Big Junior laughs. "That's Gilby's, boy. Made in Augusta, right on the Savannah River."

"It *tastes* like the Savannah. Is it downstream from the nuclear plant?"

"Hell if I know."

"You ought to. You might wake up one of these nights and see your liver glowing in the dark."

"And then I'd be out of work," he says soberly, capping the bottle.

"Right," Jacob says. They are nearing the college now. Ahead, he can make out the lighted cupola of Memorial Charity Hospital, all-hours beacon to the city's injured drunks and battered wives. He has never thought before that any of them would be reluctant to seek its shelter. "So are you good for this? I can make it an even hundred for the job."

After a moment Big Junior begins nodding. "All right," he says. "But where your shovel, man? Can't even fit a suitcase in this car."

"It's at the school. Got a real pretty one just waiting for us."

NEARING FIVE A.M. now and only two of the garbage bags are full; Jacob is beginning to think that this job is hopeless. In half an hour they have covered only a few yards of the basement, sifting through the loose clay, sandy and striped with old lime in layers above each new set of bones. Big Junior seems to be moving slower by the minute. Once he nearly fell over when they uncovered a skull with its dome neatly sawed off. Jacob is sympathetic. Before they started, he had allowed himself one more drink, and now, with another belt of Big Junior's gin in his system, this task is seeming more surreal by the minute.

Jacob has a tibia in his hands when they hear sounds of movement outside, drifting in through the grated casements just above ground level. Quickly he stuffs the bone into the black garbage bag by his side and motions for Big Junior to be still. He hears the great front doors swing open, followed by the chirp of the security system he disabled when they entered. He curses himself for not rearming the alarm as footsteps sound on the boards above. Big Junior looks like he is ready to swoon for certain this time.

On his hands and knees, Jacob stares up the steps as the first-floor door swings open on its creaking hinges.

A pair of oversized hiking boots appears on the stairs, followed by white legs and knobby knees capped by tan Bermuda shorts. Above a Sam Browne belt, the visitor wears a khaki shirt as well. When the man's face comes into view, it is owlish behind huge spectacles resting above a red mustache that would have been more appropriate for the previous century. All he is missing, Jacob thinks, is a safari hat and a butterfly net.

The man claps his hands together as he surveys the basement. He seems delighted by what he sees, the gold shovel in particular. "What a splendid welcome," he says. He takes the remaining stairs two at a time and crosses the dirt floor toward Jacob, talking all the way.

"I worked all night to get a team together, and let me tell you, traveling in the wee hours, taking the back roads from Clemson wasn't even necessary. We made excellent time on the roads." He sticks out a hand, and Jacob slowly rises to shake it. "David Sanburn," he says as he pumps Jacob's hand. "Forensic anthropology, Clemson University."

He wears the thickest eyeglasses Jacob has ever seen. Behind the Coke-bottle lenses his eyes are refracted, so that when he speaks it seems he is addressing not Jacob but a point a few inches above his left shoulder.

"Professor Claybaugh, I presume?"

Jacob smiles bitterly. "No. I guess Adam is sleeping in. I'm Jacob Thacker, the college's public relations officer."

Sanburn takes another look at the gold shovel and the plastic bags, as if truly seeing them for the first time.

"And I'm sorry to tell you, Doctor Sanburn, but the party's over already. There's nothing here to merit your interest."

Sanburn takes off his glasses and begins to wipe them on the tail of his shirt. Without them, his eyes look tired and sad. "I had hoped there would be minimal friction in this matter, but perhaps I can head off some unpleasantness by telling you that Professor Claybaugh gave an entirely different account. So different, in fact, that I took the measure of notifying the South Carolina Historical Society last night, immediately after his phone call. Their offices are here in Columbia. There will be a delegation here at nine o'clock to determine whether the site is as extensive as Doctor Claybaugh indicated."

"Not possible. This is a working building, and under construction to boot. There won't be any visitors."

Sanburn smiles as he puts his glasses back on. "An office building, yes. But this building and its grounds are also a designated historical site. Which means that a discovery of archaeological significance places it under the aegis of the Historical Society until such discovery can be properly researched and catalogued."

Jacob begins to speak, but Sanburn raises a hand to silence him. "I mean you or the school no disrespect, sir. I am merely citing state law on the preservation of sites of cultural importance. We will work as quickly as we can, as I can see there is a construction schedule to be maintained." He looks over the basement. "Salvage archaeology. Far short of ideal conditions, but we must do what we can."

"I'm guessing there's no legal avenue to stop you."

Sanburn shakes his head. "I could refer you to a number of precedent cases, all of which dragged out in the courts and resulted in great expense for the plaintiffs. The interests of science prevailed in each case." Jacob would like to say a thing or two about science, but the man never seems to pause long enough for him to break in. "Medical College of West Virginia, 1980. Boston University, 1988. And Ann Arbor just last year. But that was only a disposal pit. Nothing of this magnitude. Disarticulated remains, clandestine medical practices in those cases, as here, but nowhere near the scope this looks to be."

"You seem almost happy about it."

"I'm happy whenever fugitive history gets a proper hearing."

Jacob snorts. "You're happy, all right. So you can write your article or what have you."

"Article?" Sanborn gives a dry laugh. "This is not the material for an article, my friend, but for a book."

"Good for your career, no doubt."

"That's incidental."

"The hell it is. Nothing is incidental."

Sanburn seems to think this over. "Perhaps I misspoke. Ultimately, I suppose, nothing is incidental. I stand corrected."

There is more activity upstairs. Jacob hears the front doors opening again, and soon the steps are full of people, mostly graduate students he guesses, coming down with shovels and picks, boxes and wooden stakes. Sanburn begins giving them their various assignments as efficiently as if he has spent days down here, dispersing them in groups to begin their work. A camera starts to flash, strobelike in the near darkness.

Jacob picks up the shovel, its gilded blade nicked and scraped down to the humble steel, and motions for Big Junior to follow him out. Sanburn interrupts his shouted instructions to thank him for his cooperation, and his assistants all turn their attention to the departing white man with his hulking black companion and gold shovel. Curious sensation: Jacob feels his cheeks burning as he files past all the quizzical faces with the shovel clutched tight in his fist. Unbidden, a phrase from the past has come into his mind: First, do no harm.

Upstairs, he hurls the shovel into a supply closet with a clang, knowing that neither he nor McMichaels will be wanting to see another shovel for a long, long time.

JACOB FIDGETS THROUGH the entire Wednesday staff meeting. He has cleaned himself up tolerably well, with a shower and shave and a charcoal suit fresh from the cleaners, and he tries to keep his hands clenched so that no one will notice the half-moons of dirt under his fingernails. But his head is still cloudy with fatigue and the lingering effects of the cheap gin, and the meeting seems to crawl through its agenda at a glacial pace. In practice he could have seen a half-dozen patients in as much time. These strange gatherings, a mix of all types from the college's spectrum of officials, have always amused him—the striking conglomerate of research scientists like Kirstin Reithoffer seated next to business officers, grabby development people trying to explain the subtleties of an "ask" to surgeons—but not today. Although he and the dean seem to be the only ones aware of it, things have changed; this meeting to discuss the school's weekly forward momentum is more pro forma than any of the others could imagine.

For the past hour McMichaels has fiddled with a glass paperweight, a gift from a local Kiwanis group, that he seems to find fascinating. Toying with it behind the huge mahogany desk, he looks like a superannuated child, just waiting for the meeting to grind to a halt. "Anything else?" he asks, squinting at the refraction of light through the milky glass.

Jacob glances down at his planner. Its agenda seems like the material of a fairy tale to him now, none of it significant. "The alumni magazine," he says. "We still haven't selected anyone for the cover."

"You send me a memo on that, Jake?"

"Sure. Week or so ago."

"Elizabeth." McMichaels sighs, as though his secretary's name alone were explanation for the sheaves of papers he has misplaced over the years. He sets the paperweight down on the desktop gently. "What about Branson Hodges? When was his last contribution?"

In the back of the room, Bennett rifles through a stack of papers. "Uh, '84, sir. Alumni annual fund."

The dean snorts. "Tightwad. Yup, put Hodges on the cover. Class of '82. He's got the biggest plastic surgery practice in Savannah. And still single. He's capable of a big damned gift. Put Hodges on the cover and see what he coughs up. Are we through here?"

Jacob checks his notepad. "That does it."

The dean nods all around, and the suits and white coats leave the table. "Good. I'm due on the fairway in fifteen minutes." He shucks his arms out of his suit jacket and hangs it on the coat tree behind his desk. "Jake, make sure your photographer gets a good shot of old Hodges. Lighting, touchup, whatever they do." He mimes a golf swing and winks at Jacob as the imaginary club comes to rest, perfect form, behind his back. "I want him to look good. Make the son of a bitch look just like Paul Newman."

Jacob nods and the dean casts an eye toward the door as it closes after the last faculty member.

"Jake," he says quietly, "what the hell happened this morning?"

"We got bushwhacked, Jim. Apparently Adam Claybaugh put in a call to Clemson yesterday. This Sanburn is connected all the way up. I've been on the phone all morning with the Historical Society. Looks like our hands are tied because the building's on the historical register. Best I could do was get him to commit to a two-week time frame. And no press, at least not yet. The Legal Department is drawing up the papers today."

McMichaels shakes his head sadly. "Claybaugh, you say?"

Jacob nods.

"That Anatomy Department is going to be the death of me." His brow knits as though he were working out a complex problem. Then he shakes his head again. "Can't touch him, damn it. He's tenured."

Jacob is shocked by the implication. "You'd fire Adam?"

McMichaels's eyes are burning fiercely when he speaks. "You're fucking-A right I would. This is a disaster for the school," he hisses. Then his face softens. "Claybaugh is a PhD anyway, Jake. He's not one of the brotherhood."

There is a long silence before Jacob speaks. "I'm not sure there isn't a way to spin this positively, sir. We've got a pretty big surplus in the capital fund. What if we set some of that aside? I could get to work on it. Maybe the key is to face this head-on. We could arrange a symposium on it, something commemorative. Get the ball in our court."

McMichaels looks at him incredulously. "Are you back on the Xanax? All the black community will think of is Tuskegee. Syphilis, for God's sake." When he sees the change in Jacob's face, he puts a hand on his shoulder. "Ah, Jake. I'm afraid the strain is getting to me."

The hand squeezes Jacob's shoulder, then drops. McMichaels

moves across the room to open a closet and pulls out a bag stuffed with golf clubs. Its strap creaks on his shoulder as he turns to leave.

"Someone's going to have to take a fall if this goes public, Jake. You'd better be thinking about Claybaugh. That's a viable option. There aren't many others left."

JACOB HAD TOLD himself that a midday drive would clear his head, that a few miles on the road with the top down might help him sort out whether what McMichaels had said was truly as ominous as he feared. But before he had even crossed the Gervais Street bridge over the Congaree, he realized it was no accident that his break from routine had taken him away from campus and headed west.

And now, twenty miles into the piney Midlands on the Old Chapin Road, he takes the cutoff to Lake Murray without a second thought, though he has not driven this stretch in half a dozen years. The lake comes into view on his left, through the trees, stretching across the horizon vast and green under the hazy sky. A half mile out, a motorboat churns the water, towing a skier, but otherwise the lake's surface is placid, as though in surrender to the August heat. When he pulls into the gravel lot of his aunt Pauline's store and shuts off the engine, the only sound is the lapping of water against the clay banks.

The store is built shotgun-style, long and narrow like the

mill house he grew up in, only larger. It stands on brick pilings a yard above the ground, its white-painted clapboards weathered and flaking. When he climbs the steps to the porch and reaches for one of the two screen doors, he can already hear the chirring of crickets inside.

The door slaps shut behind him and he takes it all in, all of it as he remembers: the long shelves along the walls built from two-by-fours and plywood, stocked with all manner of country sundries, from paper towels to boxes of ammunition. In the back sits an old ice cream freezer that has been covered with window screen, where the crickets are singing, and next to it a water tank topped with Styrofoam minnow buckets, a net for fishing out the minnows hung on its side. And there, behind a little cash register set on a glass case stocked with spinner baits and plastic worms, sits Aunt Pauline, a cigarette burning in one hand while she tots up figures in a spiral notebook with the other. She looks up from the notebook, squinting over her readers, and smiles at Jacob.

"We're fresh out of night crawlers, doc."

He smiles back at her. "Do I look like a worm fisherman to you, Pauline?"

She takes a long drag off her cigarette and stubs it out in the ashtray next to the register. "No, honey, you look like big money. Come over here and give me a hug, you weasel. I haven't seen you in ages."

He goes to her, wraps his arms around her skinny shoulders, inhales her scent of smoke and coffee and cheap perfume. Then she holds him at arm's length and looks him over.

"Yes, sir. Your daddy would be proud. You cleaned up real good."

"I'm sorry I haven't been around. I stay too busy for my own good."

"Appreciated the Christmas card last year. That's one good-looking girl you been going with."

Jacob smiles. "Kaye's Jewish. So it's not supposed to be a Christmas card. They're called holiday cards now. You know, to be more inclusive."

"Well, goddamn," Pauline says. "Times change."

"I guess they do."

She drops her eyes long enough for Jacob to look at her face. Pauline is nearing seventy and looks every year of it. Though her eyes are still bright, her cheeks are wrinkled beneath them, and fifty-odd years of sun and alcohol and nicotine have weathered her skin to the hue of a tobacco leaf. No wonder Pauline and his mother never got along: she must exhale smoke in her sleep.

But she is moving before he can think on it further, pulling up a stool for him next to hers at the counter and motioning for him to take it, asking questions about his job and life all the while. Before he sits, he pulls the folded paper out of his back pocket and straightens it on the glass countertop. Pauline's eyes settle on it for a quick moment, then cut away as she lights another cigarette.

Jacob stares down at the photocopied picture of the lecture room, at Professor Johnston and his slave, at the nurse.

"This is from the school's archives," he says. "It's probably from the 1860s. I can't get it out of my head that the woman looks like Dad."

Pauline looks at the picture again and sets her lighter down carefully. Jacob feels suddenly foolish for bringing it here. "It's crazy, I know," he says, reaching for the paper.

Her hand stops him, her fingers splayed across the paper, pressing down on the creases where he had folded it. When he looks up to meet her eyes, he sees that they are fixed on the nurse's face.

"I guess every family's got skeletons," she says, still looking down at the picture. Then she exhales a plume of smoke and looks at him tenderly, a deep sadness in her pale gray eyes.

TEN MINUTES LATER Jacob is sitting on the porch of Pauline's little bungalow out back of the store, his foot tapping against the floorboards while he waits for his aunt to return from inside. She has been moving slowly since she locked the store and flipped its OPEN sign around. He listens to her rummaging around inside the little house. When she emerges from the front door, he sees that she carries a small black book and two Budweiser tallboys. He shuts his eyes as she settles into the chair next to him and pops the can of beer open. Then he feels the cold aluminum pressed against his hand.

"Thanks, but I've got to be back at work."

Pauline ignores him. "Take it. Go ahead."

He takes the beer and tilts it back, a token sip. Pauline opens hers and gives it a long pull before setting it down on the porch floor and opening the little book in her lap. It is old, the gilt of the cross on its cover and the edges of the pages nearly worn off. She shows him the title page—the Book of Common Prayer—then flips through it to the back and pulls out a handful of old pictures. She shows him snapshots of his father and herself as children, then an older picture—not black-and-white now, but sepia—of men in straw hats and suspenders at a picnic beneath live oaks.

"That's my granddaddy James, grown then." She shuffles the picture to the back of the stack. "Here's one when he was a boy." She shows him a shot of a boy in a cart drawn by a goat.

"And here's one of James with his mother, Sara, when he was I reckon one year old."

Jacob looks at the portrait and sees a little boy in a christening gown perched on the lap of the woman from the school picture.

"Sara Thacker," Pauline says. "The midwife."

Jacob studies the eyes in the portrait. "All right. But I'm not getting it. What's the secret?"

For answer Pauline turns the Book of Common Prayer back to its front, the pages for baptisms and confirmations. He sees that James Thacker was baptized at Saint Mary's, Lexington, on April 18, AD 1867. The name and dates are written on the page in flowing script. But though there are two lines reserved for parents' names, only one is filled, with Sara Thacker's small signature.

Jacob looks up and sees that Pauline has been watching him intently. "Your daddy never told you because he never wanted it spoken of. He was ashamed."

Jacob shakes his head slowly.

"She was what you nowadays call a single mother," Pauline says. "Only they didn't call it that back then. What they called it was a disgraced woman and her bastard son. Can you imagine what it was like for Granddaddy James growing up? He probably had to whip every boy in school, every year. But they made a life of it. Granddaddy James never turned mean, bless his heart. And people loved Sara. Loved her. They say she birthed half the babies in Lexington County."

Jacob looks down at the blank line again. "So who was the father?"

"She never did say."

Jacob shakes his head again. "You have to have some idea."

"Nope. She wouldn't say. You think she was the first poor girl to get herself in trouble? But she never told who the father was, not even to James. Never married, either."

Pauline shuts the book gently, traces the cross on its cover with her finger. "And that is the Thacker family tree. I wish you wouldn't be angry with your daddy. He wanted a better life for you."

She lights a cigarette and stares out across the lawn at the lake. "Back in the forties a bomber plane went down in that lake, couple miles from the dam. A B-25. They flew them on training missions out from the army air base down in Lexington. There's a rich doctor up in Greenville's been raising money to bring it up, put it in a museum. He's been at it for years. A lot of folks think he's crazy. It's down deep, and it's been down there a long time."

"I think I see what you're saying."

"I'm just telling you, a lot of things in the past are just plain gone. Sometimes it's more trouble than it's worth going after them."

Jacob takes a deep drink from his beer. *Immoral conduct*, he thinks as the Budweiser turns bitter in his mouth. "I still don't see why Dad never told me about her—especially after I started at the school. It makes no sense."

"I'm thinking," Pauline says, tapping the cover of the book in her lap, "that nobody knew about the school. Granddaddy James used to tell stories about Sara all the time, about her and all those babies. But he never said anything about the medical school. I've never heard mention of her working anywhere but West Columbia. I thought you were the first Thacker up there. Hell, you were the first one of us to even go to college."

Jacob rises from his chair and stretches. He can feel the alcohol beginning to seep into his bloodstream.

"They're going to be looking for me at the school if I don't get back there soon. It's been a hell of a lunch break." He sighs. "And I've got an afternoon full of meetings."

As they walk back to his car, Pauline surprises him by taking his hand, holding it in hers like a girl. When he opens the car door she hugs him tightly.

"You take care of yourself," she says in her Marlboro voice, "and don't wait so long before you come back out here again."

He kisses her cheek and gets in the car. As he pulls out of the lot, he watches her in his rearview mirror turning the store sign around again, looking frail through the glass. When she is gone from his view he reaches for his cell phone and punches in the number for the school's directory so that he can call Janice Tanaka and ask her where in the hell one goes to find a 130-year-old birth certificate.

Fernyear: 1864

JOHNSTON WOKE WITH HIS HEAD ON his desk. His lamp had burned down to the last threads of the wick and the sky outside was at its blackest pitch. He pulled out his pocket watch and looked at it: 3:50. Nemo should have been back with the MacCallan woman by two or three at the latest, but he was late—never a good omen for a resurrection man.

Johnston gathered his coat and hat. He was trying to plot out the shortest route to the colored cemetery when he heard the scrape of the back door, followed by the thump of a heavy bundle being dropped on the wooden floor. He sighed and put his coat back on the wall hook. Rolling up his sleeves, he started down the hall.

In the dissecting room Nemo had laid out a body on a table and was cutting the cords that bound a second bundle at his feet. His knife severed the hemp cords effortlessly and he lifted the sheeted body to its place with a grunt.

"Two?" Johnston said. "In one evening? Extraordinary." He pulled the sheet off Ossie MacCallan and brushed dirt from her cheek. "What is your guess here? Do you think the colored doctor got it right?"

"Looks it, sir." Nemo stretched the other body across the next table and rested a hand on its ample belly. "Might as well warn you now, boss. Got a white man here."

Johnston gave a start. "That is strictly off-limits. What do you think we are?"

"He's a no-count, sir, just an old buckra off the rail line. Confederate deserter's my guess." Nemo's hand hovered over the covered face. "You ready?"

Johnston nodded. Nemo rolled the covering back to reveal a begrimed face, black whiskers, and a trail of tobacco juice— apparently permanent—at one corner of the mouth. The face still wore a grimace, and a delicate open line ran halfway across the neck beneath the chin.

"I can tell you cause of death right now, sir. Going to be exsanguination by a severed carotid artery. You find a puncture wound to the left kidney under this stain here." He gestured to a darkened patch on the sackcloth shirt.

Johnston turned the man's jaw to have a better look at the slit throat.

"It's that neck that done it. Kidney weren't more than a warning."

"Nemo, this man's flesh has not yet cooled. There is no sign of rigor. He can't be even a day old."

"No, sir. He ain't but two, three hours old. I'll get the formalin directly."

"Wait. I suspect there is foul play involved here. Where was he buried?"

"Didn't say he was buried, sir."

Johnston covered his face. "Out with it."

"Well," Nemo said, drawing the word out, "I did find him in Cedar Vale, indeed. At Mrs. MacCallan's grave, matter of fact. Digging. He weren't about to be discouraged by my claim." Nemo leaned against the table and put his hands in his pockets. "Naturally, we articulated about it for some minutes, but his voice kept rising. Rose quite a bit when I showed him my blade. Weren't a thing to do but the expeditious thing, so I done it."

"You cut his throat?"

"Don't forget about that kidney. He had his warning."

"This is murder, Nemo."

Nemo laughed his mortuary laugh. "No, sir. Now don't go getting excited. It's done now, and there's one less speculating sack-'em-up man in the world and one more study for the college. He'll do some good in the world now."

"My God. Nemo, you are *colored*. You have killed a *white* man. No matter his station in life, this is—"

"Wasn't at the station, sir. Had of been, he'd still be there."

"Damn it, Nemo!" Johnston's cheeks had blanched. "You would be hanged for this. Hanged before they did worse to you, if you were lucky. You know well that merely assaulting a white man is a capital offense."

Nemo's voice was soft when he spoke. "He won't be missed, sir. He really was no-count. Check his pockets. Nothing in them but a fork and a heel of bread, and wasn't no more in them when he was breathing."

Johnston laid his hands on the table and looked down at the dead man as though he were a kinsman.

"You never turned me in, Doctor Johnston. Never. Because you know the things I've done, I've done without no say in matters."

Johnston looked up at Nemo. "Not a word of this. Not the first word of how he was procured."

Nemo smiled. "I'll get that formalin now. I mean it now, Doctor Johnston, don't you fret it a minute. Cedar Vale's my graveyard. I can't tolerate no freelancing in there. Next thing you know, bottom rail be on top."

Johnston watched his broad shoulders disappear down the stairs. *Bottom rail, pshaw,* he thought. *You are on top of the whole game.*

FROM HIS CORNER of the dissecting room, where he watched the students bent over their cadavers, busily at work, Nemo judged the scene before him to be a beautiful sight this spring afternoon, a veritable vision of plenty. The twenty-five men so hastily concluding their training as Confederate surgeons were matched, each of them, with a cadaver of their own—better than two dozen white male specimens culled from the Union dead in the Shenandoah Valley. With the war going so strong and Lee and Stonewall Jackson still tearing up the Federals in Virginia, it seemed that his digging days were finally behind him. Twice this month he had been sent up to Raleigh to meet Champ, the University of Virginia's man, at the midway point between the schools to gather up a wagonload of dead boys who had fallen far from their homes in Ohio, Wisconsin, or Maine. And they were fine specimens: young men in good health and well fed, perfect save for the odd missing limb or the angry-looking rash left on their abdomens by grapeshot. These days, Nemo's procurement chores were hardly less pleasant than buying handkerchiefs by the carton, to cover the faces and genitals of the dead.

This afternoon, however, the handkerchiefs over the cadavers' faces had been removed for the dissection of the brain. With the tops of their skulls removed, the bodies looked oddly shortened, but Nemo was satisfied with the progress he observed as the students separated the lobes of the brains and traced the intricate network of the superficial cerebral veins. In his practicum lecture he had demonstrated the need for steady but light cutting, pointing out the thin coat on the veins from the median section along the longitudinal fissure to their termination in the sinuses. Seeing the students intent on their task, he settled back with a copy of Emerson's *Nature*, reading it for perhaps the fifth time, content among the usual busy sounds of the dissecting room, punctuated now and then by a muttered curse or the tinny clang of a dropped instrument.

"Boy, what you want to be reading Emerson for?"

Nemo put a finger in the book to mark his place, just below a passage he had underlined in India ink the last time: "Even the corpse has its own beauty."

"Beg pardon, Mister Cullen?"

"I said, why are you wasting your time with Emerson? That Yankee don't know shit from apple butter."

"Emerson been good to me."

"He'll put a lot of fool ideas in your head, is what he'll do. The *Messenger* said it best. Called that last book of his 'spasmodic idiocy.'"

One of the other students laughed. "A man in your line of work ought to be reading Poe."

"I've read him. Read 'The Premature Burial' twice. He got it about right," Nemo said, smiling. "But now, Poe seem to me to be the spasmodic one."

Cullen stiffened. "You wouldn't be reading the Sears catalogue if it was up to me."

"Yes, sir."

Cullen seemed ready to say more, but another student was calling out and beckoning to Nemo.

"Nemo! Help me here with this dura mater, will you, boy?"

JOHNSTON SHIFTED IN his chair, wishing he were anywhere else in the building except for this office, where the presence of Sara Thacker seemed to make the order of this familiar room, his carefully arranged books and diplomas, fade to inconsequence. Nearly a minute had passed since either of them had spoken, and still he found himself struggling for an adequate answer to her question. Every time he looked up into her gray eyes his resolve to answer her manfully collapsed.

"I'll say it again, then," she said. "Three years."

"Yes," Johnston said, stroking his beard.

"And has the condition of the Negro hospital not improved dramatically? Has Doctor Evans not been pleased with my work?"

"But Sara, I have admitted you to several lectures."

"And do you know how many babies I've delivered myself, when Doctor Evans's affairs detained him at the Five Points Tavern? Seven breech babies I've turned in the womb. Seven!"

"Your midwifery is to be commended, Sara."

"Midwifery! Doctor Evans would have put those women under the knife. Surely that demonstrates my ability to take the obstetrics course at the very least."

Johnston's brow furrowed. "Can you imagine yourself among those boys in the dissecting laboratory? Can you imagine the disruption it would cause? There is already opprobrium enough for us, having a woman nurse on the staff. It can go no further, I am afraid."

Sara ignored him. "Elizabeth Blackwell graduated from the Geneva Medical School in 1849," she said. "Three women have been admitted to Syracuse since. There is talk of a medical college being opened in Pennsylvania solely for females."

"Yes. In New York and Pennsylvania. Both of them a long way from here, Sara. But why not apply to them?"

For the first time, Sara's eyes faltered. "Would you have me leave?"

"No. But what you are asking is simply impossible at this time."

Then her cheeks flushed. "You know I do not have the means. I can study here or not at all."

Johnston rose and walked behind her chair. He placed a hand on her shoulder and kneaded it softly. "Change comes slowly to the South. Give it time, my dear."

Sara dropped her head. "I believe you mean more time than I am likely to have."

"Patience, dear. The day will come."

"But when? Surely, Frederick, you know that I am capable."

"There is capable, and there is feasible. If we took a stand on the principle, we would lose the bulk of our enrollment. What good would it do to be a graduate of a defunct institution?"

"It would do me a great deal of good, Frederick. But I can see how the institution figures in this."

Johnston put a hand on Sara's other shoulder and bent down to kiss her sandy hair. But the gesture was awkward, for Sara was slowly shaking her head from side to side.

SUNDAY MORNING, MAY 10, 1864, and Nemo Johnston was a spectacle of superfine raiment and bearing. His haberdashery was all in place, from the fine felt bowler just arrived from the Bloomingdale's catalogue to his wool suit with a subtle stripe accented by a silk pocket square of the finest ivory hue. All of it set off by the gold-handled cane he had retrieved from Colonel Lamar's coffin last week. He made his way leisurely down this public street dressed finer than most of Columbia's white citizens, grinning like a death's head.

The Columbia *South Carolinian* folded under his arm bore news of a slave uprising down in All Saints Parish, two plantations over from Drake's Windsor. With the Union gunboat blockade just off their shore, the rice aristocrats were losing control; two overseers had been killed—one shot, the other hanged—and there were now armed slaves loose in the low country. The newspaper compared the uprising to those of Denmark Vesey and Nat Turner, reminding its readers that upwards of fifty whites were dead before they brought Nat down. The *South Carolinian* writer, in fact, seemed nearly hysterical. Nemo had already read the article twice over his breakfast, but had decided that the news was so good he would carry the paper all day.

The morning was especially fine, so he detoured from his usual route, drawn by singing in the Episcopal Cathedral on Gervais a block away. Rare indeed for the devil's right hand to darken this door, but this was an extraordinary day. He slipped through the great doors and climbed the steps to the slave balcony soundlessly.

Upstairs was full of the smell of starched cotton and sweated wool, black faces gleaming over the busy fans that could never cool these upper reaches in the Carolina heat. A nearly electric tension followed him as his brethren marked the appearance of the slave quarters' boogeyman in this sacred place. He squeezed into an open seat beside a teenage girl—Tyree's niece, he thought—who dropped her fan to the floor and stared at him, her head wobbling slightly, as though a timber rattler had come to service and alighted beside her. He showed her a mouthful of white teeth.

The singing ended and the rector rose to the pulpit, bespectacled and albed and looking especially stern. Without preamble he leaned upon the great Bible propped before him and read: " 'Woe unto you, scribes and Pharisees, hypocrites! For ye are like unto whited sepulchers, which indeed appear beautiful outward, but are within full of dead men's bones, and of all uncleanness. Even so ye also outwardly appear righteous unto men, but within ye are full of hypocrisy and iniquity.' So says Christ Jesus, in chapter twenty-three of Matthew's gospel," the rector said, "and it is a text with particular application to the congregation gathered here today."

Nemo leaned forward in his seat, hardly believing his luck. Years now since he had last emerged from this building with the bilious taste of its bland hypocrisy in his mouth, and he had sworn then that he had quit this godforsaken place for good. But now, on his first day back, the white preacher had welcomed him with a homecoming message, the truth at last. He gazed down upon the rows of white parishioners below and thought, *You had it coming and now you going to get it, and all your chattel up here to witness it.*

"For it has come to be known here in Columbia—and throughout the South—that conditions within our domestic sphere untouched by northern aggression are not so blessedly tranquil as they have lately seemed," the rector said. His face was tilted upward, as was Nemo's; Nemo was beginning to wonder if the God he had heard discussed so warmly since he landed in Charleston might not be showing his presence after all. But when he lowered his gaze from the timbered ceiling, Nemo saw that the preacher's eyes were raised not to heaven but to the balcony.

"My sable brethren, these dry bones are not just the sins of the gambling house, the saloon, the bedchamber of your neighbor's wife. These dry bones of iniquity are also the hardness of heart you may feel toward your masters, for as our Savior Christ has told us, we are all servants, and should be humble, gracious, obedient. This is no less true for the benighted child of Africa than for the sons and daughters of Europe—nay, it is even more so."

Nemo leaned back, settling against the pew heavily. It seemed that the preacher had read the morning paper too.

He allowed himself to drift for a few moments then, knowing he had been burned again by this great white machine, all-powerful, with its plotting and knowing tentacles stretched out a half mile farther down any road he had yet chosen to travel. So for some minutes his mind was elsewhere, as it often was on moonless nights in Cedar Vale, prospecting among the remains of his people for forage to sneak through the back door of the medical school. As he did then, he thought not of this steaming southland but of vast dry plains far away, of mile-wide suns setting savannahs afire with the orange glow of sunset.

But the man's voice kept bringing him back. And the eyes, the pale blue eyes quick with life. Every time the preacher looked up from his text they rose to the balcony, scorching and accusative. When Nemo knew that Doctor Ballard, down front and center in the pews, had just performed an appendectomy on the rector's daughter, Margaret, cauterizing the wound as he'd practiced on the body of Berenice MacCallan's mother—and Berenice herself sitting two rows behind him now.

Nemo thought back to assisting at the dress rehearsal of that procedure in the anatomy laboratory—the suturing and tying of Mrs. MacCallan's dead appendix—when the preacher's voice returned to him, the words seeping into his consciousness like the bite of formalin in the nose.

"And hear me well, you servants, destined for a higher station in the glorious hereafter," the preacher said—always, always, Nemo thought, a better place once dead. Poor Mrs. MacCallan hadn't got there yet, as far as he could see. "Repentance never comes too late. I urge you to bring your dry bones into the light, to confess the sins of your plotting against your masters. I say to you, my black brothers, come forward and confess your sins and even the scribes and Pharisees among you will be forgiven."

He felt it welling up inside him, stronger than anything he had felt in years. Maybe it was Doctor Ballard sitting down front in his white suit looking innocent as a lamb, pure as a whited sepulcher. Maybe it was Berenice MacCallan murmuring "Yes, Lord" behind him, knowing nothing of the busy week her mama had had at the college, picked over by a third of the faculty before he laid her in the basement under a thick coat of lime. Maybe it was even the news from All Saints, turning the tide down by the Waccamaw, swapping bone for bone. Probably it was all these things. He saw it all now—this sermon, this moment—as the punch line to a great cosmic joke, two hundred years of irony echoing across the oceans from Africa to Columbia. And because he could do little else, he began to laugh. A chuckle at first, and one of his pew mates shushed him, but the preacher was off again on the dirty bones and Nemo, bone man himself, cackled aloud. Bowing over with it, he saw that he had clamped a hand on his neighbor's knee—that of Tyree's niece, who sat walleyed, transfixed and petrified by this contact in spite of the indignity.

"No, child, I ain't no Satan. Devil's in the good seats," he said, his throat hitching. "Downstairs. On the ground floor."

He was gone then, beyond restraint. A basso roar, peals of his laughter cascaded down from the balcony. Faces turned up toward its source, reddening—none of them redder than Ballard's when he spotted Nemo. A handful of men rose and made their way up the aisle. In seconds he could hear them pounding up the stairs.

"That's right, white folks, send up the deacons!" he shouted before exploding again.

There was a shuffle behind him, and Nemo felt hands hooking him under his arms. He had only a second to dab his glistening cheeks with his handkerchief before they hauled him up.

Downstairs they hurled him clear of the nave steps onto the sidewalk. Rising, he replaced his pocket square and adjusted the bowler back to its steep angle. He set out for home with the gold cane tapping the sidewalk bricks smartly, evenly, his head held high. He was smiling again, for Nemo Johnston was superfine, a man among men, and despite the rough handling, entirely beyond their reach.

EDWIN WINSTON SAT on a stool behind the wooden dispensing counter of the apothecary, his eyes intent on the pages of the ledger spread open before him, blissfully content among the familiar scents of calomel and castor oil. The morning was quiet, the only sounds at this moment the scratch of his pen's nib against the paper and the creaking of the wooden stepladder on which Nemo stood, above and behind him, reaching for another bottle of patent medicine on the apothecary's tall shelves. They had been at this work for an hour now, the professor of chemistry tallying off inventory as the slave called out quantities of Burnett's Cod Liver Oil, McMunn's Elixir of Opium, Dr. Wistar's Balsam of Wild Cherry. Winston wrote out each number carefully in his ledger, periodically pausing to press a blotter on the pages to soak up the fresh ink from the fountain pen. The room was filled with lambent autumn light, dust motes dancing in it, and the light glinted off the doctor's spectacles as he nodded at the figures in the ledger.

"Barnes's Magnolia Water," Nemo said, "two quarts."

"Very good. That leaves only Winston's Baby Syrup. How much?"

Nemo shook a bottle, its liquid contents sloshing against the brown glass. "Just one half pint, Doctor Winston, near empty."

Winston smiled. "Going like hotcakes, is it not? I'll mix up a new batch this evening. Ballard tells me he can hardly keep enough on hand for new mothers with colicky babies. The morphine is the ticket." Winston looked up at Nemo. "I say this in the strictest of confidence, of course. The blend is proprietary. I am expecting word from the Patent Office any day now."

Nemo nodded as he descended the stepladder. "Congratulations to you, sir."

"Missus Winston is nearly beside herself with pleasure," he said, blushing. He cleared his throat and looked back at the ledger. "All is satisfactory except for the laudanum count. One expects the students to dip into it from time to time, but this year's boys are setting the record, I am afraid. Have you seen anyone back here more than usual?"

Nemo shrugged his shoulders. "They a few claiming stomach ailments."

Winston seemed about to inquire further, but before he

could speak again the door opened and Johnston entered, looking flushed and triumphant. He shut the door behind him carefully and smiled at Winston and Nemo as he leaned against it.

"We have a most propitious new enrollment," he said at last.

Winston shut the ledger. "This late? The term began two
weeks ago."

"Trust me, Winston, you will be happy to make whatever
adjustments are necessary. Our new man is a refugee from the
low country, a gentleman who has lately vacated his lands for
fear that Sherman's march will proceed to the seaboard. Nemo,
do you remember a Mister Albert Fitzhugh from All Saints
Parish?"

Nemo stiffened slightly. "Two plantations over from Windsor, I recall." He remembered much of the Fitzhughs, from
what he had heard at Christmas visiting-time from the slaves
five miles down the coast. Fitzhugh, it was said, had shot a field
hand named Monday in the face for working too slowly at har-
vesttime. He had left the body in the fields as a reminder to the
others, who watched it picked over by crows as they hoed the
nearby rows. Two nights later, some of them had stolen out to
the field and buried the body in a levee. "Folks said the old
gentleman was a Christian man."

Johnston waved a hand in the air. "He may have been, but it
is the son I am talking about. He spends money like a pagan."
Johnston crossed the room and set a paper on the counter in
front of Winston.

"Check those figures, Winston. I negotiated special terms

for his admission. It seems there is no accredited high school in the parish. Certain tuition adjustments were thus in order to make his matriculation amenable to our standards."

Winston's eyes widened behind the glass lenses. "By what terms did you arrive at these fees?"

"He will need tutorials to bring him up to speed. His mathematical ability is atrocious, his chemistry even worse, Winston. We will all have to take a special interest in his progress." Johnston turned to Nemo. "I am placing his success in the anatomy course in your hands, Nemo."

Nemo began to speak, but the doctor turned on his heel and motioned for the slave to follow him. "To the dissecting room, Nemo. Mister Fitzhugh expressed an interest in beginning the course of study immediately."

After a moment's pause, the slave followed him, hurrying to catch up so that he could hold the door open for the doctor. Johnston was already talking again, a stream of words pouring forth that Winston did not hear. Neither did the chemist note the silence that ensued once they had gone beyond the shut door, so intent was he on scribbling ratios of morphine, sugar, and corn syrup on his shirt cuff, all the quantities doubled from his last production run of Winston's Baby Syrup. He could hardly wait to share the news with Mrs. Winston.

NEMO MOVED QUIETLY down the midnight-dark cobble-stone streets, the moon dim above him through the blanket of fog that had settled over the town and its river-basin valley as though it meant to choke out all the life there. The fog was packed densely between the buildings, spilling out of the alleys and into Harden Street, damping the usual glare of the street's opulent gaslights to irregular flickers little stronger than candles. Against the stones, his footfalls were strangely muted by the close air, short echoes tapering quickly into the fog and dying there.

How strange, this near silence. Ten years ago he could not have imagined a city the size of Columbia, but he had grown to love it—its colors and noise, so many sounds, even at night, from the horses and milk cows in their stalls on every block to the ruckus of the red-light district down on Huger, near the river, throwing up its bawdy roar into the wee hours. A steady din that rivaled the slave quarters at Christmas, every night. It had always made his work easier. But tonight, it seemed, he alone was stirring.

He paused to check the address written on his hand against the numbers he could just make out on the iron placard fastened to the front of a brick townhouse. When he was certain the address was correct, he stepped up to the front door and gave the brass bellpull two short yanks. After a moment he heard sounds of movement inside, and the door was thrown open to reveal Albert Fitzhugh in a silk dressing gown. Fitzhugh's eyes seemed unaccustomed to the darkness outside; for nearly a minute he only stared at his caller, as though without recognition. Nemo saw that behind him the parlor was heavily furnished, its walls adorned in a flocked wallpaper against which hung an oval portrait of an aristocratic-looking white woman. When his eyes fell again to Fitzhugh's face, he saw that it had reddened.

"My God. You are at my front door." He looked up and down the street in spite of the fog and the hour. "Are you insane, boy?"

"Doctor Evans said—"

"Go around back." The door slammed shut.

Grinning, Nemo stepped off the narrow porch and hooked around its banister into the alley, waving at the fog as he had once swiped at spiderwebs in the dense thickets of All Saints. This new boy had become his cross to bear, certainly, but even this cross came with certain amusements. He remembered the day Johnston had introduced them in the dissecting room, how they had found Fitzhugh sitting on top of the demonstration desk in the midst of a monologue to the other students about the gout that had regrettably kept him out of this great fight, about the lodgings he had secured for himself and his mother on Harden Street, about his and his mother's decision that he could best be of service to the cause as a Confederate surgeon. At his feet had lain a mottled hound with brown ears and doleful eyes. The dog had risen, growling, when Nemo entered the room. Johnston had settled a hand on Nemo's shoulder then, smiling uncomfortably.

"Mister Fitzhugh, tell us again the name of your companion."

Fitzhugh had dropped off his perch on the desk and begun scratching the dog under its jowls.

"Stonewall. He's an English pointer. Best bird dog in the low country. I paid a hundred Confederate dollars for him and he was worth every penny of it."

Nemo had suppressed a smile. He had just read an article in the *South Carolinian* reporting sorrowfully that the Confederate dollar was now trading nine to one against gold. This dog was depreciating fast.

Despite Fitzhugh's ministrations, the dog still growled at Nemo. "Doesn't like niggers, though," Fitzhugh said thoughtfully. "Might want to keep that boy clear of him."

"Perhaps he may not have a place in the dissecting laboratory," Johnston had said carefully.

Fitzhugh straightened to his full height. "He goes where I go."

Johnston cleared his throat. "Very well, then. But this Negro is your preceptor in anatomy. Some compromise will have to be reached."

Fitzhugh had nearly quit just then, but at Johnston's urging, and with assurances from the other students of Nemo's abilities, Stonewall had been retired with a kick under the table set aside for his master. Yet even after Doctor Johnston had gone, the dog still growled and yipped as Nemo set out Fitzhugh's dissecting knives and saws, and nipped once at his ankle. Fitzhugh laughed, so Nemo had thrown the sheet off the dead corporal from the Wisconsin Regulars a little more abruptly than usual, to showcase the bruising on the dead man's collarbones and around the bayonet wound in his chest, which was now leaking pale formalin. Once Fitzhugh had recovered from his pallor, he spoke almost reverently.

"My first patient."

"Don't look like he's going to make it."

Fitzhugh had glared at him. "I used to own niggers down in the country," he said.

Nemo had folded the sheet evenly. "That a fact, captain?" he had said, already moving away with the folded sheet, glad to put some distance between the dog and his ankles.

"And I believed in the whip," Fitzhugh had said to Nemo's back.

He could hear the dog now, barking furiously in the kitchen at the rear of the house. Fitzhugh was waiting for him there in the open doorway, one hand against the jamb and the other knotted into the ruff of Stonewall's neck.

"What in God's name are you doing here, and at this hour?"

"I was saying that Doctor Evans want you down to the Negro hospital to watch a live birth. Woman's been in labor two hours and he can't hold the baby off much longer."

"You woke me for this? A nigger live birth?"

"Doctor Evans say it's time for you to start your obstetrics training."

Fitzhugh seemed too furious for speech. He caught a flicker of movement in Nemo's eyes and turned. Behind him, on the townhouse's back staircase, stood a middle-aged woman in a voluminous satin robe, her hair bundled under a linen sleeping cap. Nemo recognized her as the woman from the portrait in the parlor, only heavier and with more pronounced cheekbones than the portraitist had recorded. She clutched the stair railing nervously as she looked down on them.

"Albert, what is it?" she said, her voice giving way to a heavy cough.

"Get back to bed, dear," Fitzhugh said gently. "You should be resting."

With a worried glance, the woman climbed the steps out of sight. Fitzhugh turned back to Nemo. "The town air disagrees with Mother," he explained, "and the last thing she needs is a strange nigger interrupting her sleep."

"You want I should send Doctor Johnston out for her? Cough sounds deep."

"I'll attend to Mother, thank you," Fitzhugh said archly. He looked down at the dog, whining in his grip. "I'm inclined to turn Stonewall loose on you for bothering her."

Nemo did not budge, only raised his hands in a gesture of strained patience. "What you want me to tell Doctor Evans? That woman can't wait long."

The door was already shutting on Fitzhugh's response. "Come back when you have a paying patient," he said.

Nemo turned to make his way back to the school. He had taken perhaps a half-dozen steps on the courtyard bricks when a shape came out of the fog in front of him, too quickly for him to reach into the pocket where he kept the knife. A face pressed close to his before he could see that it was female, and smiling.

"I knew that voice. You Cudjo from over on Windsor, ain't you?"

The face was not only smiling but beautiful, a honeyed brown the color of deep amber, yet he squared his shoulders just the same.

"Who's asking?"

"It's Amy, Mister Cudjo. Don't you remember me?"

Nemo felt his shoulders loosen, remembering a thirteen-year-old with ribbons plaited in her hair, fanning rice from a grass basket into one of the hollowed-out trunks that served as mortars after the harvest, her smile as bright as the sun.

"Toby and Maria's Amy?"

Her smile broadened. "That's me," she said, nodding. "Come up with Mister Albert and Mrs. Libby. Ain't this a fine town?" She held out a hand to him, almost formally, and he took it. Her touch was cool and warm at the same time.

"How come you didn't stay with your mama?"

"Daddy said she too old to travel. Sent me instead. I'm so glad to be out of them All Saints fields I don't know what to do with myself."

Nemo placed his other hand on top of hers, encircling it with the darker skin of his own.

"Well, you out of the frying pan, girl," he said, sighing as he looked back at the townhouse. "Let's just hope you ain't landed smack in the fire."

Nemo sat on his front porch in his favorite rocking chair, reading a week-old *South Carolinian*, warming his bones in the weak afternoon sunlight that bathed his west-facing house. This December had started breezy and cold and showed no signs of letting up any time soon. Twice this week he had begun his mornings by breaking ice on the surface of his well, dropping the bucket hard to crack through the icy skim, which shattered like glass in the predawn stillness. But this afternoon was warm enough, just barely, to sit outside and take in some fresh air, to watch the sun play out its hues over the rooftops of Rosedale and read a little news of the war.

All the news this month, like most of November's, was of William Tecumseh Sherman. His name had been anathema to the southern press since Meridian, and now, with Atlanta and Savannah burned to cinders, the *South Carolinian* seemed to be straining to find epithets enough to heap on the Yankee war criminal. Charleston would be next, the paper said gloomily; all Columbia could do for its sister city was offer consolations from its safe distance up in the Midlands, clear of the sea and too insignificant to burn. Yet still the city was shrouded by an anxiety he could feel in the air, could sense in the quick gait of people on the streets, the quiet apprehension of the horses and livestock.

Maybe it was the newcomers who spread the unease; half of Charleston and Savannah, it seemed to Nemo, had been here since the harvest moon, fleeing Sherman's swath of destruction with as many of their belongings as they could carry. The city was loud with their low-country accents, all the boardinghouses full. They had brought their things, and they had brought their money too: Nemo saw an article on the front page announcing that Columbia was now home to fourteen banks, when just five years ago there had been only three. He reminded himself to point out the piece to Doctor Johnston, who would be pleased by the growth potential the article indicated. Lately the doctor had been nearly disconsolate over the progress of the war.

Nemo heard the rasp of metal on metal out at his front gate. Without moving the newspaper held in front of him, he dropped his left hand to the pocket of his overcoat. He felt the cold steel of his knife there and pulled it out slowly, placing it at the proper angle across his lap.

He folded the paper over to the second page, lowering it, and as he did so he caught sight of a group of figures at his front gate, silhouetted in the orange light of the lowering sun. He counted five of them. He was about to speak when he saw one of them drag a stick along his fence pickets. It rattled against the fence and fell silent.

"Say, Mister Nemo. You really the booger-man?"

The speaker's head just barely cleared the top of the fence.

"Who that out there projecting in my yard?"

His deep voice startled a couple of the boys, who stepped back closer to the road. But the speaker pressed forward, through the open gate, and walked a half-dozen slow steps up the walkway. Nemo saw that his feet were swaddled in old croker sacks against the cold, and that he wore no coat.

"I say, you really the booger-man?"

"Step closer, child. I can't see your eyes."

"Ain't afraid. Mama tell me you going to hell."

"Come closer, child. I got to be able to look you in the face."

As if emboldened by invoking his mother, the boy stepped up nearly to the porch. Nemo saw that he was standing on one of his pansies, the croker-sack binding on his foot crushing the flower, which had been holding out strong against the winter cold, still blooming purple and yellow.

"Mama say you going straight to hell. She say the plat-eye going to get you and take you down there hisself."

"I got something to tell you, child," Nemo said, setting the newspaper down and leaning as far forward as the rocking chair would allow, his chin poised over the porch rail. "I *am* the plat-eye." He raised two fingers in the direction of the boy's eyes and wriggled them like brown snakes.

The wail seemed to begin deep within the child's body and rose in crescendo as if to match his widening eyes. In seconds the sound reached a full-pitched scream, and he turned and ran down the lane with his shirttail flapping. The others followed him like a Greek chorus of woe in rapid transit, pursued by Furies.

Nemo rocked back and laughed deeply. "Oh, my," he said, wiping his cheeks.

Just at the edge of his yard, by the bare crape myrtle that marked the property line he shared with Mrs. Thompson next door, the boys parted like a stream around a woman coming down the sandy walk. He saw that it was Amy, and he laughed again at her expression of consternation as she shut the gate behind her.

"Oh, me," he said by way of greeting. "What a man's got to do to keep his property private."

Amy shook her head, but he saw the wisp of a smile on her light-brown face. "That was Aunt Sampson's boy. You gone catch hell from her tomorrow. Tonight, if she get mad enough."

"I ain't catching nothing. Ma Sampson ought to keep her mouth shut around that boy. He got a big enough mouth without putting gossip into it."

"Least we know he gets it natural." Amy settled languidly down on the top step, at Nemo's feet. The paper lay on the boards beside him, forgotten as he latched his fingers between hers, but he put the knife back in his coat pocket quietly. Almost two months of Saturday visits from Amy now, since the night at Albert Fitzhugh's place, and still he marveled at how his heart raced when he was near her, pounding through the mellow tenor of these afternoons.

"What you reading in that paper?"

"Nothing much. Says Wade Hampton got Columbia all stitched up tight. Says Sherman going to get Charleston sure, Augusta maybe, but we holding tight."

Amy looked up at him sharply. "How old that paper?"

"Monday."

"Need to get you a new one. Roony come by the Fitzhughs' this afternoon saying Sherman's going to be across the Congaree at the New Year."

"Naw."

She nodded. "Wait and see."

"Lord, Lord," Nemo said. "He'll burn Columbia all right."

But Amy seemed unconcerned. "They say he's taking freed slaves with him as he goes. Whole train of them, just following behind, heading north." She hooked an arm around his leg, like a child would. "Let's you and me pack it up and take off, Nemo. Or leave it all, just take what we can carry."

"Where'd it go better for us, gal? Where you think we'd have a better stake?"

Amy smiled, her eyes dreamy. "Chicago. New York. Boston." She said the names as though they were incantations. "Or we could go back. Across the water. I hear there's boats leaving out of New York for Liberia every week now. I've got some pennies saved up. I know you do." She hugged his leg a little harder.

Nemo shook his head. "Ain't no way I'm crossing that ocean again, child. Not Nemo." He closed his eyes against the idea, remembering the barked orders of the pirates and the ceaseless heaving in the hold of their *Fair Dealer*, the endless tossing that grew frenzied when the storms came. He still remembered the sloshing of the waste tubs and once, with the timbers groaning as though the ocean meant to rend the ship to kindling, a child smaller than himself being pitched headfirst into the filth.

He shook his head again. "You don't know about it. You was born in All Saints. Can't know."

The two of them were silent for a moment, staring out as the sun dipped below the last tarpaper roof across the way. Finally Nemo spoke.

"We got plenty of Africa here. All that rice culture down in the low country ain't nothing but Africa. The levees, the drainage ditches. Who you think taught the buckra how to work it all, how to keep the harvest flow water fresh? It was Africans, Amy. Senegalese. I reckon if we can make it this far, we can see how much farther the road going to go."

But his words sounded hollow and he felt he had spoken too much. Optimism, he had found, could be a dangerous thing, like a cutting tool that could just as easily turn on its wielder. To break the leaden silence, he asked the question that was never far from the surface of his mind.

"Mister Fitzhugh been leaving you alone?" he said, embarrassed.

She responded too loudly for his liking. "He left me alone since you gave me that conjure powder. Old possum don't bother me as long as I put it in his food."

Nemo smiled. "Wasn't conjure nothing, child. Just old saltpeter. Keep his manhood down like it ought to be."

Amy leaned close to him and whispered, "I know it ain't conjure powder, but Mrs. Thompson over there don't know it.

You notice you ain't heard her broom on the boards since she come out. She ain't missing a word you say."

He looked across to the porch next door, where Mrs. Thompson stood with a broom in her hands, eyes down to the floor.

Nemo rose and held out his arm for Amy. "Let's walk uptown, see what's doing," he said, then whispered as she took his elbow, "You good for business, child."

Thursday

The MORNING SUN IS SLANTING THROUGH the blinds when Kaye begins to stir. Jacob has been awake, propped against the headboard, since three. For the last half hour he has stared through the blinds as the sun has risen, watching the night give way slowly, the sky going from black to bruised shades of blue to the nearly blinding whiteness that is now filling the room, superseding the light cast by the little lamp on his nightstand. Before that he had read—read with an intensity he had not known since his days in medical school, when a biochemistry or internal medicine book had been, for the long night before exams, the tangible key to his future. Because Abraham Flexner's *Medical Education in the United States and Canada: A Report to the Carnegie Foundation* had had the opposite effect of the soporific he'd hoped for. Instead of being bored back to sleep, he'd felt something begin to turn inside him, as if heating up. It was ever thus, Flexner may as well have been saying. In chapter after chapter he exposed charlatanry and worse, puncturing the thin veneer of piety laid over it all. There had been many Nemo Johnstons, used and discarded. And perhaps many more like Sara Thacker. Only once the sun had begun to come up had Jacob set the book down—laid it across his chest as if to trade the darkness within its pages for the sunrise.

The sheet is pushed down nearly to Kaye's waist. She lies facing away from him, and the slatted light from the window blinds stripes her gorgeous back. With his finger, he traces the line of her spine up from the rise of her hips to the mass of tousled black hair on the pillow, tucking a few loose strands behind her ear. He leans over to run his finger under her fine jawline and kisses her ear. Her eyes are closed but she is smiling.

"*Guten Tag*," she says.

"Welcome back."

"So you said last night."

"I'll keep saying it."

Kaye opens her eyes. She gathers up the sheet and turns over to look at him. "How long have you been up? You've got circles under your eyes."

"I'm fine, Mother."

"I'm serious. You'd think you were the jetlagged one."

"I had a dream about my dad. He was standing with your father." Though he takes care not to mention Meyer to Kaye more than he must, he has thought about the old man almost every day of the past year. He is glad Meyer did not live to see him brought before the Physicians' Task Force, glad that Meyer did not have to stand up for his protégé at the hearing. The last time Jacob saw Meyer was at Beth Shalom, where Meyer had lain wrapped in white linen from head to toe, looking like a corpse from another time in history, which to Jacob seemed appropriate. When the rabbi spoke the last words in Hebrew and let the dirt sift through his fingers, Jacob had cried as hard as the family.

"They were together?"

"Together."

"And?"

"There's nothing else. They just stood there, looking at me."

"How strange."

"We are both thirty-something orphans, Kaye. That's strange in itself."

"I'm twenty-nine," she says absently, and pushes her bangs out of her eyes. "Is that the book Daddy gave you?"

Jacob nods. "The one. I hate to admit it, but I never read it before. Didn't seem to have the time." The reprint of Flexner's 1910 *Report* is an odd book—so odd, in fact, that Jacob had at first thought it a joke when Meyer presented it to him after he'd passed his boards. Meyer had scrawled an inscription on its title page: "To Dr. Jacob Thacker, May 1990, with all best wishes. Read it, Jake, to remember we are as much about art as science—and still have a long way to go."

He picks up the book from his chest. "It's amazing, Kaye. I had no idea. Most of the medical schools at the turn of the century were run for profit. I mean, for profit alone. You can almost see that in the school records, but Jesus, not like this guy Flexner tells it. They'd let anybody in. More students meant more cash flow." He begins rifling through the pages, looking for those he has dog-eared.

"Get this—the typical southern school spent more on advertising than on laboratories. They almost had to; there were seven medical schools in South Carolina in 1900. *Seven*. They were churning out doctors like hairdressers. Listen to this: 'It is a singular fact that the organization of medical education in this country has hitherto been such as not only to commercialize the process of education itself, but also to obscure in the minds of the public any discrimination between the well trained physician and the physician who has no adequate training whatsoever.' "

"Sounds like the law school."

"Funny. But this is worse." He reads again. " 'The Carolina anatomy room, containing a single cadaver, is indescribably foul. The cadaver on display was in such a state of advanced putrefaction that—' "

"Okay, enough."

"All right. One more thing, though: 'The situation at Columbia is utterly hopeless. The university ought not much longer permit its name to be exploited by a low-grade institution, whose entrance terms—if the phrase can be used—are far below that of its academic department.' Can you believe that? Jesus, Kaye. The shit they shoveled down our throats. The shit I've been shoveling." He taps the page with his finger. "There's no glorious history in here. Just a bunch of dirty laundry, things the school should never have gotten away with. McMichaels is full of shit. He's got to know that. I ought to blow this whole basement thing wide open."

Kaye reaches out a hand to his and closes the book gently. "What do you think Daddy would tell you?"

Jacob shuts his eyes and shakes his head. "No," he says. He can feel her eyes on his face, so he says it again.

"No. I've worked too hard."

When she speaks again, her voice is next to his ear, soft. "No one has ever said otherwise."

He closes his eyes tighter. "One more year. That's the deal. Then I'm out."

Then, before he can push it away, a memory of Meyer comes to him, from one of the many times Jacob had gone to his mentor's office ready to quit. Meyer had sat him down and listened.

That morning, on rounds, Jacob had diagnosed a fever of unknown origin in one of his patients. His supervisor, Dr. Sanderson, had nearly exploded.

"Let me guess," Meyer replied. "Too vague?"

Meyer had stood up and pulled a copy of Tinsley Harrison's *Principles of Internal Medicine* down from his bookcase. He flipped through the pages a moment, then set it down on the desk, opened to a page of diagnostic diagrams with symptoms on one side and diagnoses on the other.

"Tinsley Harrison was a friend of mine, Jake. A good man

and a hell of a doctor. This book of his is used across the country. Which means that somewhere out there, right now, some intern is looking at these pages, as nervous as you, hoping this little diagram will prove him worthy as a diagnostician."

Jacob said nothing. He had looked at the same diagram himself the day before.

"Do you really think it's this simple?" Meyer said. He sat down and shut the book. "John Sanderson does, and that's what makes him weak. The need for absolute certainty. No great doctor ever has that need." Meyer leaned back in his wooden office chair, tapped his chest. "The great ones make the connections here."

"Right. But you can't go into surgery without some certainty, Meyer."

"True. But you can't go in with absolute certainty, either. I am not advocating lassitude. I am advocating a combination of knowledge and gut instinct. Do you know, Jake, that there are twenty-seven different procedures for an appendectomy, all equally viable? I imagine that keeps Sanderson awake at night."

Meyer leaned over the desk and fixed his eyes on Jacob. "What falls to the great ones is to make the connections others cannot see," he said. "Half knowledge, half gut instinct. Those are the connections no book can teach you."

Jacob opens his eyes and stares at the ceiling, wondering why his head is so full of memory this morning. This past of his, so distant most days that it seems threatened with fading out entirely, is on him like a fever. He turns on his side and looks deeply into Kaye's eyes. "No," he says, "One more year. Too much sacrifice to waste it now."

Kaye sighs. It burns him that she has always been more rational than he, has always possessed the ability to reconcile decisions and consequences better than he ever could. "Your choice," she says, as though this were at its root a problem as solvable as an equation. "A year, then. But it's your year, Jacob. If you stick it out, you'll have to do your job." She pushes the book aside. "You have to let this go. You'll have to forget it."

"Sometimes I worry that I've forgotten too much already. Like the school." He takes a deep breath, his eyes still on the ceiling, and says, "I went out to see Aunt Pauline yesterday."

Kaye props herself up on an elbow, leans closer.

"At her combined grocery store and bait shop."

Kaye smiles. "Quite a combination."

"Indeed. A lovely establishment." But he hates the tone of his voice as he says it.

"How long has it been?"

"Six years. Dad's funeral. She's getting old, Kaye."

"Is that why you went?" she asks quietly. He can tell she is trying not to push him too hard.

"I just don't have that many connections left," he says. He starts to tell her more, tell her everything, when he feels her hand on his chest, soft and warm.

"You have me."

"I do," he says, swallowing hard. "And that's enough. Forget the rest."

Kaye glances at the clock beside the bed. "I'm not due in until nine. Can you go in a little late today?"

"Sure. Time is all I've got."

Kaye sits up now, not bothering to adjust the sheet that has fallen to her waist. "Come here, then. Let me help you forget for a while."

Soon enough he is forgetting it all.

THE CLERK AT the Lexington County Courthouse is everything Janice Tanaka is not: from his scuffed comfort shoes to the oily comb-over on his head, he radiates the kind of Deep South indolence that is implicitly banned on campus. Jacob stands at the counter of the Birth Records Division for nearly a minute waiting to be acknowledged, watching the man read *The State* at his desk and sip from a coffee-stained mug as though unaware of his presence. Just as Jacob is reaching to ring the little bell on the counter, he rises from his chair with an underwater slowness and makes his way over.

"Help you?"

"Yes, thanks. I need a birth certificate from 1866. Do your records go back that far?"

"Oh, they go way back," the clerk says, waving a hand at the stacks of shelves behind him. "You doing a little genealogy? It's usually just little old ladies come in here."

"It's nothing personal," Jacob says, hoping the county won't require him to fill out a form, to give his name. "It's a birth that probably had no father listed. The infant was a James Thacker."

"Genealogy is simple," the clerk says, "if you got a paternal name."

"I told you I don't."

The clerk nods, smirking. "That kind of genealogy is what we call woodpile research."

"I know the joke. I'd rather not hear it."

The clerk returns Jacob's look sourly as he pulls a spiral notebook from his shirt pocket. "Spell that out for me?"

"James Thacker. Should be 1866."

The clerk writes it down, scratches his jaw, and then disappears into the shelves behind the counter.

He is gone nearly half an hour, leaving Jacob to sit in one of the plastic chairs that seem to be made expressly for the state government in order to make long waiting times as uncomfortable as possible. Jacob is checking his watch for the fifth time, thinking about the drive back to his office, when the man emerges from behind the stacks. Jacob meets him at the counter and takes the certificate from his hand.

"Nothing personal, huh?"

Jacob cuts his eyes at the man. "No. Just in a hurry," he says, then looks down at the paper.

The man makes a sound that seems meant to convey that Jacob is making his morning difficult. "Copies cost a dollar-fifty."

"I don't think I'll need one," Jacob says without looking up.

He is thinking of Meyer as he holds the old document in his hand, thinking of gut instinct and the dance of possibilities before the elements fall into place, before all the disjointed symptoms cohere into a diagnosis. A likely diagnosis, he reminds himself. But he can almost hear Meyer's voice in his head. *What does your gut tell you?*

He knows the answer, can feel it in his stomach, in the coppery taste in his mouth. For though the line for "Father" is blank, the birth certificate has been signed in the delicate and precise hand of the attending physician, F. A. Johnston.

WHEN JACOB GETS back to Johnston Hall, Elizabeth is waiting for him at the top of the stairs. She begins to speak, breathlessly, before he is halfway up the staircase.

"Oh, Jacob, where have you been? I was hoping Doctor McMichaels was with you."

"Haven't seen him yet. What's up?"

"These men are in your office, Jacob. I told them to wait, but they barged on in. This man's secretary has been calling all week. This morning she's called every half hour. He said he couldn't wait any longer."

Now that he is level with her, Jacob can see that several long strands of Elizabeth's hair have come loose from her hair band. She tucks them behind her ear like a schoolgirl.

"Who is it?"

Elizabeth looks at a scrap of paper in her hand. "Reverend

Marcus Greer, from the Ebenezer Methodist Baptist Episcopal Church." She sounds out the unfamiliar cluster of words carefully.

Jacob knows the church. It is the best building on its block, a half mile from Mary's house, immaculately kept and with a neon cross out front that glows twenty-four hours a day, as if in proud defiance of its impoverished surroundings.

"In my office, you said?"

Elizabeth nods.

Jacob is already moving down the hall. "All right. I'll handle it. Let me know if Jim comes in, will you?"

The inside of his office is, for once, cramped when he opens the door: four black men are crowded against the walls, standing with their backs to the window and the bookcases, all of them big men and clad in dark suits that make them look even larger. They are ranged around the room shoulder-to-shoulder, in the stance of the Secret Service, with their hands crossed at their waists. One of them, to Jacob's surprise, is Lorenzo Shanks, whose massive chest seems to strain against the fabric of his brown suit coat. However impressive his pectorals, however, Lorenzo's face looks humble, even a bit cowed.

Jacob reaches out a hand to him. "Lorenzo, what a surprise." He looks down at the suit and smiles. "You clean up mighty well."

Lorenzo shakes his hand absently, his eyes over Jacob's shoulder, looking at the man seated in the chair opposite Jacob's desk. The man rises slowly and turns around. He is shorter than the others but wider, built like a football lineman past his prime. Unlike those of the others, his suit is silk, blue and double-breasted, with a faint pinstripe. When he reaches out a hand for Jacob to take, an onyx cufflink emerges from his sleeve. His handshake is cool and fleshy.

"I would say I'm glad to meet you, but we have no time for hollow pleasantries," he says in a baritone. "My name is Marcus Greer, and I'm here to talk with you about the remains of our brothers and sisters in your basement."

Jacob sets his portfolio down on the desk carefully and settles into his chair. It requires some effort not to cut his eyes toward Lorenzo.

"All right. Let's talk, then. As Lorenzo has probably told you, a renovation crew found a number of bones in the cellar earlier this week. The exact number will take some time to determine, but we're confident at this time that the remains are human."

"And African American."

"That is yet to be determined."

"Yet?"

"We have a forensic anthropologist from Clemson University working on the site right now. He has assured me he will prepare a full report on what he finds."

Greer shifts in his chair to look at the other men. "On the site now, you say? I wonder why the basement is so quiet. We checked the cellar door. It's locked."

Jacob only shrugs. "I don't keep his schedule for him."

Greer pulls a handkerchief from his breast pocket and dabs

at his forehead with it. "And you-all will be content with this report? When it is published, will that conclude the matter for you?"

"I can't give you a definite answer on that right now. This is a highly unusual situation. At this point, the school is measuring its options as carefully as possible before we proceed. We want to be sure to take the appropriate course of action."

The reverend replaces his handkerchief carefully before he looks up at Jacob. "I think your preferred course of action is inaction, Mister Thacker, just as it has always been. Or should I say, inaction where the citizens of Rosedale are concerned. Just this week I have had my secretary calling the dean's office since Monday afternoon, when Brother Shanks came to talk with me. Not a single call has been returned."

"I was not aware of that. Had I known of it, I would have contacted you myself."

Greer arches an eyebrow. "Is that a fact?"

"It's my job."

Jacob begins to say more, but Greer cuts him off with a wave of his hand. "I know the party line. I know you could go on all morning about the old Negro hospital, the Charity Hospital, the free clinics. But all of that is just covering, just a salve on the wounds of racial injustice that are as much a part of your school's history as the buildings themselves. A salve over an old wound—a wound that your basement tells me has been festering for a hundred years."

One of the men by the bookcases makes a noise of agreement. Things are getting out of hand. Jacob reaches for his port-folio on top of the desk gratefully and takes out the envelope from the archives. He opens it and passes the photocopy of Nemo Johnston's picture across the desktop.

"Take a look at this, if you will, reverend, and tell me what you see."

Greer takes the paper and glances down at it for a moment. "I see a brother from another time, an ancestor, a grandfather. A man with dignity in spite of the trials and tribulations that show on his face."

"I agree with you. But what you also see there is the man we think is responsible for every bone in that basement. Nemo Johnston was his name. He was the school's resurrectionist, a body snatcher. What they used to call the men who procured the specimens for gross anatomy. So this matter isn't as simply black-and-white as you seem to think it is."

The reverend's face darkens a hue. He hands back the photo-copy as if it has contaminated his hand.

"He stayed on with the school after the war, after emancipa-tion," Jacob says, letting the silence in the room gather weight. He looks down again at the photocopied image of Nemo John-ston before he puts it back in the envelope with the others, carefully, willing his hand to stop trembling.

The reverend is speaking with an effort at composure. "I am not here today to debate what a brother may have done, or been forced to do," he says. "I am here today to demand a hearing—a public hearing—about the remains of our brethren downstairs.

Since your dean has been so reticent in meeting with me, he will meet with the public." Greer shoots his cuffs and places his hands on his knees, leaning forward in his chair.

"Saturday morning my congregation will assemble at Ebenezer at dawn. We will march down Gervais, past the statehouse, to the very door of this building. Our banners will proclaim the event as a reparations march. I will tell the press that since dialogue has failed us, we have no recourse but to pursue civil litigation. I believe the news coverage will be extensive."

Jacob can feel the sweat, which had begun under his arms the minute he entered the office, begin flowing in earnest.

"If you think coming in here and hot-boxing me with these guys is going to change how the school conducts its business, you're mistaken. Your march won't do much better."

Greer leans back in his chair and smiles. "And there we have it. Your business. Your business has been conducted on the backs of my people for generations. But the times have changed, Mister Thacker. Your business is now our business."

"Doctor," Jacob says, hating himself for it but unable to keep his tongue. "It's Doctor Thacker."

"Doubtless it is. But from where I stand, a white coat and a white hood don't look all that different." The men—all but Lorenzo—chuckle as Greer rises from his seat.

"I implore you to talk with your dean about this. If we can get no justice from official channels, we must agitate in the streets. Thirty-six hours from now, we will march. And the march will have a historic impact. Your school will feel it for years."

He turns on his heel and steps to the door, already being opened by one of his men. They follow him in silence, single file. Lorenzo is the last out the door, lingering on the threshold.

"Didn't know you were a religious man, Lorenzo," Jacob says.

"I meant to come by yesterday," he says, almost apologetically. "But Bowman's got us working over on the East Campus."

"You do what you have to, I guess," Jacob says, trying to smile. "I've seen you down at the gym. Hell, I'd want you in my corner too."

"Brother Shanks!" the reverend calls from the hallway. With one last glance at Jacob, Lorenzo is gone.

THE BMW CLINGS to the curving driveway of the Dean's Mansion like a lover, its humming engine echoing off the low stone walls that border the neatly sealed blacktop beneath a canopy of dogwoods and magnolias. Except for its narrowness, this route could be confused with a road, stretching as it does over a winding quarter mile from the estate's iron gates on Beltline Avenue to the circular turnaround in front of the antebellum manse, where the asphalt gives way to pea gravel that is neatly raked each morning by the grounds crew. As often as he has been out to the mansion, Jacob can still hardly believe the grandeur of the place.

Yet this evening, with the day ebbing into plum-colored twilight, he has anything but beauty on his mind. All afternoon he tried to reach the dean, who has steadfastly refused to carry a cell phone or beeper since the day he left private practice. On his way home from the office, Jacob tried the mansion once more from his own cell phone, breathing an audible sigh of relief when the familiar voice of Bitsy McMichaels answered and told him that Jim was just back from the golf course and would see him if the matter was urgent. He assured her that it was.

He pulls into the turnaround a little too fast, pea gravel clattering in the convertible's wheel wells. Hurrying up the steps, he has a hand out to ring the bell when the great door swings open from the inside to reveal Bitsy standing in the great foyer. She is, as ever, immaculate, a former debutante who has never quite lost the easy grace of her youth, though her sandy blond hair is now streaked with gray and her suntanned face is beginning to show wrinkles at the corners of her mouth. When she smiles, the wrinkles first deepen, then disappear.

"Jacob, please come in," she says, extending a hand. "I have to say, you've got me worried, though. I'm afraid something terrible has happened."

"No, no, nothing terrible," he says, straining to smile. "You know how the first week of school goes. Lots of little fires to be put out."

She leads him through the ballroom, where the catering services staff is setting up tables and chairs for tomorrow night's year-opening banquet. Their voices reverberate off the high ceilings of the room.

"Jim is in his study, having a drink," she says, and gestures toward a high oak door that has been closed against the noise of the caterers. "Go on in, and I'll bring you boys something to eat in a minute."

He begins to tell her not to bother, but she cuts him off and places a hand on his arm, light as a bird. "You know it's no trouble, sugar. Make yourself at home."

Jacob finds Jim in the study, which is paneled in oak from floor to ceiling, with built-in bookshelves of the same wood flanking a brick fireplace. The dean is hunched in an old leather armchair that looks like it has been sandblasted, pulled up close to a small television set on one of the bookshelves. On the screen David Hasselhoff is being held at gunpoint in a locker room. Hasselhoff wears his trademark red swimming trunks and nothing else; his hair looks like a living thing.

"Jake, have a seat," Jim says, eyes never leaving the screen. "Mitch is in trouble."

"*Baywatch*? You should be grateful I'm not a donor. Not the kind of fare one expects from the dean."

Jim leans over and cuts the television's volume. "I don't watch it for Mitch," he says. And as though to corroborate his claim, within seconds the screen fills up with the mutely bouncing curves of Mitch's colleagues, jogging to his rescue.

Jim is looking at Jacob and grinning. "Guess you noticed the improvements in our basement today."

"It's quiet. And padlocked."

Jim leans back in his chair and stretches out his legs, clad in

Scottish plaid golfing pants, before him. "Quiet, and it'll stay quiet. I had to call in a whopper of a favor, but by God, our property's going to stay ours."

"Sanburn's gone?"

"For good. We ran his ass back to Clemson this morning. I'm sorry you missed it. You know Buddy Armistead?"

Jacob smiles. "I've never met him. But I know who the lieutenant governor is."

"Right. Well, Buddy and I go back many years, all the way to Charleston Academy. He was good enough to walk over from the statehouse and have a sit-down with this Doctor Sanburn. Seems Clemson's Anthropology Department is looking at some potentially serious budget cuts next year. Buddy volunteered to intercede on its behalf."

"Jesus," Jacob says.

"Yep," McMichaels says. "He's on our side, son." He rattles the ice in his glass and looks out the window. The television flickers, and Jacob realizes it is the only light on in the room.

McMichaels rises and steps to a wet bar set into the bookcase next to the television. "Get you anything?"

"Sure. Whatever you're having."

McMichaels speaks over his shoulder while he pours two glasses of scotch. "So that's today's good news. I have a feeling you're here to tell me about another kind of news. These things come in threes, don't they?"

"I guess they do. A black preacher came in today. Name's Marcus Greer."

McMichaels shakes his head as he hands Jacob his drink. "Never met him."

"He's the pastor at Ebenezer M.B.E., over on Pulaski Street. Somebody told him about the basement and he's all over it. Says he's got a march set up for Saturday morning."

"A march, for Christ's sake?"

"He called it a reparations march, from the Ebenezer church to the front door of Johnston Hall."

"The fuck he will."

"We can't keep him off the campus if he gets a permit."

"And how in hell is he going to get a permit by tomorrow?"

"I guess he's connected. Maybe he goes way back with someone at city hall."

McMichaels shoots him a look, then walks over to one of the tall windows that overlook the back gardens. He stares out on the palmettos and azaleas as though looking for a solution outside, in the gathering dusk.

"I know," Jacob says. "Bad for the school."

"Very bad," McMichaels repeats, shaking his head. "What kind of man was this Greer?"

"How do you mean?"

"I mean, how was he dressed? How did he act?"

"He's a dandy. Double-breasted suit. French cuffs. Lots of rings."

Jim almost smiles. "Just how Elizabeth described him. He's the one. We had some trouble with him back in the eighties.

Some kind of dustup over the physical plant laborers." McMichaels nods slowly at the window.

"I thought you'd never met him."

"I haven't. But it's my business to know a little about everybody. I had Austin Malloy pull together a file on this Greer today."

Jacob takes a deep breath and makes an effort at speaking calmly. "That raises some significant confidentiality issues."

But the dean seems unconcerned. "We're well past confidentiality now. Besides, I want you to know what kind of man you're dealing with." With the dean facing out the window, Jacob can see only half his face. It is expressionless.

"John Beauregard handled the physical plant thing, if I'm remembering it right," McMichaels says.

"That was before my time."

"Yes it was. Beauregard was an asset to the school."

Jacob shifts in his chair, remembering Beauregard's retirement party, when Jacob had been officially introduced as the old man's replacement. He'd felt like a usurper all evening among the old guard gathered over cocktails to wish Beauregard a fond farewell. Six months later Beauregard was dead of an embolism that laid him out on the ninth fairway of Augusta National, midway through another sub-par round.

McMichaels steps back to his leather chair and bends behind it. When he rises, Jacob sees with a sinking sensation that he holds a plain manila folder. "And he didn't have this." He drops the folder in Jacob's lap, where it rests with a leaden weight.

"Use it only if you have to. Otherwise, we're going strictly by the book on this."

McMichaels crosses the room to his mahogany desk and opens a drawer. He takes something out of it and pulls the chain on his desk lamp. Under the green light of the banker's shade, Jacob sees that it is a checkbook.

"Reparation march, my ass," he says. "Don't fall for the man-of-God routine, Jake. This Greer is a petty hustler, a shake-down artist. Lucky for you, Beauregard got his number ten years ago." He begins to scribble on the checkbook as though writing out a prescription. "I'm writing you a check from the dean's discretionary fund. I want you to go see this reverend, get this taken care of."

Jacob looks down at the folder in his lap, and at the glass in his hand, realizing he had forgotten it. He takes a long drink from it before he speaks.

"I don't think I can do that, sir."

McMichaels waves a hand in the air as he might swat at a mosquito. "Nonsense. It must be done." He looks over the green lampshade at Jacob intently. "It's a tax-deductible donation. If I can't rely on you, Jake, who have I got?"

"You're talking about a bribe, sir."

McMichaels's eyes flash as he comes around the desk. He jabs a finger at Jacob, the check held loosely in his hand as he points toward Jacob's chest. "You never use that word around me, son. Never. Spend a few more years in this business and you'll see there's no such thing. Do you think a school gets built—clinics, hospitals set up—without quid pro quo? This is the rule, Jake, not the exception."

"I still think we should take this head-on. I've been finding things in the archives, Jim, about this slave named Nemo Johnston. Amazing stuff. He was likely the first black anatomy professor in the South. Or hell, the country. If we've got this money, we can afford a symposium on this Nemo Johnston, maybe even a center. You know Sanburn would eat it up. We'd be beating Greer at his own game."

"Nemo Johnston?" McMichaels said, shaking his head. "No, no. Sanburn is gone now. And so is the past. Stand up, son. I want to show you something."

McMichaels has moved to the window again, and he motions Jacob over to him. "Let me tell you what I've learned in my time, Jake. It's all about end results, long-range thinking. That's how you build a legacy. And I'll be absolutely goddamned if my part of that legacy should end up in a scandal. I'll retire in two or three years, Jake. I will not be remembered by what's in that basement."

McMichaels gestures toward the window, the flush on his face beginning to fade. "Take a look out there. Just take a look at this place."

Jacob looks out over the rear grounds in the twilight. The exterior lights have been turned on, all of them, from the ground lamps along the brick pathways to accent lighting under the crape myrtles, spotlights in the live oaks. It looks like a vision of the Old South set up by a Hollywood scene artist.

"All of this was started with slave labor, then carried on through Reconstruction and into this century by workers paid damn near slave wages. No point in dredging all that up again. But just look at it now. Now it's maintained by tax dollars, for the greater good. Today, anybody in South Carolina who can make the academic grade is welcomed to this medical school. Black or white, rich or poor, it belongs to them. Hell, even foreign students. And that overrides whatever concessions were made to get us here."

McMichaels reaches out an arm and hooks it around Jacob's shoulder. "You're one of those people, Jake. Do you think I don't remember you from years ago? I do. I remember Jacob Thacker, up from West Columbia to make something better for himself. I remember reading through your admissions file and saying to myself, Sweet Jesus, we've got somebody here who'll crawl through broken glass to be a doctor, somebody with real guts." He hands Jacob the check. "You still want to be a doctor, don't you, Jake? Do what you need to do."

Jacob looks down at the check, all the zeros in its sum, the dean's scrawled signature. McMichaels has written "501 (c) (3)" in the memo line. "You didn't make it out to Greer. That line is blank."

"Talk to the man. See if he wants it made out to the church, to a scholarship fund, whatever. I'll leave that part of it to your discretion."

Jacob is about to speak when he hears a soft knock at the door. Bitsy enters with a tray of cheese and crackers and smiles as she sets it on the coffee table. McMichaels moves to help her. His face seems to light up in her presence.

"What a woman, huh, Jake? Still as beautiful as the day I met her on the beach at Edisto," McMichaels says, stuffing a cracker in his mouth and putting an arm around his wife.

Bitsy blushes and laughs shyly. "And he's still carrying on like a fool," she says.

Jacob stuffs the check in the pocket of his jacket and sets his drink on the table, then reluctantly picks up the folder. He smiles and reaches out a hand to the dean. "You are a very lucky pair of people," he says.

"Can't you stay a while longer, Jacob?"

"No, ma'am. But I'll be back tomorrow night with everyone else. Thank you for your hospitality."

And with that he leaves them, standing together in front of the cold fireplace as though posing for a portrait in one of the southern lifestyle magazines, the expensive ones, as modern-day exemplars of a kind of feudal grace, long ago lost. A couple from another time, in whose kingdom he has briefly interloped.

Fernyear: 1866

NEMO STOOD IN DOCTOR JOHNSTON'S DOORWAY with the bloodied handkerchief pressed against his face, as he had for nearly five minutes now, with his shoulder leaning against the jamb and his eyes on the doctor, who had not yet looked up from the clutter of papers on his desk. Beneath the handkerchief his nose still throbbed, but the sharp pains had ebbed and he was nearly certain the bleeding had stopped. Nevertheless, he kept the stained cloth in place. He wanted Johnston to see it.

As though finally giving up on the problem before him, Johnston shuffled the papers into a single stack and set them aside. He looked up at Nemo wearily, then ducked his head an inch to peer over his spectacles at the man in his doorway. His eyes narrowed.

"Nemo, my heavens. Have you been in some kind of a scrape?"

"Same kind of scrape I've been having. Albert Fitzhugh."

Johnston rose from behind the desk and stepped up to Nemo's face. He lowered the slave's hand and touched the nose gently, squinting at the clotted blood in each nostril. His fingers pressed gently against the bridge of the nose, testing it. "Not broken," he said. "But we should get you a cool cloth for the swelling."

"Albert Fitzhugh fell out in the surgery theater not halfway through an amputation. Fainted dead away. Mrs. Harris lying there on the table, half asleep with the ether, and him just cutting his eyes from the saw to her thigh. Doctor Evans telling him to go on and make the cut and Mrs. Harris starting to cry and Mister Fitzhugh's eyes cutting back and forth like a possum's. So Doctor Evans takes his arm to guide him, and when the saw blade makes the first cut he's greening up around the gills, and when he hits the bone he faints and falls right on top of Mrs. Harris. I laid him out on the floor and commenced to patting his cheeks. Minute later he wakes up and cocks me across the face." Nemo raised a finger of his own to the injury. "You seen what he done."

Johnston turned and walked back to his desk. He sat down heavily, and Nemo could hear the leather seat of his chair creak as he leaned back in it.

"I apologize on behalf of Mister Fitzhugh," he said after a long pause.

Nemo said nothing. His hand clenched and unclenched around the handkerchief.

"This is unprecedented," Johnston went on, "and unacceptable. Perhaps it might alleviate your anger to know that Mrs. Fitzhugh is down with her rheumatism and a grave case of the flux. Her situation is dire. Could it not be that the mother's illness is weighing heavily on her son?"

Nemo stuffed the handkerchief in his pocket, next to his knife. He looked down at the floor for a moment before he spoke.

"If it were Mrs. Fitzhugh would be one thing. But this ain't a matter of one thing. This is his second *year* here, sir. He ain't never going to pass the obstetrics course. He failed the cesarean practical last week. Tore old Addie Kennedy's uterus all to pieces. And you know what he told me? Told me to bring him a white cadaver and he wouldn't have no problems. Said a nigger cadaver's naturally defective."

Johnston was staring at a spot on the ceiling when he spoke. "Could you get him a white cadaver?"

Nemo felt like laughing. "I could get him Helen of Troy, he'd still botch that surgery. Can't even do a basic amputation. What happened in the theater today, most of the students could make that cut with one eye closed. You and me could do it in our sleep."

Nemo thought he saw the doctor stiffen slightly at the last phrase, but he could not help himself from speaking once more. "Why can't he just *go*?"

Johnston leaned forward and rested his elbows on the desk, then removed his spectacles and rubbed the red spots where the glasses had been resting. "I am afraid it is not so simple as that," he said. "There are financial exigencies involved." He sighed. "Let us see what changes another month will bring."

"That's what you told me in February, sir. And February last year."

"Well, he cannot keep repeating the course in perpetuity, can he?"

Nemo arched an eyebrow, and Johnston caught the gesture. "No," he said, in answer to his own question. "He cannot. Twice is the most I can allow him to repeat and still live with myself." He turned his spectacles in his hand and stared at them, bemused. "But there should be some recompense for this indignity you have endured. I will raise your salary two dollars a week, Nemo, in lieu of a more formal apology. I would do more, but that is all I can manage at present." He looked up at Nemo with a weak smile.

"Didn't come asking for a raise, sir."

Johnston set the spectacles back on his nose, tucked their wire loops behind his ears, and pulled the stack of papers to him. "Two dollars a week it is, then. That will surely make matters more tolerable for you."

He pulled a sheet of paper covered with figures from among the others and tapped it with his forefinger. "This is a notice from the Roth Brothers' apothecary supply house in Charleston. It is on the brink of receivership and financial ruin, it says, and is no longer able to offer delivery service to the Midlands." The doctor sighed. "Carolina may never recover from last year's destruction, Nemo. We are still feeling it. These are hard times for all of us. But we must take them as our portion and persevere."

"I guess I'm dismissed, then?"

But Johnston seemed not to have heard the question. He only stared down at the invoice, the shadow of a smile starting around the corners of his mouth.

"Say, perhaps there is a silver lining here after all," he said, lifting the paper. "How would you like to go down to Charleston in my stead, to gather up our supplies? The scenery would do you good, and a few days' vacation would allow matters with Mister Fitzhugh to cool somewhat. Yes indeed, this sweetens the deal considerably. I would make the journey myself, but Mrs. Fitzhugh's condition truly is dire. From what Ballard tells me, I doubt if she will last the night." Johnston paused and cleared his throat. "A delegation from the school will be expected at the funeral. So, what do you say to a trip to the coast?"

"Supply house still down on Queen Street?"

"Indeed it is. The address is here on the letterhead. I shall attach Doctor Evans's requisition list and write out a pass for you if you agree. I think it would be a capital diversion."

Fifteen minutes later Johnston had completed a draft of the pass assuring any and all interested white men that he allowed and guaranteed Nemo Johnston's free passage from Columbia to Charleston and back, for this second week of March in the Year of Our Lord 1866. He signed the paper with a flourish and escorted the Negro to the door with his papers. At the threshold he paused and rested a hand on Nemo's shoulder.

"The world moves at its own pace, Nemo, however we wish it to proceed. Someday Mister Fitzhugh will be gone, and you will still be with us. In the meantime I advise forbearance and patience. Patience, Nemo, for this too will pass."

Nemo took the papers and nodded, eager to be gone. His footsteps sounded dully on the floorboards of the empty hallway. He was at the front door when he heard a soft voice behind him: "You should go away."

He turned and saw Nurse Thacker leaning against the foyer wall, deep in the shadows, with a bundle of linens under one arm. One of her feet was propped up against the wall behind her, like a girl would stand, making her look even younger in the dim light than she did in the daytime.

"Yes, ma'am," Nemo said. "Going now. Don't you fret it."

She came off the wall and closed the distance between them in an instant, then took hold of his arm with a nervous strength.

"Don't play the Negro with me, Nemo," she said, her grip on him tensing. "When have I ever talked down to you?"

"You haven't, ma'am."

Her voice softened. "Then hear me now," she said, pulling him toward one of the front windows. "Look around this place. Do you remember what it was like before?"

He remembered much from the years before she came: the foot-deep mud right up to the Negro hospital's front door where now there burned twin gaslights over a path of pea gravel, flanked by azaleas beginning to bloom; remembered the scant candlelight that once flickered in the gloomy interior, now flooded with light that gleamed on the hard-polished windows.

"Do you think Doctor Johnston remembers? It is not in his nature to remember. And so we do the work and the fruits of it pass us by. You really should go."

"All due respect, Miss Sara, some ain't as free to come and go as others."

Her eyes drifted away from the hospital toward some undefined point in the darkness. "And others," she said, "are not as free as they seem."

Her fingers fell away from his arm and he stepped away from her toward the door, taking a long look at this strange white woman who stood like a daydreaming child in the two-story foyer, a bundle of linens pressed tight against her belly.

Outside, he patted the papers in his coat pocket, thinking of destinations farther than Charleston, wondering if Nurse Thacker dreamed as he did of places beyond the reach of the mapped world's compass, where all the men like Albert Fitzhugh might find their authority revoked, stranding them in some new realm of justice and reckoning.

CHARLESTON, AS EVER, sang with a level of activity that beggared belief, even at suppertime on the last day of the week. Nemo's ears rang with the din as he and Ben Joyner loaded up his wagon at the curb in front of the supply house.

Traffic thundered against the paving stones as delivery wagons like his hurried to complete the day's runs with their red-faced drivers yelling at their horses for more speed. The racket echoed off the storefronts and mingled with the cries of the fishmongers who had taken their carts in hand to roll them inland from the street corners at the harbor, anxious to be rid of the last of the day's catch before it spoiled. On this block alone, three taverns had thrown open their doors to the street. The raucous sounds from within them seemed to be intensifying by the minute.

As Ben loaded the last clinking crate of medicine bottles onto the wagon, a jet-black barouche flew by with its iron-rimmed wheels clattering against the cobblestones. The pair of white faces in the back seemed especially pale in the bracing late-winter air. Their Negro chauffeur rode high above the pavement, haughty in his livery, and cracked his whip over the horses' heads as they passed. Nemo watched the fine carriage speed eastward down Queen Street, at the end of which he could see the two-story Slave Market standing tall. It was now home to the Reconstruction government of the city, Ben had said, but it still looked as evil as the day Nemo first saw it. Its whitewashed stucco walls reflected the pastels of the setting sun in the gloaming, the colors shifting slowly.

"You needing anything else?"

Nemo turned back to the wagon bed, then looked at Ben. "Got enough in there to dope up Columbia till July. What else I be needing?"

Ben smiled slyly. "Oh, something under the table. Something else a medical school might need." He leaned in close. "Specimens, you know."

"I reckon they still dying in Columbia, Ben." He held out his hand, and Ben took it.

"I'm talking about a white one," Ben said. His grip was firm and insistent. Nemo nodded and Ben leaned a little closer.

"Man come by here this morning wanting to unload a white woman. Old man Roth run him off, said he ain't in no body-snatching business. Heard him say something about the Grand Mark Hotel. Ain't but two blocks over, on Broad Street."

"Why you telling me this?"

Ben smiled as broadly as a child. "Always ready to help out a friend, brother. And plus, I hear some coin jangling in your pocket." His smile narrowed. "Them Roths don't pay me enough to starve proper."

Nemo took a gold dollar from his pocket. Ben looked intently at the Indian head balanced on the broad palm and reached for it. The hand clenched shut.

"You got me a name?"

"Pollard. Don't know no first name, but you won't need it. Everybody knows Pollard. He's around town right regular."

Nemo placed the dollar in Ben's hand. Ben stepped off the curb and started toward the tavern nearest them, his gait sprightly as he spoke over his shoulder.

"Pleasure doing business with you, Mister Nemo. Anybody asks me, I tell them Nemo Johnston's first-rate, yes I do."

Nemo climbed up to the buckboard wearily and shook the reins. The horses started forward, toward Meeting Street, where he would take a right over to Broad. The Slave Market glowed ahead of him, its rainbow hues fading now as the sun departed, leaving the façade only coral against the blackness of Charleston Harbor, and beyond that, the blue Atlantic.

He sat on the cold marble floor of the Grand Mark's lobby with his back against a stone column and his hands dangling between his knees, only half interested in the desk clerk, who kept his eyes on the black man as though he might steal the great column itself the moment his back was turned. Twice the man had told him there were no rooms here for colored before he had heard the name Pollard and sent a bellhop upstairs to summon the guest. Now Nemo sat a full five yards from the warmth of the roaring hearth fire as he counted off the minutes of his wait.

The bellhop reappeared at the counter, a little breathless, and pointed out Nemo to the white man who followed him. Nemo felt his stomach tighten as the man started across the lobby, his boot heels clicking on the marble. He was white trash, no doubt, no matter the bright pattern of the satin vest he wore. His hair was black, long, and thinning, with a mustache of the same color drooping around the corners of his small mouth. When he was close enough, Nemo could see that the toes of his boots were scuffed through the polish and that the vest was frayed at the seams. He looked down at Nemo for a long moment before he spoke.

"You here for the package?"

"I reckon I am."

"Well, come on, then. Ain't got all night to stand around jawing."

He turned and started toward the grand stairwell, his heels tapping fast on the marble before Nemo could get to his feet.

"I say again, the boy can't have a room here," the desk clerk called after them.

"It's all right. He's just going to haul some luggage for me," Pollard said without turning, then, under his breath, "So shut the hell up."

Nemo followed him up three flights of carpeted stairs, then down a gaslit hallway that was close with the fumes from the lamps. Pollard stopped at the last room and opened it with an iron key, a few stray hairs dangling over his forehead as he worked the lock. "This is going to be forty dollars," he said as he turned the knob. "You got that kind of money, boy?"

Nemo took a deep breath. "Got it. But don't know as I can part with it."

Pollard looked up and smiled, and Nemo could see that his teeth were yellowed and that one of his bicuspids was missing.

"You take a good look at this one and you'll part with it, all right." He pushed the door open and nodded for Nemo to enter first.

The room was a study in disarray, with an unmade double bed in one corner and a half-dozen whiskey bottles standing empty on the dresser. A pile of dresses rested beneath the single window, as though thrown there. Cigar ashes dusted the carpet and a week's worth of newspapers lay sprawled beneath the room's single armchair.

The woman lay on the divan beside it. The red velvet fabric of the couch offset her alabaster face and the faint flush of her cheekbones such that she looked almost alive. One of her hands dangled toward the floor, motionless, the knuckles just touching the carpet. The other lay across her breast with its fingers splayed against her collarbone, near the soft fall of her golden hair.

She was completely nude, and Nemo could see that although she was thin, she was not too much so. Her breasts were firm and taut, and her pelvic bones, though visible through the flesh, were not pronounced. Her abdomen looked full and healthy, offset by a small tattoo of a rose just above the triangle of hair covering her pudenda.

Nemo took his time studying her, assessing the risk. He watched the breastbone for any sign of movement, studied the tattoo to see whether it rose or fell.

"Yeah, boy," Pollard said behind him. "I think you in love."

"You check her pulse?"

"Shit. She's dead, boy. You blind?"

"You mind if I check it?"

Pollard stepped forward as if to move between Nemo and the woman. "You don't get to touch her till you buy her."

Nemo raised his hands deferentially. "All right. How'd she die?"

"Fever. Had it all week, couldn't work a lick. She just laid in here and burned up, I reckon."

"When?"

"Sometime in the night. I checked on her about dawn and she was gone."

"You didn't call a doctor?"

Pollard looked at the dead woman disgustedly. "Don't have a lot of cash flow right now. Even the damned room's on credit. You want her or not?"

"Why I pay you forty when I can get one free?"

"You can get a nigger for free, yeah. Dead niggers is always free. But this one ain't no nigger, is she?"

"No, she ain't." She wasn't a Negro and she wasn't even common; she was beautiful. Nemo thought that next to Amy, she was the most beautiful woman he had ever seen. He knew that in Columbia she would be eagerly received.

"What's that, boy?" Pollard's lip had pulled back from the missing tooth. "You say 'sir' to me, boy."

Nemo nodded absently. "No, sir," he said. "No sir, she ain't." He nodded again. "Where you find her?"

"Find her? She's been with me six years."

"She your wife?"

The man sneered through his blackened teeth. "No, boy. You stupid or what? She's my girl. She's a whore."

Nemo stared at the man.

"You ask too many damned questions. If you want her, ante up. Else get the hell out."

"Forty, you say?"

Pollard nodded. "Forty. And you do the toting."

HE HAD SMELLED it ahead of him, the pungent odor of charred wood and old charcoal, carried for miles on the southeasterly breeze, and the smell had kept him awake for the last hours of his ride into Columbia. After two full nights without sleep, and with the wagon groaning under the weight of his supplies and the woman's body, he had welcomed the smell of his hometown as it incited him to stay awake, to keep going, these eighty-odd burned blocks of Columbia seeming to urge him back via the night breeze. As the wagon rumbled beneath him, Nemo thought back to the year before, remembering the drunken Federals smashing store windows, remembering Johnston feverishly hoisting a yellow hospital flag out front of the school to save it from the invaders. Later that night the fires had started and stray wads of burning cotton had blown pinwheeling down the streets like infernal sagebrush, some of them borne aloft on the February wind like comets. Toward midnight, anxious to catch a glimpse of the northern harbinger of fiery destruction, he had watched as Sherman himself rode past the school on a roan charger. He had seen nothing very intimidating about the man; he looked like any other sun-burned cracker with half-crazy eyes.

But still, well into 1866, Sherman's legacy of fire remained in the air and in the white-hot memory of the whites. Outside Cayce, Nemo had seen what he took to be an omen that he would reach his destination: a gray wood barn in a fallow field, one of the few left standing, on which had been painted "Sherman Fucked a Cowe," the dripping whitewashed letters ghostly in the moonlight.

He had known then that he was close, and now, with the dawn a half hour away, he rolled into the courtyard of the school and up to the back door of the building, quietly so as not to wake the students sleeping in the dormitory across the way. He climbed down from the buckboard with his joints popping and pulled the woman's body, wrapped in the soiled hotel sheets, to him. When he had her hoisted over his shoulder, he hooked a thumb into a two-gallon jug of formalin from the wagon bed. He pushed the back door open with his foot and stepped inside, the heavy oak swinging shut soundlessly behind him.

In the dissecting room he laid the woman out on Albert Fitzhugh's empty table and left her covered while he went to the cellar for his rubber tubing and an empty jug. He brought a candle back with him as well, its flame low and flickering on the walls but just light enough for him to work by. He rolled the sheets back from the body without looking at its face and placed the end of one tube into the empty jug and pulled the knife from his pocket and made the first cut on the upper inside thigh, where the femoral artery rose closest to the skin's surface.

He always made the thigh cut first, and as he had done so many times before, he made the inch-long incision cleanly through the artery and the blood came fast. It came too fast, and in pulsing gouts, jetting out from the thigh with the regular rhythm of a heartbeat.

Nemo stared at it, his bloodshot eyes hardly registering what they saw. After a long moment he shook his head and reached for the woman's wrist, feeling for a pulse, his own blood racing. He could barely discern a fluttering of blood beneath the pale skin of her wrist.

"Oh," the woman said. "Oh."

"Oh, damn," Nemo said.

He had heard talk of comas, of death-sleeps. Once he had even opened a casket to find the underside of its lid clawed a half-inch deep, broken fingernails embedded in the wood from the frenzied struggle of a last hour spent in rabid claustrophobia. But never anything like this. The woman had been cool when he had carried her down the servant's stairwell of the Grand Mark, and cool this morning. She had never stirred during the long ride back over the rough country roads, through the cold night. It was impossible that she was still alive.

"Oh, *God*," the woman said, her voice rising in volume as though fighting its way out of her chest. "Oh, God, I hurt."

Instantly Nemo was making shushing sounds to her and reaching for a cloth to press against the wound in her leg. His hand settled on a box of the handkerchiefs used to prepare the cadavers for their first viewings, and he snatched out a handful of them and wadded them against the woman's thigh.

"Oh, God help me," the woman said, and for the first time Nemo allowed himself to look her in the face.

Her eyes were wild with fear and pain and the confusion of this sudden reveille. They rolled in their sockets twice, the milky blue irises revolving drunkenly, then fixed on his face.

"Don't scream, honey," Nemo said. "More you scream and writhe, more it bleeds."

The woman's eyes widened further, this time with anger rushing into them. Her jaw clenched as she spoke. "Get your nigger hands off of me!"

"I'm going to stitch it up, ma'am. But you got to hold still."

"Don't touch me again, you black bastard. Murder! Murder!"

Across the courtyard Nemo could see a lamp flare to light in a dormitory window. He looked down at the woman and saw that her hands were beginning to flop on the slate table as she tried to work life back into them.

"Ma'am, ma'am! You going to bleed to death we don't stop that blood. Just lie back." He put his hands on her shoulders and pushed gently.

"I never did no nigger and never will!" she screamed. "Where's Reggie? Oh, God, get those black hands off of me!"

"Ssh, ssh. Ain't nobody going to hurt you. Just try to settle yourself." He pressed against her shoulders until he felt her resistance give way. "That's better," he said. "Tell me your name, child, while I tend to you."

He removed his grip on her shoulders and pulled the handkerchiefs away to check the wound. He was looking around the room for the nearest needle or suture when one of her arms lifted from the table with the suddenness of a catapult and slapped across his face. He stepped back, his eyes watering. The woman's chest rose as she took in a great breath. "Murder!" she screamed.

Outside, Nemo could hear a door slamming, and when he looked up to the adjacent building he saw that two more windows were now lighted. From the courtyard came the sound of footsteps. He looked from the windows to the woman lying beneath him and saw that her chest was rising again with another inhalation. Quickly he grabbed the wad of bloodied cloths and pressed it against her mouth.

The woman gagged and he loosened his grip on her jaw, letting his hand go just slack enough to muffle her voice. Her eyes widened again and he hissed, "Be quiet. If you don't be quiet it'll only get worse."

The woman nodded. Both of them listened as the footsteps crossed the courtyard and sounded on the back stairs. Nemo felt like weeping when he heard a dog's whine following them.

"Anybody home? You boys ain't having a cockfight without me, are you?"

Nemo heard the door slam shut and he shook his head at the woman to lie still. When the footsteps began to sound on the boards of the rear anteroom, she erupted into a fit of thrashing on the table, her voice keening through the cloths. Nemo pressed down, gripping her face harder.

"Sure sounds like a cockfight to me," Albert Fitzhugh said from the next room. "Could have sworn I heard my old Dan tearing into some damn rooster."

The dog whined sharply and there was the sound of a body hitting the floorboards. "Goddamn you, Stonewall, you stupid mutt. Where's a light in this place?"

His eyes still over his shoulder and on the dissecting room door, Nemo began to sing. The song was one of Amy's favorites—"Roll, Jordan, Roll"—and he sang it in a falsetto, loudly, as Fitzhugh fumbled at the door and finally jerked it open.

Fitzhugh stood in the doorway, the dog beside him, its hackles raised. He looked unsteady, and Nemo could see that his eyes were even more red-rimmed than his own.

"Good morning, Mister Fitzhugh," Nemo said.

Fitzhugh listed to his left for a moment, then straightened up. "Well, I'll be damned," he said. He looked down at Stonewall as if the dog could offer a commentary on the scene. Stonewall only growled.

"Stonewall never has liked you, you know," Fitzhugh said. "Can't say I blame him. In here with your embalming stuff and a dead one and hardly enough candlelight to see your own hand in front of you. Damned creepy."

Nemo forced a smile. "I suppose it is, Mister Fitzhugh. Just getting a jump on the day."

"And my God, that singing. You've got a voice like a busted fiddle."

Nemo only smiled, his teeth and eyes glistening in the candlelight. Fitzhugh took a step into the room. "What have you got there? Looks like a hell of a pair of legs."

"She's not ready yet, sir. Still working on her."

"Let's have a look. She looks like something special."

"No, sir. She's not too special yet. Need another little while to get her ready."

"Oh, come on," Fitzhugh said, smiling. "I doubt she'd mind." He took another step forward.

Nemo had to strain to make his voice level. "Can you come back in a half hour, Mister Fitzhugh?"

Fitzhugh weaved and reached out a hand behind him, his fingers settling finally on the door he had opened. He rocked back and forth with it for a moment until he caught his balance. He looked at Nemo for half a minute and then shrugged. "Why not? I've got to take a shit anyway."

Then he was gone, the outside door banging shut behind him, and Nemo could hear his footsteps tramping to the outhouses. The dog whined alongside him.

Reluctantly, Nemo turned to look down at the woman. Her eyes had rolled back, all whites beneath the painted lids. He bit his lip and bent to check the cut in her leg. The blood was seeping slowly from it now. He looked back to her face and realized that his left hand, as though of its own accord, was still clamped firmly around her mouth. He bent close and removed the handkerchief. A slow exhalation of air, like the faintest of cellar breezes, brushed past his ear. He heard nothing else.

He held his ear against her mouth for a full minute, hoping, before he rose slowly and reached for the tubing again, slipping the rubber hose into the unresisting thigh. He picked up another hose and held it ready as he cut the jugular and inserted it. He bent over the woman as he rubbed her body, kneading the blood toward the incisions and into the tubing, down to the jug at his feet. Had Fitzhugh still been in the room, he would have seen the silent tears streaming down Nemo's face as he took up the old song again, calling over Jordan more softly this time, singing it now in the tuneless voice of the damned.

THE DISSECTING ROOM was filling fast with morning light and the students roused by it as Nemo sat on his stool in the corner, yesterday's *South Carolinian* held out in front of his face. He tried his best not to hear the comments the students made about the new woman, tried not to watch as Fitzhugh, bolstered now by two pots of coffee, pantomimed his reenactment of finding Nemo hunched over the woman. As his story wound up to its crescendo, the dog beneath the dissecting table began to bark, the sound earsplitting in the big room, until Fitzhugh finally settled him down.

"What's the order of the day, Nemo?" Fitzhugh called out as

he patted the dog's head. "Might I have a few moments alone with this lovely lady before we begin?"

Nemo chided himself for leaving the woman's face uncovered, though he doubted they would have granted her that dignity for long anyway. He rattled the paper, turned a page. "First procedure is the cesarean," he said. "Abdominal exposure and incision into the uterus. Mind you don't make the cuts too deep."

"Right, right," Fitzhugh said, either too preoccupied by the dead woman or still too drunk to catch the reference to Addie Kennedy. He picked up a scalpel from his tray and began. Following Fitzhugh's lead, the others too began to get down to their business, and Nemo settled back gratefully into the familiar, wordless hum of the busy laboratory.

Fitzhugh made the cut on the abdomen just below the rose tattoo. The blade sank into the soft flesh, and as it did Nemo and the others heard a long hiss of gas escaping. One of the students nearby coughed. Fitzhugh stepped back and put a hand to his face. "Are you sure she's well embalmed?" he asked.

"Same as the others," Nemo said.

"I may need some assistance here."

The *South Carolinian* rattled again. "Can't help with this one. Doctor Johnston told me expressly." He wet his fingertip against his tongue and turned another page, over to the obituaries, and started when he saw Mary Elizabeth Fitzhugh's name at the top of the listings in large type. Her name was followed by a long list of her ancestral relations and a history of her debut in

Charleston, then her married years with Albert Fitzhugh, Senior, among the swaying rice fields and gentle ocean breezes of All Saints Parish.

Nemo lowered the paper and peered over it at Mary Elizabeth Fitzhugh's sole surviving relation. His mother just barely gone and him raring about drunk all night, looking for a chance to gamble on roosters killing each other. Nemo could not understand it. Yet he knew that Doctor Johnston would explain it as some kind of expression of grief.

He could see that Fitzhugh had pared back the epidermis and was cutting at the underlying fat with slow, deliberate strokes. If he ever had to perform the surgery on a living person, Nemo thought, the woman would need a double dose of ether and a blood transfusion. Beneath the table, the dog panted, its tongue lolling out of its mouth. Fitzhugh had clamped the tip of his own tongue between his teeth as he concentrated on the delicate work.

"There!" he cried. "Or almost. I think I can see the uterine wall."

"Make your lateral incision," Nemo said, his voice distant.

Fitzhugh made the cut and frowned down at it. He set the scalpel aside and reached into the cavity with both hands. When he raised them the others saw that they were full of scarlet and white tissue, latticed and perforated with decay. In his hands the tissue fell apart, dissolving between his fingers like dirty snow melting. His face was contorted with disgust.

"Something's wrong," he said. "Is this some kind of joke?"

Nemo rose from his stool. "Yep, something wrong. Haven't seen nothing like that before."

"You haven't, have you?"

"I have not."

"Why do I wonder?" Fitzhugh said, his cupped hands still half filled with the diseased tissue. "You bring me niggers that are no good, so I ask you for a white specimen. You bring me a white woman, and her insides are eaten up like an old cheese." He held the ruined uterus aloft as if to present it as evidence. "Something is wrong, all right. The problem, I am beginning to see, is you, Nemo. I will speak with Doctor Johnston about this in the clearest of terms. You are sabotaging my medical career."

"Doctor Johnston going to tell you that you don't need my help with that."

Fitzhugh made a growling sound of inexpressible rage and flung his hands at Nemo. The fragments of the dead woman's uterus flew across the space between them and hit Nemo full in the face. He heard the impact as much as felt it as the tissue struck wetly against his skin and dripped down from his forehead to his shirtfront, then the floor. He wiped at his eyes and closed the distance to Fitzhugh in two strides. Stonewall was barking wildly now and rocking back on his haunches, ready to lunge.

"Stay away from me," Fitzhugh shouted. "You crazy nigger, stay away from me or he'll tear your throat out."

Nemo pulled the knife from his pocket and held it out. He

turned the blade until it glinted in the room's light. "Any dog that comes after me going to be a dead dog in a minute's time. You take him by the collar now and walk him out and you'll live to see another day. Don't, and I'm going to make a specimen out of you right here."

Fitzhugh had backed up to his table, his buttocks against the slate top and his hands out behind him. "You would, would you? In front of all these witnesses?"

Nemo registered the movement of Fitzhugh's hands too late. The white man's right arm arced out toward him with the scalpel pointed downward and raked across his chest, leaving a burning line behind it. Nemo raised his own knife from his side and lowered his head to go in, his eyes on the point of Fitzhugh's shirt just below the sternum. His knife was still rising when he felt someone take hold of his forearm and yank back. Nemo pulled, already sensing himself stronger than this new antagonist, until he caught the scent of talcum powder and, behind that, a sweetish wisp of ether.

"You know I cannot overpower you, Nemo. Allow me to appeal to your reason," Johnston said behind him. "And you, Fitzhugh, put down that scalpel or I shall expel you this afternoon."

Nemo and Johnston hung poised in the strange embrace as Fitzhugh reluctantly tossed the scalpel aside. One of the students handed him a cloth and he mopped at his face with it, then wiped his hands on it violently.

"Your future, Nemo," Johnston whispered in his ear. "Think of the opportunities you will squander with this violence." The doctor squeezed Nemo's arm almost tenderly. "I implore you to use your reason," he said.

Slowly, by degrees, Nemo allowed his muscles to relax. When he felt Johnston's hand slip away, he placed the knife back in his pocket and lifted his hand to the long cut on his chest, assessing its depth. His eyes never left Fitzhugh's face.

"You saw that, Doctor Johnston," Fitzhugh was saying. "With your own eyes. He took up a weapon against a white man, sir, with a clear intent to murder. I demand you contact the authorities this instant."

"Oh, shut up, Fitzhugh," Johnston said. "We are the only authority needed here." He stepped around Nemo and toward Fitzhugh. He glanced at the open abdomen of the dead woman and his gaze stopped there, as though his intellect had been aroused despite the uproar. He picked up a scalpel and prodded the tissue, his brows knitting. "Tragic. What kind of abortifacient was used, one can only imagine," he said. "Probably chemical. Come here, Fitzhugh, and have a look at the fetus."

"I don't want to see it," Fitzhugh said sullenly.

"No. Of course you do not." He turned and stretched to his full height, until his eyes were level with Fitzhugh's. "That is because you are an imbecile. Another student with even a hint of scholarly curiosity would have treated this scenario as an opportunity. You, however, have rendered it an occasion for unmanly complaint and common violence."

Fitzhugh's mouth dropped open. Beneath the table, Stonewall whined sympathetically.

Johnston looked down at the dog and gave it a sharp kick. "Out, out with this cur. I have let things go too far. Mister Fitzhugh, you will accompany the animal out of the building. If you choose to grace our hall with your presence again, it will be at seven o'clock sharp tomorrow morning. I will supervise the remainder of your dissection practice myself."

Fitzhugh stood as if struck dumb until Johnston made a flicking motion with his hand. Then he bent and took a handful of the dog's ruff and dragged him away. A few paces from the doorway he turned and shouted, "I'll have your job yet, boy! I'll get my justice!"

"You might," Nemo said quietly. "You just might have it yet." He looked down at his chest. The cut was not deep, but he knew it would scar.

In the heavy silence that followed, one of the students cleared his throat. "The boy did assault a white man, sir."

"And was he not assaulted first? Round and round we go, and where does it get us? Surely I do not need to furnish you with an answer. Today's business goes no further than this room, gentlemen. Am I clearly understood?"

There were murmurs of assent, most of them reluctant. Johnston turned to Nemo.

"And you, Nemo, will atone for your lapse of judgment by having another female specimen on this table by seven tomorrow."

Now it was Nemo's jaw that slackened.

"But Doctor Johnston," he said. "This poor woman—"

"Is dead, Nemo. Neither our pity nor our sympathy can help her one iota." He raised his voice to address both Nemo and the students. "Our business, as I have told each of you a hundred times, is the living."

"The living," Nemo said.

"Yes, the living. The dead teach us, yes. But beyond that, their value is negligible."

Johnston seemed to be waiting for Nemo's assent. But Nemo only stared at the floorboards beneath his feet. On one of them lay a fragment of gossamer tissue, white and delicate as a dogwood petal.

One of the students, Mullins, finally broke the heavy silence. "Alma Bodifer died Sunday. They buried her yesterday. I know because her sister cleans my room."

"And of what value is that?" Johnston said too quickly. His eyes were still on Nemo's face.

Mullins glanced at the others, looking as if he wished he had not spoken. "I just mention it because she's white, sir. And, uh . . ." Parks strained to find the proper words. "And not likely to have gotten into this kind of condition. She was common, but she was a churchwoman. That's what her sister says."

"Thank you, Mister Mullins," Johnston said. "Nemo, I trust you can manage the procurement?"

Nemo sniffed once and nodded his head.

"That's my good man," Johnston said, smiling, and reached out to pat him on the shoulder. "Please see to it that she is here and in good condition for tomorrow morning."

"I'll give it my full attention, Doctor Johnston. And I want to thank you, sir."

"For what?"

"For teaching me what I know."

Johnston blushed, and Nemo thought he saw his shirt-front puff out a fraction of an inch. When he turned back to the remaining students, he was already rolling up his shirt-sleeves. "Gentlemen," he began, his voice restored to its former composure, "we now return our attention to the great art of anatomy."

Nemo could hear the whittling of the blades clear out the rear door.

ROBERT MULLINS WAS standing beside the dissecting table with the scrap of newsprint in his hand, scanning its four lines of close type, when he and the others heard Albert Fitzhugh's whistling outside the building, followed closely by the sound of the dog pattering across the packed-dirt yard behind its master. Quickly he tucked the clipping back under the woman's left shoulder where he had found it and returned to his own table. Alma Bodifer had enjoyed no such greeting as her predecessor the day before, and little wonder, he thought, as he took another glance at the new cadaver: she was as ample as her surviving sister, the fact made even more evident by her nakedness in the unforgiving morning light. Against the black slate, her abundant flesh seemed ghastly white, grossly pallid, with her ponderous breasts sagging toward her armpits and the excess skin on the backs of her arms and legs pressed flat against the tabletop. Beneath the edges of the handkerchief over her face, Mullins saw her cheeks drooping downward as well, gravity pulling the fat there earthward.

"What time have you got, McEwan?" he said as he took up his scalpel.

"Ten till. He made it, by God."

"He'll not make it ten minutes when Johnston gets here."

"Now, Turner," Mullins said, grinning, "Old Fitz may just pull through yet."

"So long as his next check don't bounce."

Mullins was casting about for a response when the laboratory door flew open, framing Fitzhugh in its bright opening. He paused a moment for the dog to precede him, but the animal stopped at the threshold as though galvanized, with its head raised and its long tail poised erect over its hindquarters. Fitzhugh looked down at it for a moment, then burst into a laugh.

"My God, what a dog! Do you see that, boys? He remembers. Memory like an elephant's." He bent and scratched behind the dog's ears. "Of course you will wait outside, old boy. What a good dog he is." He made cooing sounds of approval, then shut the door slowly, its lower panels stopping an inch shy of the dog's rigid snout.

Fitzhugh strode into the room magisterially and up to the

table where his third obstetric cadaver lay. "What have we here? Quite the heifer," he said. There was a smattering of laughter as he picked up the obituary.

"'Alma Bodifer, aged forty-two,'" he read. "Says she made the best cornbread in Cotton Town." He chuckled as he wadded up the paper and tossed it aside. "Can you believe that?"

"Looks like she ate every bit of it."

"Heifer means more cutting, Fitz."

"By God, there is a lot of her, but I'm ready, boys. This is my last day with these bitches."

"Third time's the charm, Fitz," Mullins said from between the splayed brown legs of his cadaver.

"The next time I explore the female nether regions, gentlemen, it will be on my own time and at my own leisure."

The ensuing laughter stopped abruptly with the sound of the door being opened again. Fitzhugh blushed as he looked up to see Johnston shutting the door on the immobile dog with a quizzical look on his face.

"Mister Fitzhugh," he said, "I trust you have already begun your incision into the abdominal wall?"

"No, sir. I was just assaying my equipment."

Mullins snorted into the perineum of his cadaver. Johnston's neck flushed as he looked down at the Bodifer woman.

"First the legs must be spread to access the perineal region," he said. "Proceed."

Fitzhugh struggled for a moment with the heavy thighs,

then looked up at Johnston meekly. "Her hips don't seem to move right."

"Stand aside, then." Johnston pushed against the cadaver's thighs, trying to spread them. Neither leg would budge.

"Ideally, the thigh and gluteal region would have already been dissected," he said between breaths, "affording easier articulation. We must be able to abduct the thighs to expose the perineum." He stood and nodded at the tray of instruments at the foot of the table. "Two incisions through the thigh muscles near the genitalia, Mister Fitzhugh, to render the right hip mobile."

Fitzhugh made the incisions in the right thigh. When Johnston nodded, he pushed at the leg again. It spread open with a cracking sound.

"Doubtless Nemo has been over this ground with you before, but next is the abdominal incision." He watched intently as Fitzhugh carved a foot-long crescent on the cadaver's lower belly, pulling back against the flesh as he cut deeper through the layers of orange fat. A film of sweat formed on Fitzhugh's upper lip when the tissue of the uterine wall came into view.

"Good, then. Now, a light incision into the membrane of the uterus." He winced as his student cut deeply into the organ.

"If this were in fact an actual cesarean operation, the uterus would be enlarged, with far more vascular tissue."

"Swollen, you mean?"

"Enlarged enormously, yes. Which would give you a bigger target, would it not? Perhaps then you would need stitches only for the mother, and not her newborn as well."

If Fitzhugh heard the insult, he ignored it as Johnston went on. "In practice you would follow with the removal of the fetus, cutting of the umbilicus, closing the uterus, et cetera."

Fitzhugh looked relieved and moved to set his scalpel back on the tray.

"Now," Johnston said. "Two birds with one stone. Proceed with a hysterectomy, as you would if you were to encounter tumors or a naturally ruptured uterus."

"Nemo never said nothing about a hysterectomy."

Johnston looked at him evenly. "You failed under Nemo's tutelage. Now you are under mine." He picked up a long needle and began threading a length of suturing through its eye. "Dilate the opening in the vesicouterine pouch laterally."

Fitzhugh looked at his tray of tools helplessly. Johnston leaned over the body's open cavity impatiently and stuck his hand inside it. "With your fingers, thusly," he said. "The uterus remains attached to its surrounding organs by the broad ligaments alone. See?"

Almost imperceptibly, Fitzhugh nodded. Several of the other students were now standing in a loose circle around the table, anxious to see the next step of the surgery. Johnston handed Fitzhugh the needle dangling its length of catgut. "Pass this needle through the ligaments and set a firm ligature for each. Mind you steer clear of the Fallopian tubes for the third suture."

The room was silent as Fitzhugh labored through the procedure. A bead of sweat dropped from his forehead into the open abdomen as he worked.

"Your suturing should be more expeditious," Johnston said. "Imagine a live woman under your knife. In her place, would you not want the operation to proceed more rapidly?"

"This is quite difficult enough as it is, sir."

"Not nearly so difficult as watching you perform it, Mister Fitzhugh."

But Fitzhugh pressed on, sweating freely now, and even Johnston began to nod as he finally pressed the needle through the last gray band of ligament and tied it off firmly. Johnston handed him a pair of steel snips and he clipped the tissue cleanly.

"Very nice," Johnston said as Fitzhugh lifted the pear-shaped uterus clear of the orange fat and set it down on the slate. "Final suturing of the peritoneum and abdomen is next. Carry on." He pulled out his pocket watch and consulted it while his student made the final stitches. "Eight minutes. A frankly amateurish time, but you will improve with practice," he said, his voice trailing off as he completed the sentence. A minute later Fitzhugh looked up at him expectantly, and clearly considerably relieved, as he tied off the last knot on the cadaver's belly.

"The final step is to plug the vagina with gauze," Johnston said, "to stanch the drainage."

"We have no gauze, sir," Fitzhugh said in a light voice.

"Where the devil is Nemo when we need him?" Johnston

said as he pulled the handkerchief from the cadaver's face and handed it to Fitzhugh.

But Fitzhugh did not take the cloth proffered to him. His eyes were fixed on the face of the cadaver lying before him, and they widened and contracted as if the muscles around them had become suddenly spasmodic.

"That's not the Bodifer woman," Mullins said quietly.

Fitzhugh's jaws were working like those of a man trapped underwater. Johnston looked down at the face of the dead woman, at the flesh sagging beneath the high cheekbones, with a faint sense of recognition, then turned back to his student. Fitzhugh was gasping now, and sounds of choking came forth from deep within his throat. Still his eyes stuck fast to the cadaver's face. For an instant they left it, darting down the naked torso to the crosshatched lines of sutures on the abdomen and the pubic mound below them, and back to the face again. The sounds in his throat redoubled in volume, and he turned aside and vomited onto the floor with one hand set out for balance on the table. When he straightened, he saw that his fingertips were splayed against the dissected uterus.

"Her womb," Fitzhugh said in a quavering whisper.

His throat hitched again, but he did not retch, only drew in a great shuddering lungful of air and pressed a hand to his face as he stepped backward and screamed, "Mother! Oh God, Mother!"

Fitzhugh's eyes rolled backward and his body followed them, arms thrown out as he collapsed, dragging down a tray of clattering scalpels and forceps as he fell. A long second of silence passed before Johnston and the others moved to assist him and the laboratory filled with their cries and the sounds of Stonewall scratching against the door, his barking panicked at first, then rising by degrees to a crescendo of hysterical fury.

He was still barking when they carried Fitzhugh out.

Friday

THE SLATE-BLUE CROSS ATOP THE steeple of Ebenezer M.B.E. sputters and hisses, its old neon coursing through the glass tubes wearily, as though the chemical reaction between the neon and the electricity has reached its last half-life. Its glow, so bright through the darkest predawn hours, is now giving way to the sunlight filtering through the trees and bungalow roofs to the east. By degrees the streets are illuminated in hues of gray below the church set high upon its little knoll at the corner of Hardin and Pulaski, looking down regally on the barren landscape of inner-city blight that surrounds it.

Across the street, Jacob's car idles in the lot of an old service station with boarded windows, beside the abandoned gas pumps. The top is up, the air conditioner running, its condenser kicking in every few minutes as the fan drones and fills the car with cool air. Inside, Jacob has cranked his seat back as far as it will go, and he lies against the cool leather, dozing fitfully. The manila file folder he spent most of the night reading and rereading lies closed in his lap, a smear of grease on its tab still damp from its short tenure in his kitchen garbage can, where he had thrown it just after midnight. Three hours later, finally giving up on the prospect of sleep, he had risen and showered and snatched it out of the can and climbed into his car, bone-weary but anxious to have this errand over with before he could give it more thought.

The digital clock on the BMW's dashboard shifts over to six-thirty as the engine's fan whirs to life again. Jacob twists in his seat, sweating despite the rush of cool air. He is deep within a dream.

He is walking from the school toward the house where he grew up in West Columbia. It stands alone with the vast plain of the Midlands stretched out behind it, the scrub pines and rolling hills forming a scant topography, as though huddled, cringing, beneath the merciless sun. The rest of the neighborhood, the whole town, is gone. Between him and the house, the Congaree winds and flows, a big lazy mass of water on which the curls of eddies and waves glint like copper in the sunlight. There is no sound. His family is gathering on the front steps as if they intend to meet him. But no—there, with the surreal logic of the unconscious mind, is Jacob himself as a boy of five, the last out the storm door to stand on the brick porch with his parents. Jacob waves to himself as he comes down the hillside toward the river, his stride impossibly long and limber, like the gait of an astronaut on the moon. He is stopped by the water and waves again, his family's features somehow clear across the distance over the currents. His father gathers his mother and the young Jacob around him on the front steps. The wind is up and the collar of his father's plaid shirt flaps against his chin; under his callused hand, tufts of the boy's white-blond hair lift in the breeze.

Jacob can see no color in them through the metallic atmosphere of the dream; the scene is in sepia except for the sky above—a magenta backdrop against which the cumulus clouds scud and scurry in cottony haste, harried by the wind.

There is a camera in his hand, and he realizes the reason for this tableau: his father has brought them out to be photographed. The camera is a relic, older even than the Polaroid his father let him play with back in the seventies until he broke it. It is a nineteenth-century contraption of wood and glass, a tripod-mounted box complete with a black curtain to shield the photographer and his exposures from sunlight. Jacob sets it up and checks his family's position through the glass. When he is satisfied with their pose, he pauses to look on this vision of himself from those years long ago.

Such a beautiful boy! Jacob thinks. The cheekbones so delicate, the skin so clear and firm, seamless.

But his family stands there looking as dour as Puritans. His father will not meet his eyes; his mother seems distracted, as if worried that she has left the gas stove alight or a door unlocked. The boy looks at him as though he doesn't think much of what he sees.

Jacob pushes aside the camera's curtain and looks at them directly, trying to encourage them to make a good portrait. "Smile!" he shouts over the water, flapping his arms, but their expressions do not change. He gives up and tucks his head under the cloth once more, looking through the viewfinder again to be sure they have not moved out of the frame. "Suit yourself," he says, and clasps the bulb that will discharge the flash. He is just about to take the picture when the boy speaks.

"I never hurt you," he says to the grown Jacob through the camera's lens.

"Christ!" Jacob spits as he bolts upright in his seat, bumping his head against the metal frame of the convertible's top. He raises one hand to his forehead and the other to his eyes, rubbing them. "Christ," he says again as the dream's force dispels in his mind.

The interior of the little car seems to him suddenly close and airless, and he reaches for the door handle in claustrophobic haste. As soon as the door swings out he stands, spilling the folder and its contents from his lap to the oil-slicked asphalt. A bell inside the car dings manically. For a moment he only stands in the cool morning air, trying to breathe it all into himself. But the papers begin to turn and shuffle in a low breeze and he bends to gather them again into the file. When they are back in some semblance of order, he reaches into the car and turns the key in the ignition, sets the alarm, and crosses Pulaski without a look for traffic in either direction.

REVEREND GREER IS the first to arrive at the church a half hour later. He pauses a moment on the stairs below the church's front doors and studies Jacob. After a moment he seems satisfied with what he sees and proceeds up the concrete steps heavily, pulling a key ring from a pocket and nodding to his visitor, who steps aside.

"We'll talk inside," is all he says by way of greeting.

The sanctuary is painted robin's-egg blue, with lavender carpet that matches the cushions on the wooden pews. The morning light falls gaily through the stained glass windows, which are small but busy with colored glass, rainbow hues from Noah's story set off by a single white dove, the serene face of a black Christ looking down through yellow rays. The room smells of flowers—lilies, Jacob thinks—and their scent hangs in the air with the oppressive weight of the odor in a funeral home. Greer moves silently over the carpet toward the back of the sanctuary and opens a white door. Jacob follows him through a threadbare hallway of Sunday school rooms and up a narrow staircase where someone has fitted a homemade rail fashioned out of plumbing pipe to the wall. At the top, Greer opens the door to his office, where an oak desk sits squarely in the middle of the room, and steps to the window. He turns on the air conditioning unit there, takes a seat behind his desk, and stares at Jacob wordlessly.

Jacob stands helplessly for a moment until Greer nods to

a chair. He sits and crosses his legs, tapping the edge of the file folder against his ankle idly while he tries to decide how to open the conversation. A wisp of the dream flashes in his mind—the brick porch, his father's upturned collar—and he pushes it away by speaking.

"The school is prepared to make a donation to the church."

"A love offering," Greer smiles.

"You can call it what you want, just so long as the march doesn't happen this weekend."

Greer nods for him to go on.

"I've been authorized to negotiate a contribution. A substantial one. For you and your church, your colleagues, to do with as you see fit. We suggest a scholarship endowment. I'll work with you to set one up if you wish to pursue that course. I can write out a check this morning for twenty-five thousand dollars."

Again Greer nods, and Jacob lets the silence play out.

"But this is a one-time offer. The administration can see that this is a delicate and special situation, but this case will not set a precedent. I'm authorized to make one contribution, today. No more."

"No march tomorrow or ever, you mean?"

Jacob shrugs. "No march tomorrow, no more talk about the basement."

Greer picks up a letter opener from his desk and tests its point against an index finger. "I do not like ultimatums. To me, they smack of bygone days, of masters and servants. Of orders given and obeyed."

"This is a business transaction, nothing more or less," Jacob says, the words thick in his mouth. He can hear movement in the church below them, the sound of the organ in the sanctuary being warmed up, a major scale tentatively played.

"I'll take it under advisement," Greer says, setting the letter opener back on his desk.

"There isn't time for advisement. I need your assurance that your church members won't be on campus this weekend."

Greer's mouth tightens. "My people have operated without assurances in South Carolina for four hundred years. A few hours will kill neither you," he says, "nor any of your *colleagues.*"

But he seems to have heard the organist too. He rises and motions for Jacob to follow him. They descend the narrow staircase. At its bottom Greer turns toward the back of the church, keys the lock to a rear door, and throws it open to a playground, where particolored swing sets and slides litter the concrete pavement, the entire play lot surrounded by a chain-link fence six feet high. Greer indicates it all with a wave of his hand.

"It's nice," Jacob says after a moment.

"Perhaps it is. But look closer." Greer's hand drops toward the base of the fence and Jacob sees on the concrete there a number of tiny glass vials and, in one back corner, two syringes lying on the pavement. Their plungers are orange-handled—the same sharps used at the hospital. He sees that the reverend is watching him intently, so he nods grimly.

Greer seems pleased. "Quite different from the playgrounds of your youth, isn't it, Mister Thacker? Perhaps you can see why I am not so eager to step and fetch at your school's behest."

Jacob can feel the blood rising in his neck, in his cheeks. "The school has nothing to do with this," he says. "And you don't know the first thing about me."

Greer steps away and begins picking up the little vials. They clink together in his broad palm as he collects them. "Our youth operate in a world entirely bereft of your opportunities. Where you have networks and connections, they face closed doors and impossible odds. There is a great debt to be redressed."

"I was no more connected than your youth," Jacob says. "I worked my way up. Nobody ever offered me a handout."

Greer pauses in his work to look over his shoulder with one eyebrow raised. "Oh? No decent schools in your neighborhood? No resources for a letter of recommendation? No community to see that you succeeded?"

"My community was West Columbia Textiles. My family poured their life into it."

"Earning a living wage while my people were digging out from under Jim Crow."

"It wasn't much of a wage. And they didn't do much living."

Greer seems not to have heard. He picks up the syringes and studies them. "Addicts," he says, shaking his head. "What's an addict? Somebody who's given up on living. Who's given up on the Lord."

Jacob barely suppresses a snort of disgust. The file in his hands seems ready to leap from his grasp.

"Or," Greer is saying, "someone who's faced obstacles so daunting you can only imagine them. Do you honestly expect me to be moved by the fact that you were born to a linthead family across the river?" Greer smiles, his eyes feline. "If I had a nickel for every cracker up-by-my-bootstraps story I've ever heard, I'd be a wealthy man. Am I supposed to feel sympathetic?"

Jacob is moving toward him across the concrete before he finishes the question. He holds the file out and slaps it against Greer's chest while the man takes a step back.

"I don't care a damn how you feel. Fuck you and your sympathy and your sanctity. Read that file. It's a copy of your record from the treatment clinic. A very interesting account of cocaine abuse and recovery. Confidential, up to now. But if it were to be leaked to the press, it would become public in record time. You'd be back down to your bootstraps in a week."

Greer drops the syringes and the vials, a few of which shatter on the ground. He clutches the file against his chest weakly. "This is malpractice," he says, his voice nearly a whisper.

"This is hardball. You dealt the play."

Jacob turns back toward the church, already reaching into

his pocket for the car keys. He feels the folded check in his pocket and stops, turns back to face Greer.

"And the donation," he says, "is rescinded." He is improvising now, well past the boundaries of the plan McMichaels gave him last night, but the freedom feels viscerally good. "I've taken it under advisement, and I don't think much of our contribution would actually reach your youth. We'll pursue other avenues for making a contribution."

He leaves the reverend there, alone on the forlorn playground, looking for all the world like a soul lost in a purgatory of his own making, a shade wandering in a familiar, bitter landscape.

For the first time in weeks, Jacob immerses himself totally in his paperwork, spending more time on each form and press release and e-mail response than is really necessary, trying to smother the aching thoughts in his brain with the mass of administrative minutiae as though his very sanity depended on it. Which he supposes it does: every time he allows his mind to wander, it flashes back to the Ebenezer church or to the image of McMichaels holding out the manila file folder. Or to the thought of a woman left deserted and on her own over a century ago, in this very building. And every time he has glanced up from his desk, his eyes have met the damning smiles of his parents in the snapshot on his bookshelf—or, worse, the group portrait of the class of 1860, from which Frederick Augustus Johnston stares down like an enigma. So when he hears a soft knock on his door he only burrows deeper into the budget form in front of him, hoping the visitor will come back later.

Instead, McMichaels's secretary, Elizabeth, sets a thick manila envelope on his desk, on top of the budget report.

"From Janice Tanaka," she says.

He picks up the envelope. "This isn't a campus mailer," he says, peeling a Post-it note from the heavy package.

"Janice delivered it this morning. Herself."

Jacob realizes he has never thought of Janice outside her warren of filing cabinets at the archives. He imagines her blinking in the sunlight and the open air of the campus on her journey to Administration.

"I think you're growing on her, Jacob." Elizabeth smiles.

He holds the Post-it note close to his face so that he can make out Janice's tiny, cramped script. "There is a good deal of material here," it reads. "I hope you'll review it carefully. I've noticed administrators tend to read cursorily at best." Another schooling from Janice Tanaka. The Completist.

"And Yara Nasir is here to see you," Elizabeth says.

"What for?"

"For her interview."

Reluctantly, Jacob looks up. "I thought that was next week."

For answer, Elizabeth bends over and taps a manicured fingernail on his desk calendar. And there it is: "Yara Nasir" penciled in neatly at his noon slot in Elizabeth's careful hand. "You don't remember, do you?"

Jacob rubs a hand over his eyes. "No. When did you tell me?"

"Wednesday, in the meeting."

"Right." Wednesday morning seems like years ago now. He looks up at Elizabeth meekly. "I need to ask a favor. Can you tell her something's come up?"

"And what could be more important than Miss Nasir?"

"Nothing. I just can't talk to her today."

Her brows knit. "Why not?"

Jacob gives a desperate little laugh. "Do you really want to know?"

He stares at her as her eyes drift toward the window. "No," she says quietly, "I don't suppose I do."

He stuffs the envelope from Janice into his portfolio, then rises and steps around the desk, pats Elizabeth gently on the shoulder. "I'll owe you one, Elizabeth," he says. He glances across the open hallway to the glass-paneled door of the dean's office, where he can see a portion of Yara Nasir's beautiful face as she sits in one of the overstuffed chairs talking to Austin Malloy, who looks as flushed as a frat boy when he speaks to her.

"I'm just going to step out for a while," he says to Elizabeth, his eyes never leaving Miss Nasir's face as he sidles toward his office door. He wants to slip away unnoticed.

"Jacob?" Elizabeth says. He turns and sees that she is holding out his suit jacket. "Don't forget this."

She holds it for him as he slips his arms into the sleeves, then pats his back as he steps out the door. He turns to wave to her as he goes down the stairs and sees her shaking her head at him, but not in the usual bantering way. She looks almost sad.

Outside, Jacob breathes the open air gratefully, not certain of his destination but glad to be free of the hush of the administration building. On an impulse, he pulls his cell phone from his pocket and calls Kaye's office, on the off-chance that she might have a rare hour free for lunch. But the phone rings and rings until he hears the line click over from Kaye's direct phone to the firm's receptionist, who tells him that Kaye will be taking a deposition all afternoon. She has left word that she will meet him at the Dean's Mansion tonight for the banquet.

He presses the off button on the phone and stops for a moment. Ahead of him, where the brick walkways terminate on Gervais Street at the gates of the university, he sees Lorenzo Shanks standing at the corner crosswalk. His broad back is turned to the campus, so Jacob waits until the traffic light shifts to green. But Lorenzo does not move with the others across Gervais. Instead he begins pacing in front of the gates, checking his watch once as he walks in nervous circuits in front of the brick pillars and the palmettos planted before them. On his third pass he looks back toward the school. When he sees Jacob, he raises a hand.

For a second Jacob thinks of turning on his heel and heading back in the opposite direction. But he resumes his walk, forcing his stride to look normal. He will speak to Lorenzo, he thinks, then go on across Gervais as soon as the light turns again.

"How about it, Jake?" Lorenzo says when he is within earshot.

"Doing all right. You?"

"Making it," he says, and holds out a hand. Jacob takes it with an eye on the traffic signal.

"Thought you were down on East Campus."

"We are," Lorenzo says, nodding. "But I'm meeting somebody."

"Great," Jacob says, looking away.

"Meeting Reverend Greer. He and I are supposed to map out the route for tomorrow."

"Great," Jacob says again, idiotically. To his vast relief, the traffic light has turned yellow. He already has a foot on the pavement.

"But he's late."

Jacob pauses for a moment, even though the signal is now flashing *Walk*, and Lorenzo takes hold of his arm. His grip is like a vise. "I'm sorry it had to go down like it did, Jake. I really am."

"I'm sorry too."

"It's nothing personal."

"I know what you mean." Because he cannot meet Lorenzo's eyes, he stares at the light. He shuts his eyes for a moment when it shifts again to red.

"Lorenzo, listen," he is beginning to say when a white pickup truck with the seal of the university on its doors slows in front of them and stops a dozen feet beyond. The driver honks the horn and throws on the flashers, and the truck jerks as its transmission is dropped into park. A second later Bowman's head juts out of the passenger side window, his face red as he glares at Lorenzo. It seems to take him a few seconds to compose himself for speech.

"There you fucking are, Shanks," he says finally. "Sonny Jesus, boy, you're damn near an hour late. What kind of a lunch are you having?"

Jacob can hear Lorenzo's measured breathing beside him. The two of them stare at Bowman until his face reddens another shade.

"I'll tell you what kind of lunch," Bowman yells. "Your last fucking lunch on my payroll if you don't get your ass in this truck. I ain't running no drop-in business." He throws the door open and wriggles across the bench seat behind the steering wheel. After a moment he gives the horn three more taps.

Lorenzo sighs and walks toward the open door. He looks back once at Jacob, his face inscrutable, before he settles into the truck and shuts the door. The flashers cut off and Bowman puts on his left turn signal and pulls back into Gervais, heading east. Jacob watches the two of them through the rear windshield, the white man and his stoic black passenger, until the white tailgate disappears in the lunch-hour traffic.

When they are gone he pulls his phone out again and begins dialing the number for the dean's office, to tell Elizabeth that he will not be back in today. He is hoping that a few hours at the gym might go a long way toward soothing his conscience, the dull ache there. As the phone begins to ring, he thinks that but for his obligatory presence at the banquet tonight, he would be spending the weekend as far away from campus as he can.

ROSEDALE JUST AFTER quitting time seems to be breathing a collective sigh of relief. Cars cruise the streets more slowly than usual, with sinewy black arms dangling out of their windows, the front seats pushed back so far the drivers' heads are obscured by the doorframes. While Jacob and Mary wait at the light at Harden and Devine, an old Oldsmobile painted bright blue rumbles past with a primordial thumping of bass blasting out its open windows, the booming noise enveloping the vehicle like a sonic cloud.

"Wonder why they ride around with the windows down in this heat?" Jacob asks.

Mary looks at him askance.

"I'm serious. Do they feel obligated to share that music with the community? Why not just roll up the windows and turn on the AC?"

Mary's head is beginning a slow wobble on her shoulders. "They roll them down because they don't have air conditioning. Boy, you have got above your raising."

Jacob glances down at the vents on his dashboard, where the German-cooled air is blowing over their legs before it loses the battle with the summer heat coming in from the open top. It's wasteful, but also the only way he can stand putting the top down before dark in August.

"You want me to turn mine off? Does it make you feel pretentious?"

"Don't make me feel nothing but cool."

The light turns to green and he accelerates through the intersection. Twenty minutes now since he picked her up at his condo, and the conversation has been unusually fitful. He thinks he knows why.

"How's Big Junior?" he asks.

Mary looks away. "Gone north."

"North?"

"Yeah. He got a girlfriend there he stay with sometimes."

"Seems like the wrong time of year to head up there."

Mary shrugs. "Said he's had enough of Carolina for a while."

Jacob can think of nothing to say. As if to break the uneasy silence, Mary bends down to the floorboard, picks up his portfolio, and fusses with the loose flap of manila envelope that pokes forth from its leather.

"Going to lose something important riding around with this loose," she says. And sure enough, now that she has lifted them off the floor, the pages flutter and snap in the wind. She gathers them together and opens the clasp on the manila envelope to put them inside. She is stuffing the stack into the envelope when she pauses.

"Who this?"

He sees that she has pulled the copy of Nemo Johnston's portrait from among the other papers.

"That's the guy who ruined my week."

"What he do to you?"

For an instant he thinks of telling her everything, of filling in the gaps of whatever story Big Junior must have already told her. He looks down again at the man's face in the photocopy. Beneath the almost fierce expression there is a sadness to the eyes, if you look closely enough. "He left a mess behind him," he says finally. "I got stuck cleaning it up."

Mary nods, makes a sound of agreement. "Well. Ain't that a switch," she says. "White man cleaning up after a black man."

"I guess it is," Jacob says as he pulls the car to the curb in front of Mary's house. She sets the portfolio on the dashboard with Nemo Johnston's face sticking out of the top of it, his distant eyes staring up at the twilight sky. Mary is opening the door when Jacob puts his hand on her arm.

"Mary," he says, "that's the guy who put all the bones in the school cellar. The ones Big Junior saw." He pauses, wishing her eyes would meet his. "Tell me something: why would he do that to his own people?"

Her chestnut eyes fix on his for a moment, then she turns back to the door. She has one foot planted on the asphalt when she looks over her shoulder at him. "What makes you think he had a *choice*?"

The car door shuts heavily behind her and he hears her feet padding across the asphalt. His eyes are still riveted to Nemo

Johnston's when he hears her screen porch door swat shut. Slowly he reaches out for the portfolio to tuck the black face out of view. He is stuffing it into the envelope when another photocopy in the packet catches his eye. He pulls it out, glancing at its familiar arrangement of five vertical figures arrayed around the horizontal cadaver.

But Nemo Johnston is not present in this photograph, and as Jacob narrows his eyes he can see that the men have posed not on the ground floor of Johnston Hall but in the basement. In a corner of the frame he can just make out one of the grilled casements of the cellar.

He flips through the papers behind it, shaking his head as he thinks of Janice Tanaka and her obsessive yearning to know the complete record, how lonely it must be for her to hoard this much information to herself. What it must have taken for her to share this knowledge with him.

He looks at the faces in each photograph. Some of them could almost pass for the nineteenth century, with their heavy sideburns, until the hand-lettered dates at the bottom of each shot proceed to the eighties, when the faces are shaved clean, the hairstyles short. And though every photograph includes a haggard cadaver and some emblem of the skull and crossbones, Jacob sees in most of the shots the familiar faces of the recent past. He recognizes John Beauregard in the 1971 portrait; in 1979, a young Austin Malloy mugs for the camera.

And indeed, it seems to Jacob that there is no small measure of bureaucratic courage in Janice's decision to slip these extra pages in among the ones he requested. For in every shot from the early seventies to the last portrait, in 1980, Jim McMichaels stands at the center of the frame, twenty pounds lighter and with a full head of hair, smiling like a prince.

With a leaden feeling in his gut, Jacob tucks the pages back into the envelope, lingering for a moment over the earliest shot with McMichaels in it, when the dean was Jacob's age. He can see that McMichaels's eyes back then were just as bright and crafty as they are today.

He sets the portfolio on the passenger seat and eases the BMW forward down Harden Street, thinking of Nemo Johnston and Jim McMichaels nestled side by side in the tan envelope. He wonders what sort of commerce the two might have had if their centuries had overlapped, wonders what his role in it might have been.

He pauses at the yield sign where Harden feeds into Huger Street, waiting for a gap in the oncoming traffic. He sees that there is a new iron marker at the entrance to Rosedale, the kind set out by the historical society: hand-painted and august, a small mound of fresh clay clinging to its base. He would like to get out of the car and read its thumbnail history, but the shadows are deepening to dark, and this is not the kind of neighborhood where a white man taking a stroll feels most at ease.

BACK HOME, AFTER he has showered and put on his tuxedo, Jacob takes a beer out of the refrigerator and sits down at the kitchen bar with all of the archives materials spread out in front of him. He arranges the Skull and Crossbones photos chronologically and places them in a stack, then begins to sort through his copies of Nemo Johnston's record. He is checking the sequence of the ledger sheets when he sees that in March of 1866, the heading for Nemo Johnston is scratched out, the column below it empty for the rest of the year. He looks at the next two years and finds no record of Johnston at all.

He flips back to 1866 and stares hard at the page, trying to make some sense of the numbers there, all the columns. Johnston was free by then to quit, certainly. But why put his name at the top of the page for March if there was to be nothing below it? Doubtful that a freed slave would give two weeks' notice, but there is nothing entered beneath the name, not even a partial payment for the month. No record of dismissal. He looks again at the scratched-out heading of the column. Is he imagining things, or is the spidery script of the rest of the ledger a little less reserved here, the crosshatched lines covering Johnston's name almost scratched into the paper?

He takes another sip of his beer. A drop of perspiration falls from the bottle and he wipes at the spot with his finger.

And then, like a gift, the numbers suddenly cohere and he can make sense of the ledger's account. Janice must be right about administrators; he seems to have gotten lazy in his reading. The content of the columns is reversed—so neatly, in fact, that he chides himself for not having seen it immediately. The month that Nemo Johnston disappeared from the expenditures column, the liquid assets column went blank. Too neat for coincidence.

"Son of a bitch," he whispers. "You cleaned them out."

❧Under the bright lights out front of the Dean's Mansion the cars are arriving in droves, their tires crunching on the pea gravel as they inch forward for the undergraduate valets to swap places with their drivers and move them to the makeshift parking lot on the huge lawn behind the estate. Jacob imagines the line is backed up halfway down the long drive, despite the hustling of the young valets. He watches them, sweating now in their Bermuda shorts and golf shirts bearing the university's seal, as they take each car away. This motley procession: the opulence of the big Lincolns and Lexuses favored by administrators and specialists is set off by the Japanese economy cars of the medical students, many of them with out-of-state plates and sporting global-consciousness bumper stickers. *Free Tibet*, one of them says. Jacob admires the sentiment but cannot help thinking that the youthful idealism will soon be fading fast.

Finally he sees Kaye's black sedan a half-dozen spaces back in the line. "The law is a jealous mistress," she had reminded him when she called a half hour earlier from the courthouse, and he had told her that he understood, straining to hear her with the cell phone pressed close to his ear in the roaring ballroom of the mansion. He had asked the black man tending bar to pour him a double scotch and then taken it outside to drink while he waited. Now he grins as her car moves up the line; he can see, in the soft glow of her visor's light, that she is putting on mascara.

He comes down the steps to greet her as the black car pulls up in front of the great house. She climbs out and says something to the young man who holds the door for her. Both of them smile.

Late or not, she looks as if she has spent the entire afternoon getting ready. Her dark hair is full and neat and her eyes are bright over the diamond pendant and black cocktail dress and stockings she wears. He cannot help admiring her legs as she comes around the back of the car; they are as lithe and long as a runner's legs, but shapely in a way that stirs something deep inside him.

"Stop staring," she says as she reaches up to kiss him.

"Can't help it," he says as he breathes in the wonderful smell of her. "If you looked like this in court, I bet the judge just handed you the case."

She takes his arm as they walk up the stairs and into the anteroom of the big house. The voices inside are nearly deafening with cheer, echoing off the parquet floors and the tall ceilings. Immediately Kaye begins nodding to faces she recognizes across the room as they make their way to the bar, easing through tuxedo-clad doctors and women bedecked with flashing jewelry. She lifts a hand to wave to a couple standing at the foot of the sweeping staircase.

"Look, the Breemans are here. Remember to congratulate them on the new baby."

"A boy, right?"

"A girl," Kaye says, rolling her eyes. "Regan."

"How could they name a kid Regan? Haven't they seen *The Exorcist*? It's like asking for trouble."

Kaye looks at him strangely.

"If they haven't seen it, they will. And then one night she'll have a bad dream and wake them up crying for a glass of water. They won't want to go."

"Jesus, Jacob. You're so weird."

He shrugs as they move up in the bar line. "I never liked Breeman anyway. You know what he calls guys like me? Fleas."

"Internists are a dime a dozen, they say," Kaye says, smiling.

"Yeah? So why don't you have a dozen?"

She laughs, so he does too, simply glad to be in her presence as they step up to the bar and he orders two scotches.

"Double again, sir?" the bartender asks.

"Why not?"

He ignores Kaye's stern look as he hands her a glass. She seems ready to say something when they hear the voice of Jim McMichaels booming out Jacob's name. Jacob looks around until he sees Jim and Bitsy standing at the back of the room, in front of the French doors that line the entire wall giving on to the brick patio beyond it. McMichaels is waving them over with one arm; the other is wrapped around the waist of Bitsy's ivory dress, which drapes down to the floor.

The dean's smile seems to fade slightly as they draw near, but Bitsy beams at Kaye and reaches to hug her as soon as she is within her reach. She plants a delicate kiss on Kaye's cheek and holds out a hand to Jacob.

"Isn't it lovely?" she asks breathlessly. "This is my favorite function of the year, every year."

"It's very nice," Jacob says, and smiles. He is having trouble meeting Jim's eyes. Behind the dean and his wife he can see a jazz trio set up on the patio, and he can just hear the music filtering in through the glass. The trumpet player blats out a raucous melody as the men behind him bend to their instruments and shake their heads in time with the music.

"Just for a minute, dear," the dean is saying quietly when Jacob turns back to the others. Bitsy looks at her husband disapprovingly for a moment before her face breaks into an exasperated smile.

"Always business with you two," she says. She takes hold of Kaye's arm. "Kaye, have you heard these boys out back? Jim says they're the best jazz band in the Midlands." Kaye smiles helplessly at Jacob as Bitsy turns her toward the patio.

"I'll have him back to you in two shakes, Kaye," McMichaels says as he puts a hand on Jacob's back and guides him toward the study. Jacob watches the women go with a sinking feeling.

It takes the dean nearly five minutes to work their way through the crowd. He is greeted by a dozen well-wishers along the way, and though he pauses to speak with all of them, Jacob can sense that he is trying to hurry each conversation.

When they are nearly to the study door, Jacob sees Austin Malloy mark their progress and slip into the room just ahead of them.

Jim shuts the door behind them and the party noise is instantly muted to a low murmur. Jacob stands for a moment just inside the threshold, looking around the room at the faces of the men arrayed there as Jim steps away from him. Malloy has taken the chair nearest the fireplace, with Parker Hauser to his left, sitting forward with his arms on his knees. The others he knows less well, but he recognizes the chair of obstetrics, Howard Roth, standing at the little bar with Bill Mitchell and Jackson Turner, the CEO of Memorial Hospital. Their conversation stops abruptly when they see Jacob.

Sitting alone on the couch, her face impassive, is Kirstin Reithoffer. For a long moment she studies the manicured nails of her left hand as though they hold a great mystery, then she looks up at Jacob with her steel-blue eyes.

"It's been a hell of a week, Jake," Jim says. He is behind his desk now, standing with his arms crossed over his chest. "A hell of a week."

"Is that what we're here to talk about?" Jacob asks. His voice sounds weak in his own ears. He swallows hard, trying to compose himself. "Because the week's over, Jim. It's history."

McMichaels nods, pensive. "We thought it was."

"This Greer had some of his people on the school grounds this afternoon," Malloy says. "It looks like this march of his could come off after all."

"And he left a message with Elizabeth, Jake. Seems he tried to get you first, but," McMichaels says as he levels his eyes on Jacob, "you were out. He claims to have a copy of his medical record. An internal file. Says you gave it to him."

"Jim, Jesus."

"If it were just his word against yours, Jake, there wouldn't be much to it. But you see, if he has the file, it raises some major confidentiality issues, the kind that can affect licensing."

"My license."

"And the school's," Turner says.

"We're into a new phase of containment now," McMichaels says. "No one here doubts your loyalty to the school, Jake, not a one of us. But there have been some lapses in judgment. We know you've been under a great strain, but there is a history to consider."

Hauser rattles the ice in his glass. "We think you're back on the meds," he says.

McMichaels looks at Hauser angrily, then turns to Jacob. "I object to Doctor Hauser's lack of diplomacy, Jake, but I can't fault his assessment. You don't seem well. All the signs are there. We're left with very little choice of how to proceed."

"Kirstin," Jacob says. "Please tell them that's not the case."

Reithoffer looks up at him coolly. "I smelled alcohol on your breath at the staff meeting Wednesday. That was ten-thirty a.m., Jacob. And all week you have displayed the symptoms of a relapse. Fatigue, irritability, disorientation. We have this information from several sources."

"Jesus Christ, Jim," Jacob says. "Tell them what's been going on."

Jacob can feel rage kindling in his chest, but McMichaels only shakes his head sadly.

"What about my urine samples? What kind of information do they give you, Kirstin?"

Reithoffer's eyes never waver, do not even blink. "The last specimen tested positive for Xanax," she says.

Jacob can feel his eyes smarting with tears, so he nods his head, hoping this will help him keep his features composed. Why not, he thinks—why shouldn't the specimen test positive? If Jim can get his hands on a file like Greer's, what's so complicated about switching a urine sample, or making a certain notation in the right file? As he raises his head and looks from Reithoffer to the dean, he feels the panic of a few minutes ago ebbing into something like grief.

"I've noticed the symptoms for years," Hauser says loudly. "I suspect you were using the stuff back when we were interns."

"Go fuck yourself, Hauser. You know that's a lie."

"Meyer Siegel kept you under his wing for too long. He babied you. I wouldn't be surprised if he was covering for you back then."

Jacob takes a step forward. He wants to put his hands on Hauser. "Leave Meyer out of this. He was better than the lot of you."

Hauser takes a sip from his drink. "So go back home and screw his daughter."

Before the others can move between them, Jacob has crossed the distance to where Hauser sits and slapped a hand across his cheek so hard he can hear the teeth clacking together. Hauser is beginning to rise when Jacob hits him again, backhanded this time, and sees the blood start to flow from his burst lip.

Then the others are moving, Mitchell and Turner pinning Hauser in the chair, Reithoffer standing in front of Jacob with her hands out, pressed against Jacob's chest. "Enough!" McMichaels is shouting over the voices of the men.

Jacob looks Reithoffer in the eyes before he speaks. "Don't touch me, Kirstin. You're getting me dirty."

Reithoffer backs away, and Jacob can see that Hauser is blotting a white handkerchief against his mouth. "I rest my case," he says. His left cheek is blazing with the imprint of Jacob's hand.

"*Enough*," McMichaels says again.

"That's right, Jim. Enough of the bullshit. I've had all I can take. Let's forget the intervention charade and call this what it is." The others look at him mutely as he walks to the door and rests his hand on the knob. "I can't believe this is all the membership you guys could scare up. Seems like you're short of a quorum." He nods toward Reithoffer. "Even if you have gone coed."

"Jacob," McMichaels says sadly. "Please, no more scenes. You're better than this." He nods to Reithoffer. "Let's get it done."

Reithoffer clasps her hands behind her as Jacob has seen her do so many times before, in clinic and at the lecture podium, and speaks.

"In view of your recent record, I cannot recommend that you be cleared by the Physicians' Task Force. We have scheduled admittance for you tomorrow morning, eight o'clock, at Midlands Rehabilitation Center. The standard twenty-eight-day program. But you must voluntarily agree to the treatment. We require a letter from you requesting a medical leave of absence, stating your recent difficulties specifically—the symptoms, the levels of medication you have been abusing."

"Tomorrow?"

Malloy clears his throat and speaks. "Tomorrow morning. If Greer does show, there'll be nobody there to meet him. School locked down. We'll let this little bit of hysteria flare up, then we'll wait it out."

"Because I'll be away."

Malloy nods.

"And if Greer doesn't let it die?"

Malloy seems unable to meet Jacob's eyes. "If it comes to it, we'll give him to understand that a member of our faculty, ah, misrepresented the extent of the medical waste to the black community. We'll mention substance abuse if we have to. Either way the basement will get taken care of. Bowman's lining up a new crew for Monday."

"And when the month is up?" Jacob asks, his mouth dry.

McMichaels will not look at him directly. "When you finish your treatment we'll reassess the situation."

"We can't afford any more mistakes," Turner says. "There

248

are accreditation issues, licensure risks. Another relapse would bring a lot of others down with you."

Jacob nods bitterly. "No guarantees, then."

But Turner does not respond. In the heavy silence Jacob looks at each of them in turn, thinking of their titles, their positions, their security. He would like to speak, but his throat has tightened again and his eyes are burning.

"I'm playing the back nine at the country club in the morning." McMichaels says finally. "I'll check in at the office afterward. If the letter is on my desk, I'll know you're with us."

"With you, right," Jacob says quietly as he opens the door to the sound of the party outside. He looks at them once more, then turns to make his way through the crowd.

He is in the anteroom, hurrying across the open space and fishing his valet ticket out of his pocket, when a smiling Adam Claybaugh comes through the front door, looming in the entrance larger than life in his tuxedo. He begins to speak, but Jacob shoulders his way past roughly, half hoping that Claybaugh will raise a fist so that he can wrap up this evening with a full-scale brawl, go all the way back down to his origins. But Adam only looks after him, shocked. Shaking his head, he turns back to the ballroom and sees McMichaels and Reithoffer coming out of the study, Malloy and Hauser filing out after them. His face clouds.

Jacob is down at the turnaround, restlessly kicking at the pea gravel as he waits for the valet, when he hears the sound of heavy footsteps behind him. Adam is calling his name almost desperately, his deep voice strained. When he reaches Jacob he grabs his arm and turns him around.

"They set you up, didn't they?"

"Leave me alone, Adam." He tries to free his arm from Adam's grasp.

"They can't do it."

"They *have* done it. It's over."

"Get on the right side of this, Jake, and the rest will work itself out."

Jacob looks up at him, smiling bitterly. "You really believe that?"

"I *know* it."

Jacob jerks his arm free. He wipes at his nose, tears starting in his eyes as he speaks. "Fuck you, Adam. I just picked up the tab for your purity. So take your Eagle Scout bullshit somewhere else."

The BMW pulls into the turnaround and Jacob starts toward it. After a few steps he turns back with a finger jabbing the air. "You guys. All the same. Always somebody else taking the fall."

Jacob climbs into the car and puts it into motion, the wheels already spinning in the gravel, before the valet can shut the door. Adam watches the little car speed down the drive until it rounds a corner and the taillights disappear.

When he turns to climb the stairs again, Kaye is standing at the top of them, her face knotted with concern as she looks down the drive after the car. "Adam, what's happened?" she says. "What have they done to Jacob?"

He is beginning to answer her when he hears the voices inside the house subside, the crowd beginning to hush. In its place, insistent, comes the bell-like sound of a knife tapping against a crystal glass: McMichaels calling for a toast.

THE BMW ROARS down the westbound lane of the Old Augusta Highway, scattering the early-fallen sycamore leaves that have piled up on the shoulder as Jacob winds the car up to 95, straining to push it into the triple digits on the straightaways. He checks the tachometer and drops the shift down to fourth gear as he clears the grove of sycamores and bursts into an open space of bottomland where cornfields stretch out on either side of the road. The wind coming in over the windshield is bracing and as strong as a hand against his face. He hears it in the corn-stalks just off the shoulders, whistling through the dry leaves that nod at his passage through the late-evening mist that has settled over the bottom. The pedal beneath his foot is taut, pressed nearly to the floor, when he sees the needle rise and hover at one hundred. His tachometer has reached nearly into the red, which suits him. He envisions blowing the engine just as he reaches the state line. And after that, he cannot say.

The little car dips and curves as the cornfields withdraw behind him and he enters more woods, this time pine and darker than the open night sky. His headlights carve a passage through the dark tunnel of branches, the xenon lamps burning like flashbulbs against the blackness framed by pine needles. The engine gives a throaty rumble as he downshifts again for a short curve, tossing the car into the turn to maintain his speed, and as he straightens into the next stretch he sees out front of him at perhaps seventy yards a deer grazing on the shoulder.

Jacob reacts with frantic swiftness, but his movements seem slowed to half speed as he downshifts again and the engine howls in protest. He moves his foot to the brake pedal, presses it too hard, and he feels the brakes clamp down. The deer is still there, just inches outside the white line, staring into the oncoming lights. He sees now, while he feels the brake disks pumping beneath his foot and hears the tires begin to whine, that it is a buck, with a rack of antlers that seems to grow larger in each half second that draws him closer to it. He tugs the steering wheel to the left, but it moves only a fraction of an inch, the warring momentum of the car and the pull of the brakes keeping him on a dead line straight ahead.

The deer's head is raised and cocked against the noise of the car when it begins to move. Jacob sees the great body gathering its strength in the hind muscles and then it is nearly aloft, beginning a leap as he closes the last ten yards before impact with the tires squealing now like wounded things. The deer's front legs rise with a glacial slowness and he is nearly under it when he hears his back wheel catch the gravel on the road's shoulder and the car begins to spin.

He throws his hands up as the deer looms outsized in front of the windshield, rising now. He feels the impact of its rear hoof on the car's hood first, then hears it as the hind leg slides down the hood to the headlight, which bursts under the pressure with a hollow explosion of glass. The car twists again, under the deer now, and in spite of himself, Jacob looks upward as it passes over the two-seater's cockpit, seeing it all out of sequence as the car spins: the thorny tangle of antlers, a black hoof trailing blood as it vaults skyward, the alpine white of its pelt below the raised tail, every bristle of the pale fur as distinct as a pixel, pristine. Then it is gone.

The BMW shudders sideways across the road and off the blacktop, hitching as the tires finally catch in the roadside gravel and it vibrates to a stop on the eastbound shoulder.

Jacob hears the clapping of hooves on asphalt, followed by a sound of crashing brush that fades quickly into the forest, leaving behind it only the ticking and humming of the engine and his own labored breathing. He raises a hand to his face, his scalp, checking for injury, but he can find none. For a long moment he stares out into the black walls of the pine trees where the animal disappeared, wishing he could see through the darkness to the deer, hoping it is all right. The vision of it passing overhead flashes through his mind again and he shakes his head at the intensity of it. No way all that could have crossed the visual cortex that fast, he thinks. Impossible.

He unbuckles his seatbelt and climbs out of the car, walks around to the front to have a look at the hood. The metal is crimped into a crease that runs down the lower third of the passenger side to the gouged pocket of the headlamp, which is dark now. Across the road he sees the shards of its glass cover lying on the asphalt and glimmering faintly. He walks over and kicks them off the road.

He is still standing in the westbound lane, parsing through the sequence of the buck's flight and trying to fashion some order from it, when he hears his cell phone ringing. Slowly he crosses the road and sits down in the car, fumbling in the light of the dashboard for the phone before he finds it and picks it up, presses the green button.

"Jacob, my God. Where did you run off to?"

"Sorry," he says. "Just had to get out of there."

"Are you all right?"

"Yeah," he says absently. "Well, yes. I hit a deer. Maybe I should say he hit me."

He can feel the tension on the line before Kaye speaks again. "A deer? Where the hell are you?"

"Listen, I'm okay. I just grazed him. I don't think I hurt him much."

"I think you're in shock. You need to get back here. I'm at my place. Come home, please."

Jacob leans his head back against the seat. Between the spindly limbs of the pine trees he can see Venus shining brightly in the night sky, like a penlight through black velvet. "Kaye, there's a lot I need to tell you. I don't think I can come back now."

He can almost hear Kaye shaking her head. "I don't care

what you have to tell me. It doesn't matter. I want you to come home."

"I got dirty, Kaye. I messed up bad with the school. I think they're going to take my license."

"No. They won't."

"Yes. They can do it." He keeps his eyes on Venus up above, but the light is beginning to blur in his watering eyes. "Without that license, I'm nothing."

"You never say that, Jacob. Never again," Kaye says sharply. "This is it," she says, her voice beginning to assume its court-room cadence. "This is it. You mark this minute. This is as low as you get, ever."

Jacob smiles as he holds the phone to his ear and watches Venus waver. This mix of Israel and the low country, he thinks, will either kill him or be his salvation.

"I know something happened tonight, and that's done. But that's not the end of it. You beat the pills and you can beat these bastards. I'm going to watch you do it, and I'm going to *make* you do it if I have to."

Jacob sniffs, quietly so she won't hear it, and waits for her to go on. There is a long silence on the line, as though she has put a hand over the receiver, before she speaks again.

"*Neshome*, Jacob," she is saying. "Remember it?"

"Let's see . . . neshome," he says, finding it doesn't take long to run through the catalogue of Yiddish he's picked up the last few years.

"Soul," she says. "Jacob, I've got someone here with me. I

want you to talk to him. Talk to him and hear what he has to say, then you get over here. *Come home*," she whispers fiercely.

Jacob hears the receiver being handed over, and a man comes on the line. It takes him a second to place the voice, and when he does he moves to switch off his phone. But the man's voice is as level and earnest as ever, almost beseeching, and talking fast. Jacob listens to him for a minute without speaking. Then he begins to nod slowly, hearing him out, and throws his head back against the seat and gives in, lets the tears he can no longer restrain course down his cheeks. He drifts for a moment until the man's voice brings him back with a question.

"Yes—yes, I'm still here," he says.

The voice carries on, talking enough for years, it seems, in a minute's time.

"Yes," Jacob says. "It's about fucking time. Yes.

"Yes," he says, "I am."

Jacob clicks the phone off, tosses it into the passenger seat, and presses forward against the shifter, forgetting the clutch. The road fills with the sound of scraping gears and he mutters as he depresses the clutch and slips the transmission into first and gives the engine gas. His tires skim in the gravel for a moment, then grab purchase and bark once as they get their grip on the asphalt. In an instant he is gone, leaving nothing behind him but the broken glass that glints in the starlight and the echoing wake of his engine as it winds eastward, until his taillights fade into the darkness leading back to Columbia.

Fernyear: 1866

THROUGH ROSEDALE THEY CAME DOWN the sandy streets in double file, two abreast in a brutal symmetry, with Johnston at the head of the column carrying a burning pine knot aloft like a flaming caduceus. His face was stern, his jaw set in a firm line as it had been since this morning. But walking behind him, Doctor Ballard thought he saw something else in the face when Johnston's head turned to check the numbers on each house they passed—that in profile, the tightness around Johnston's eyes might have held in it a shade of grief.

"What will we do, professor?" he asked. "When we get there?"

"God knows," Johnston said heavily, the words nearly drowned out by the murmuring voices of the men behind them.

"You know, sir, that these boys have violence in mind."

Johnston nodded.

"And what will you do about it, sir?"

Johnston stopped walking and the men behind him halted quickly, nearly walking into his back. "I will do what I can, Doctor Ballard," he said.

He resumed his pace and the others followed. But Ballard's question lingered in his mind, turning there like a living thing. It was the same question Johnston had posed to Sara the night before.

They had talked in his office for nearly an hour, with his curtains drawn and the lamp trimmed low. Or rather, he himself had talked, listening to his own voice, the measured cadences of it—calm, reassuring, composed. Arrangements would have to be made, he had told her. He would take care of things for her as best he could.

At the end, she had come to him and buried her head on his shoulder. "I've been a fool, Frederick."

"There, there," he said, stroking her hair. "I have been a fool as well."

"Not so great as me."

"No, no."

He was patting her head when she looked up at him. He saw that her eyes, though bright, were dry.

"No, Frederick, I am the greater fool in this," she said. "I trusted you."

From farther back in the column, at the rear, Johnston could hear others arriving, hurrying to catch up as the crowd grew, breathless but full of questions. The voices behind him grew into a cacophony.

"How's Fitz?"

"Raving. They finally woke him up two hours ago and he is still screaming, last I heard."

"My God. It's pitiable."

"Of course it is. What kind of shape would you be in? His own mother, for Christ's sake."

"It is an abomination."

"The nigger will get his, I'll vouch for it myself."

"I want a finger."

"Sure. There ought to be enough to go around."

"I'll save you an ear if you don't get there in time."

"There will be no trophies," Johnston said loudly, his voice quavering as he turned to the men behind him. "This is hardly a victory."

But the men pushed past him, seeing that they had reached the house they sought. They swarmed into the yard, crushing the picket fence beneath them, and up to the porch and into the house. From the street, Johnston and Ballard watched as lights were struck inside. A kerosene lamp flared to life in the parlor window, and they could see candles moving toward the rooms at the back of the house.

"I suppose we should go inside," Johnston said. Nodding, Ballard followed him up the walk and across the porch.

Inside, the front parlor looked as if it had been deserted long ago. Its furniture was threadbare, and there was nothing on the walls save a cheap mirror hanging over the fireplace. Johnston moved down the hall and Ballard followed him, shouldering his way through the milling students, who seemed to be growing more frustrated by the second. He saw that they had thrown open the cellar door, and he watched as a student in a bowler hat disappeared down the stairs.

The kitchen was as spartan as the front room had been, with a single plank table and chair against the west wall and a black cook stove squatting on its short legs in the opposite corner. Ballard bent to the stove, intending to see if its embers were still warm. When he opened the iron door, he saw that there was no need. The ash inside was fine and gray and a spider had woven a web in one corner. It scurried away from the light of his match.

"Sir?" one of the men said. When Ballard rose, he saw that the student was looking at Johnston and pointing at the table. On it lay, in the center, a pared-down butter knife. Johnston lifted it and felt its balance thoughtfully, as though he knew what its presence meant.

"I believe he is gone, gentlemen," Johnston said, and he sounded almost relieved.

There was a sound of hurried steps on the cellar stairs and Mullins stuck his head through the open door. "He is not here, sir."

"I was just saying as much, Mister Mullins."

"There is something in the cellar, sir. We think you should see it."

Again Ballard followed Doctor Johnston as he slowly descended the steps, as though the number of lights in the cellar and the high-pitched tone of the others' voices drew him downward. When he reached the bottom of the steps he paused, as the others had done, his attention arrested by the north wall of the cellar, by its bright colors and the intricate calligraphy of lines upon it.

The wall looked to be of sandstone and the cellar terminated abruptly against it, where Ballard guessed the builders had given up on digging farther into the earth. It was covered with words, hundreds of them, that were chiseled into the sandstone with the precision of a printer's press. Ballard stepped closer and saw that the words were names arranged in some strange chronology of Nemo Johnston's devising. He read a few of them before giving up, none of them familiar but most of them clearly Negro: names like Quash and Addie and Toby, half of them with surnames familiar to Ballard from his slave-owning patients but the rest as obscure as the southern hands' field songs had been when he first came south. Above the names, carved in larger type, was the legend "In my death, see how utterly thou hast murdered thyself." The entire wall had been painted in three vertical stripes—green, yellow, and red—and the paint had run into the letters and coated them as well. Ballard stepped back from the garish colors with the hollow feeling in his gut as pronounced as it might have been had they found a charnel house here instead.

"He really has gone mad," Mullins said. "This is the work of a demented mind."

"No, not mad," Johnston said. "The quotation is a passage from Poe. These names clearly have some significance to him. I suspect they have some significance to us as well. I recognize one or two of them. No, he has not gone mad, but he has most certainly gone."

"And what of the colors?" Ballard asked.

Johnston sighed. "The colors," he said, "are beyond my comprehension."

He turned toward the stairs, and his footsteps sounded dully as he climbed them.

"What shall we do with the house, sir?"

Johnston paused on the stairs. "Yes, the house. I suppose there is no choice," he said heavily. "Burn it."

JOHNSTON AND BALLARD stood on the sidewalk as the students ravaged the bungalow, stomping and crashing inside it. Johnston muttered to himself as the sound of glass breaking raged inside until there were no more windows left.

"Couldn't be helped, Ballard," he said, and the younger man nodded his agreement. Ballard looked down the street, watching as the curtains on the other houses parted by inches to reveal eyes looking to assess the demolition of Nemo Johnston's place. The woman in the house next door had come out on her porch and was crying loudly, begging Johnston to stop the men inside.

"Take it easy there, auntie," someone yelled from a broken parlor window. "You might be best back inside your house."

"We're not here for you, old girl."

But still the woman moaned and whimpered. When she saw the first candle put to a curtain in the parlor, she began to wail. Mullins and two of the others emerged from the house and looked at her strangely as they came to stand next to Johnston.

"They're all crazy, is what I think," Mullins said.

"That is enough, Mister Mullins," Johnston said quietly. The house was beginning to glow from the inside, amber light flickering on the shards of glass that still clung to the frames.

"Say, here comes Doctor Evans," Mullins said. They turned to look down the sand road and saw Evans walking toward them quickly, accompanied by another man whom Johnston recognized as Jonathan Bateman, from the Columbia Bank, as they drew near. Johnston seemed instantly embarrassed by the banker's presence. He walked a few steps to meet him, stopping in front of the Negro woman's porch.

"Jonathan," Johnston said, "I would have preferred that you had not seen this."

Bateman nodded breathlessly and held out a handful of papers to Johnston. Johnston squinted at them, then moved closer to the woman's house, where the light from the flames next door was stronger. He frowned down at the papers, flipping through handwritten balance statements quickly but pausing at the last page, a sheet of watermarked stationery on which had been written a figure that made him catch his breath.

"The boy brought that note in this morning, sir. Since it was written in your hand, I treated it as your request."

Johnston looked at the papers a moment longer, then handed them to Ballard and sat down heavily on the porch steps. Ballard studied the withdrawal notice, hardly believing it, then sat down himself.

"As I said, sir, it was written in your hand." Bateman looked ready to flee down the street.

Johnston smiled so bitterly that the banker had to look away. "The paper is mine, Jonathan, as must be the ink, doubtless drawn from the well on my desk. But the hand, Jonathan . . ." He looked up at the dark night sky. "The *hand* belongs to another."

Johnston's face was still turned to the sky when he spoke again. "Evans," he said, "I believe I recall your once saying, years ago, that we had mortgaged the school's future to Africa. I must now concede that you were correct."

He took the papers from Ballard and passed them to Evans. The bearded man studied them for a moment, his face coloring, then ripped them into pieces and let them fall to the ground.

"The betrayal," Johnston hissed as the flames licked under the eaves of Nemo's house and began to consume the tarpaper above. Behind him the old woman wailed like a banshee. "I never did him harm, gentlemen. And this"—Johnston lifted a hand toward the burning house and let it drop to the shreds of paper at his feet—"this is my recompense." He dropped his face into his hands.

"Ah, God, the betrayal." Johnston lifted his head, and Ballard saw that the doctor's eyes glistened in the light of the flames. "I will never understand it, gentlemen. I treated him as if he were my own."

Saturday

H E SITS ON THE BASEMENT STEPS with his elbows on his knees, moving the hasp he broke off the door above from one hand to the other. Through eyes burning with fatigue he looks down at the cellar floor below him, at the bones dug carefully out of the dirt, the orange twine snaked out tautly between the pine stakes. He has not been this tired since he was a resident, and it feels good to rest, to simply sit among the quiet of the bones and the cellar earth. His eyelids droop, wanting to close, but he wills them open so that he can witness this place— really see it—one last time.

He has decided, in this state half between sleep and waking, that the dead can be felt, if one is quiet and still enough: all of them who were here. Nemo Johnston must have traveled up and down these steps hundreds of times; Sara too was here; and the bones of those beneath him, who were brought here and never left. All of them have a claim on this ground.

He is not so certain about Frederick Augustus Johnston. If there is a blood connection between himself and the old professor, he cannot feel it.

His head bobs toward his chest and he jerks it back up. *Great-great-grandfather?* he thinks, too tired to be sure he's got the number of generations right. It sounds right. *Am I in my father's house? Tell me I'm wrong and I'll leave now.*

No answer, of course. The question itself seems to die in the dank air of the cellar.

The silence of the bones, however, is eloquent. It is a silence he can feel in his marrow.

Their unearthly quiet.

Jacob's heavy eyes close, and he sleeps, hearing.

"Jake. Jake." Someone is shaking his shoulder gently. For a moment he does not respond, preferring to linger a minute longer at the edges of sleep and let the big hand knead his shoulder. He thinks he would be content to stay here, amid the acrid smells of dry clay and cellar earth, in the mute company of those who have spent the century lying in it. But he knows he must wake. He opens his eyes to look on the kindly face of Adam Claybaugh.

Adam smiles, nods toward the bones, the orange twine. "You making some new friends?"

"Just calling on my last patients."

Adam shakes his head. "You're going to have lots of patients. This is your first day, brother."

"It's my last day as a PR man. You can count on that."

"Good riddance. Out with a bang." Adam hooks his hands under Jacob's arms and heaves him up. He swats at the red dust covering Jacob's jacket. "You may have ruined that tux."

Jacob swipes at his dusty sleeves for a moment, then decides the effort is hopeless. He looks up at Adam. "What the hell use does a doctor have for a tuxedo anyway?"

"For hobnobbing with the schmucks."

"Yep," Jacob says as he pulls off the jacket and tosses it to the ground. "Done with all that." He takes another look around the basement, at the grids that Sanburn and his students laid out so meticulously just a few days ago. It would have been a shame for all that work to go to waste.

Adam too is staring thoughtfully at the sectioned-off earth and the bones lying upon it. "Just heard from Sanburn," he says. "He's about thirty minutes outside of town."

"Did he sound ready?"

"He sounded like he was about to wet his pants," Adam says, and they both grin.

"This will make his career."

"I guess it will," Adam says. Then his face sobers as he turns to Jacob. "And how about you? What'll you do now?"

"The way I see it, Adam, my possibilities are wide open. I could look into aromatherapy or maybe feng shui. If those don't work out, probably chiropractic or physical therapy."

"Seriously."

"You know anybody who needs a doc-in-the-box, Adam?"

Adam shakes his head.

"I'm being serious. If this thing doesn't work out, I'll be lucky if I ever practice anything in South Carolina."

"It'll work out. You'll see."

"Yeah, we'll see," Jacob says absently, starting up the stairs. "Is Kaye back yet?"

Adam checks his watch. "Any minute now. She finished at the copy store at five-thirty. I sent her by your house to get you a fresh suit."

"I hope she brings the black one."

Adam laughs and they go on up the stairs, toward the light, back into the land of the quick.

HE OPENS THE heavy wooden door of Johnston Hall and steps out into the morning sunshine. It is a beautiful day, clear with a light breeze, birds singing and the late-summer light falling like gold through the trees. And it is made more beautiful by the presence of a score of reporters on the verdant lawn in front of the administration building, crowded at the base of the steps three deep, their front ranks bristling with microphones and miniature tape recorders held up to catch his words. Beyond them he sees with a feeling of triumph that two satellite trucks from the local television stations idle at the curb on Gervais. He looks into the faces below him until he spies Sabrina O'Cannon's among them. Even the heavy makeup cannot hide the circles under her eyes, but her smile is dazzlingly white.

Like the others, she answered his four a.m. phone call only after he had rung and rung her house, but here she is, among the reporters for the local papers and the Associated Press stringers, even the regional correspondent for the *New York Times*. He called them all from his dark office, working through every name in his Rolodex, and now they are here with their photographers in tow, come to see if he will make good on his claim of a historic story of racial reconciliation.

Jacob turns and looks behind him, where Adam and Sanburn stand against the building, waiting their turn to speak. They nod their encouragement. Sanburn has turned out for his big day in a starched safari shirt and matching polyester slacks, and his glasses blink in the morning light as he smiles at Jacob. Jacob nods back at him, takes a deep breath, and turns to face the press.

The cameras begin to flash as he steps up to the podium he and Adam hauled out at first light. He hopes that the photographs will not show the shadow of his beard or the darkness around his tired eyes; hopes that the image of the school's spokesman they capture will be convincing. He knows, as he spreads the page of notes for his speech on the podium, that this day's work is charged with meaning beyond any task he has undertaken since his days in practice.

For a moment he looks out over the campus, taking in what he imagines will be his last view of it from this vantage. He sees that Kaye has taken a seat on a bench in front of Park Hall, a dozen yards past the reporters. He smiles at her and she raises a hand in salute, smiling back at him, her face almost aglow.

"Ladies and gentlemen," he begins, "I thank you on behalf of the South Carolina Medical College for meeting with me at this early hour of your weekend. But our business today could not wait any longer. We are here to acknowledge a part of the school's history that has needed to see some daylight for nearly a hundred and fifty years. The college has had an illustrious past, has in fact been an integral part of South Carolina's history. But it has also taken part in the darker side of that history."

He can hear the cameras clicking as he steps over to the blowup of Nemo Johnston's portrait. Kaye has outdone herself in preparing it, setting it up on an easel worthy of a courtroom presentation, with Johnston's face nearly a foot wide, his eyes full of what Jacob now sees as equal measures of dignity and pain. He pauses a moment as Sabrina's cameraman moves to it for a close-up.

"This man is Nemo Johnston, a slave purchased in 1857 by the faculty of our school, who owned him jointly—seven physicians with legal title to the life of a fellow human being. His name had been lost to time until this week, when our Foundations for the Future renovation campaign brought his existence to our attention." He watches as the newspaper reporters scribble faster in their notebooks.

"The result has been a week of soul-searching for the South Carolina Medical College," he continues, stepping back to the podium. "During the last few days, I have been reminded of a medical term that bears particular relevance to the school's relationship with Mister Johnston: *retrograde memory*, the ability to remember recent events paired with the inability to recall events from a patient's more distant past. The South Carolina Medical College, ladies and gentlemen, has suffered from an institutional case of it."

And then he begins to hear it, faintly: the sound of singing, many voices lifted up in what he guesses is an old spiritual, coming up Gervais slowly. He smiles down at his notes, hurrying to finish his speech before they arrive.

"Given this self-diagnosis, we had a choice of pursuing two options: either to ignore this portion of our past and let it lapse back into obscurity or to come forward and acknowledge Nemo Johnston as a vital part of our school's legacy. I'm proud to say that the dean and the administration have decided on the latter course of action. It is time now for Nemo Johnston to receive his due and official recognition."

The reporters turn toward the sound of the singing as the marchers begin to file through the university's gates. At the head of the column, walking shoulder-to-shoulder, are Lorenzo Shanks and Marcus Greer. Greer's mouth opens and closes around the words of the old song and his eyes fix intently on Jacob. He dips his head slightly in acknowledgment, almost imperceptibly. Jacob nods back, standing silently at the podium as the men and women pour through the gates. For a full two minutes they come, a hundred or more of them, it seems, all dressed in their church clothes and lifting up the song in a single great voice. They follow Greer and Lorenzo as they step off the brick walkway and cross the lawn a few yards back from the reporters, forming an arc around the press and Johnston Hall. The photographers are working frantically now, bobbing and dipping for the best camera angles, and watching them, Jacob breathes more easily than he has in hours, certain that at least one of the shots they are snapping will reach a front page tomorrow.

The voices linger on the song's last note and then fade, like a tide receding, until the only sounds are the clicking shutters of the cameras and the sighing of the wind in the trees.

"The men and women of Ebenezer Methodist Baptist Episcopal Church, ladies and gentlemen," Jacob says quietly. "They are here to help us begin our dialogue with the Rosedale community in earnest." Greer squares his shoulders, and Jacob looks out across the lawn at Kaye before he continues. But Kaye is gesturing now; the arm that was raised a few minutes before is crossed over her chest as she points toward one of the huge live oaks that shade the lawn.

Behind the tree, peering around its trunk like a hunter, is Jim McMichaels. His face looks haggard and wary. As Jacob watches, he turns and steps away from the tree, walking in the other direction, back toward Huger Street, the legs of his plaid pants pumping fast.

"There he is, ladies and gentlemen," Jacob says loudly, raising a hand to point out McMichaels. "Our dean, Doctor Jim McMichaels. Let's give him a warm greeting."

Jacob begins to clap, and the others follow suit as McMichaels stops abruptly and turns to give them a strained smile.

Jacob waves him toward the podium and he comes forward slowly, moving awkwardly through the group from Ebenezer. By the time he reaches the steps, the smattering of applause has died out, replaced by murmurs from the journalists as he climbs up to Jacob and grips his hand tightly.

McMichaels smiles as he pumps Jacob's hand and says fiercely through his clenched teeth, "What the fuck is this, Thacker?"

"We're coming clean, Jim," Jacob says. "I decided it would be good for the school."

But McMichaels gives no sign of having heard him. His eyes have moved to the easel and are fixed on the image on the back of the poster board. It too is an enlarged photograph, the most recent of the Skull and Crossbones images Janice gave Jacob, and the dean's broad smile over the stripped flesh of the cadaver looks even more grotesque on the large scale.

Jacob watches him as his eyes cut from the poster to the people gathered on the lawn. "And I decided not to write that letter," he says. "I don't think I really need to. But it's your call, Jim. Say the word and I'll turn this board around."

"You touch it and I'll tear it to pieces."

"No harm," Jacob says. "I've got another copy of that picture sitting in a fax machine across town. And right beside it is a list of the fax numbers for everybody here." He pulls his cell phone out from his pants pocket just enough for Jim to get a good look at it. "Want me to make the call?"

"You're finished, you fucking runt."

Jacob only smiles back harder and throws an arm around the dean's shoulder. "I'm just waking up, Jim. I've got a feeling you are too. Smile for the people." With his arm around McMichaels, he steers them both back to the podium.

"I spoke a moment ago about official recognition," Jacob says, "and Dean McMichaels is here to make good on that promise." With his free hand, Jacob reaches into his coat pocket and pulls out the check he has carried since Thursday. He holds it up high, thinking that although it is beginning to show some wear, it should photograph well enough. "I have a check here from the dean's own discretionary fund in the amount of twenty-five thousand dollars. It is made out jointly to the Reverend Marcus Greer and Professor David Sanburn, pro tempore custodians of the Nemo Johnston Historical Fund, for the express purpose of underwriting the first annual symposium on slavery and antebellum medicine at the South Carolina Medical College."

The applause from the Ebenezer congregation is deafening as Jacob holds the check aloft. One of the photographers says something to McMichaels, and the dean nods as absently as a sleepwalker, raises his own hand to the check, and clutches a corner of it weakly between his thumb and forefinger. Beneath the clapping, Jacob can hear the cameras still snapping, recording it all for posterity, and he smiles for them with an intensity he has not felt in years.

He turns to McMichaels and sees such a deep malevolence in the dean's eyes that he cannot help speaking again, shouting over the noise to be heard. "This is the first installment of the dean's pledge of two hundred thousand dollars to this project," he says, making up the numbers as he goes and hoping they sound about right, "which we hope will culminate in a museum dedicated to Nemo Johnston and bearing his name."

The applause turns into cheers, waves of sound coming up the steps and over the podium. Jacob sees McMichaels's arm beginning to falter. He lowers the check and presses it into the dean's hands, which are trembling now, then moves aside for the dean to take the podium. When McMichaels steps up to it, he seems to be leaning on it for support, his throat working as the applause slowly tapers.

Jacob is beginning to move down the stone steps of Johnston Hall when McMichaels clears his throat and starts in on his standard thumbnail history of the school—pure autopilot. This speech is not going to be one of his best. After just a few sentences, sure enough, McMichaels begins to falter.

Jacob pauses on the steps. "Foundations, Jim," he says to help him. "All the way down."

As the dean resumes the halting speech, Jacob turns and starts to walk across the grass, the voice behind him growing fainter with every step. He can see Kaye across the lawn, see that she has stood up now and is coming to meet him. There are tears in her eyes, but she is smiling as she moves through the bands of sunlight that drop through the old oaks.

When he reaches her he will hold her for a long time, he thinks. Then he will take her hand—small and fine and pulsing with life—in his, and as they walk away from the campus they will talk of new plans for other paths, elsewhere.

But for now there is time simply to walk on the soft grass and watch her come toward him through the green-dappled sunlight; time enough to feel it all, from the great blue dome of the sky to the whispering earth beneath his feet, knowing that all of it—everything—is alive.

Fernyear: 1875

THE SOUND OF VOICES CAME TO him first, voices pitched keen with the energy of morning and the promise of the day ahead. Then, in the distance, the piercing cries of seabirds, and beneath them the sound of water lapping against the wood of docks and hulls. For a long time he lay on his back with his eyes closed and listened, trying to hear it all. He reached out a hand to the sleeping form of Amy beside him and let his palm rest on her belly, feeling its warmth in the sheets as it rose and fell with her peaceful breathing.

He opened his eyes. Morning light had crept through the muslin drapes and shot muted rays across the room. Once again dawn had come and he had slept through it, this luxury becoming habit with them now as each year the hard labor of Carolina receded further into the benighted past.

The baby too was sleeping in. Nemo rose, stretching to his full height, and stepped over to the bassinet. He grinned down at his firstborn, come late to him and welcomed twice as heartily for it. One child given to this fifty-odd-year-old ex-slave, and a son: Cudjo.

He walked to the tall windows and parted the drapes a few inches, breathing in the warm salt air as it drifted into the room. Below him, Kingston stretched out like a quilt patched together from a thousand rooftops, honeycombed with roads that widened as they neared the water. Down in the harbor hundreds of sails, bone-white in the morning sunlight, bobbed at the docks. A dozen more traversed the water farther out, their pale canvas dipping and rising on the ocean waves, coming and going as they pleased.

He loved these mornings, the quiet that was not quiet, the lull that was filled with early activity. Below him he could hear Maria as she unlocked the front door of the hospital and propped it open with the crate that would seat his late-arriving patients this afternoon, when the waiting room was full and the line stretched out the door. The last to come were the ones he was always most anxious to treat—the ones who, having reluctantly given up on the local healers, had decided to visit Doctor Johnston at last.

He breathed in the sea air again, deeply, then threw open the drapes to the brilliant Caribbean sunlight. He turned back to his family with his arms held out wide, his silhouette midnight black against the white light. Amy and Cudjo began to stir in their bedclothes, and his voice came loud and deep and clear: "Sleepers, awake!"

Historical Note

THE EVENTS OF *THE RESURRECTIONIST* ARE drawn from actual medical practice in the southern United States from the mid-nineteenth century to the late twentieth.

For historical grounding I am indebted primarily to two late scholars, Abraham Flexner and Robert L. Blakely.

Abraham Flexner was a crusader for medical college reform in the early twentieth century; his report for the Carnegie Foundation, entitled *Medical Education in the United States and Canada*, was published in 1910. Flexner's exposé of the schools of his era—many of them rife with charlatanry, operated without regulation for pure profit—ushered in a new era of medical reform. For sheer revelatory content, his report rivals any novelistic invention.

In 1989, the archaeologist Robert Blakely was called to the Medical College of Georgia when human remains were discovered in the earthen cellar of the campus's oldest building during renovations. His work, aided by the cooperation of MCG authorities, culminated in the publication of *Bones in the Basement: Postmortem Racism in Nineteenth-Century Medical Training* (Washington, DC: Smithsonian Institution, 1997). Though I have taken the liberty of changing names and locales from the scholarly account, the character of Nemo Johnston is drawn from the enigmatic biography that *Bones in the Basement* sketches of Grandison Harris, a slave purchased by the MCG faculty prior to the Civil War. Harris functioned as the school's janitor, butler, and body snatcher—or resurrectionist, in the parlance of the day. With the faculty's silent endorsement and support, Harris routinely pillaged Augusta's African American cemetery, Cedar Grove, until his retirement in 1905. Harris died in 1911, having never divulged his activities and without facing official censure for carrying out his nocturnal duties. To date, the location of Grandison Harris's remains in Cedar Grove is unknown.

These are the facts, the known historical record. With them I've attempted to tell another kind of truth.

—M.G.

July 4, 2012

Acknowledgments

My sincere thanks to Keith Stansell, MD; Robert Bailey, PA; Shelby Bailey, RN; and the late Michael Casey, PhD, all of whom provided invaluable guidance on matters of modern medical practice and anatomy.

To my many close readers and closer friends—Kristen (first, always), Amy Bowling, Nancy Sulser, Helen Braswell, Kay Largel, Floyd Sulser, Paul Rankin, Steve Yates, Scott Sutton, and Park Ellis—thank you for always asking to see the next page; it kept them coming.

For invaluable help along the way, I am grateful to my parents, Wendell and Jane Guinn, and to Kathleen Yount, Tammy McLean, Phoebe Spencer, Taylor Batey, John Evans, Maude Schuyler Clay, Langdon Clay, Thomas Ezell, Tina Brock, Jerry Ben-Dov, Sharon Ben-Dov, and the members of the Hard Times Literary and Drinking Society.

To Alane Salierno Mason, for her astute editing and for taking a chance on my work, thank you.

And to Andre Dubus III, what words suffice? Andre—thanks for everything.

THE RESURRECTIONIST

Matthew Guinn

READING GROUP GUIDE

DISCUSSION QUESTIONS

1. After reading the novel, how have your views of medical schools or of medical history in the United States changed? Which part of this history shocked you the most?

2. The act of "resurrecting" cadavers was common to Western medical education until fairly recently. What do you think of this practice, especially given that it often served the greater good? How does is cadaver theft complicated by the context of American slavery?

3. The novel is told in an alternating narrative Guinn calls "fernyear." What do you think of the technique of navigating between present and past? Does it shed any light on Faulkner's famous observation that the past "is never even past"?

4. What would you do if you found yourself in Nemo's place on Drake's Windsor Plantation? At the medical school? What ironies do you see in his unusual position?

5. Does it seem to you that Dr. Johnston—given his time and place—acts with Nemo's best interests in mind? Sara Thacker's?

6. Do you approve of Jacob Thacker's actions throughout his stressful week? Where would you have him act differently?

7. Jacob's colleagues at the medical school act on a range of motivations. What drives Dean Jim McMichaels? Adam Claybough? Kirsten Reithoffer?

8. Does Nemo's act of revenge against Fitzhugh seem appropriate to you? How does it echo what happened years earlier to Drake's foot?

9. Near the end of the book, Dr. Johnston says of Nemo, "I treated him as if he were my own." Is this choice of words revealing? Toni Morrison has said that literature should explore "the impact of racism on those who perpetuate it." Do you see that at work here?

10. The novel concludes with Nemo having made what Hemingway called "a separate peace" with his family in Jamaica. How does this resolution strike you? Discuss what is implied by Nemo's son's name.

11. Do you see a double meaning in the novel's title? Is there a sense that Jacob is a kind of resurrectionist to the departed Nemo Johnston? Or is Nemo in some way a resurrectionist to the disillusioned Jacob Thacker?

Mary Helen Stefaniak   *The Cailiffs of Baghdad, Georgia*
Manil Suri   *The Age of Shiva*
Brady Udall   *The Lonely Polygamist*
Barry Unsworth   *Sacred Hunger*
Alexei Zentner   *Touch*

*Available only on the Norton Web site